Hot Bayou Fire

by

Elizabeth Shore

Hot Bayou Fire

Contact Information: info@thewildrosepress.com

Cover Art by *Diana Carlile*

The Wild Rose Press, Inc.
PO Box 708
Adams Basin, NY 14410-0708

Visit us at www.thewildrosepress.com

Publishing History
First Scarlet Rose Edition, 2020
Trade Paperback ISBN 978-1-5092-3178-2
Digital ISBN 978-1-5092-3179-9

Published in the United States of America

Where's there's heat, there's fire...

"Autumn, hold up," a male, gravelly voice said.

A few quick strides of those hunky muscled legs and Chase stood two feet away. His black T-shirt was damp from the heat and clinging like a shadow to his powerful chest. As he stood before her, he stuffed his hands in his jean pockets, the casual movement causing a ripple along his mammoth biceps.

"We should talk." A light sheen of sweat coated his brow; a faint scent of leather drifted off his skin.

"Ah..." She fumbled to recall his question, licking her suddenly dry lips.

"Grab a beer?" He swiped a hand across his forehead. "It's hotter than hell in here, and I could sure use a cold one. It's close enough to happy hour, right?"

Ooooh. Autumn hesitated. Her "Bad Idea" radar kicked into high gear. With the way Mr. Artist made her body rev like that big ol' Harley of his, disaster seemed right around the bend. Still, with the sweltering temps outside, a cold beer sounded like heaven in a bottle. Maybe just one...

"C'mon. Follow me in that little sports car of yours. I know just the place."

Autumn gazed after him, the view from behind more than she could resist. Man-oh-man, the way those jeans clung to his nice tight ass... Her heartbeat thudded against her chest like a heavy metal drummer on steroids.

This wasn't good.

Dedication

For Dave, best brother ever. Keep making those great fires in the fireplace and be sure to get enough to eat!

Author Acknowledgments

The writing journey is rewarding, thrilling, and deeply satisfying, but when the expertise and dedication of a phenomenal editor like Trish Owens is added to the mix, the story you first thought you were writing transforms into something far greater. Thank you, Trish, for your guidance and encouragement in helping me continue honing my craft as a writer. Every book of mine you've edited has made it that much better. I'm forever grateful.

Also on my team is the best bunch of critique partners I could ever ask for. To the wonderful writers in my Hudson Valley critique group, I owe you bottomless bags of cheesy popcorn. I'm indebted to your support, your expertise, not to mention the best snacks anywhere. You ladies rock my world. Thank you.

Huge thanks to Kevin Scanlan at Scanlan Glass in Brooklyn, NY, for sharing his wealth of knowledge on the art of glassblowing and for his enormous patience while instructing me on the craft.

Lastly, no book of mine would ever get off the ground if not for the constant and inexhaustible support of my husband, Jari, who never, ever stops believing in me, even when I stop believing in myself. To the best *auto pena* in the "vörld," I love you. *Aina ja ikuisesti.*

Chapter One

Chase Durand glanced at a wall clock in the spacious lobby as he strolled through the hotel's main entrance. Although still only early morning, the Louisiana heat blasted with high noon brutality. He flicked away a trickle of sweat from his forehead as a perky girl beaming a bright smile stepped toward him.

"Mr. Durand?"

"That's me. But Chase is fine."

"Super, Mr. Durand. I'm Liesel, Ms. Boudreaux's assistant. Follow me, please." With military precision, she spun around and headed toward a long hallway, the heels of her practical pumps echoing against the gleaming marble floor.

A half smile tugged at Chase's lips. *Mr. Durand.* Like a schoolteacher or something. He shifted his motorcycle helmet from his right hand to his left and unzipped his black leather jacket. He sure as shit wasn't any schoolteacher.

As he strolled beside spry Liesel, he glanced around. In every direction, frenzied activity swirled, workers buzzing like a colony of drones. Opening day for the White Ibis Hotel was only three months away. From the chaotic, disorganized look of things, making the deadline would be tough.

"In here, please." With an outstretched arm, Liesel indicated a doorway to her right.

Chase headed toward it, but before he stepped a foot inside the expansive office, a fierce, rail-thin woman sporting a tight bun and huge smile blocked his entry.

"Chase," she boomed, taking one of his large hands in both of hers and vigorously pumping. "I'm so glad you made it."

"Good to see you, Maryanne."

Releasing his hand at last, she marched back to her desk, nodding toward the plush chair on the opposite side. "Please. Sit."

She settled into her own chair, calling out to her still-hovering assistant. "Two coffees, Liesel. Right away. And some of those raspberry cakes with that delicious red frosting." She darted a glance at Chase. "How do you take your coffee? With cream?"

"I—"

"Bring cream, Liesel. And sugar. Quickly, please."

"Yes, Ms. Boudreaux."

As Liesel dashed, Maryanne's attention redirected to Chase. She ran her hands down her red silk skirt, smoothing away non-existent wrinkles.

Chase had met her twice before. Both times she'd been decked out in clothes looking like they cost more than some people's annual salary. It seemed to be all about image with Maryanne Boudreaux, an appropriate fit with her position as the White Ibis' head interior designer.

"So," she said, flashing another giant smile with red lips perfectly matching the color of her suit. "I'm so pleased you've agreed to the terms of the contract. You ready to sign?"

Not bothering to wait for his response, she slid a

stack of papers across her desk toward Chase.

He eyed the thick pile with skepticism. "So many?"

"Oh, you know lawyers, Chase." She waved a hand through the air as if brushing aside a flitting gnat. "They get paid to write long, legal documents. But there's really nothing to it. The terms we already discussed, and your lawyer agreed to, are included."

"Somewhere in here, anyway." Chase flicked through the papers. "Two contracts," he noted. "I assumed so we'll both have a copy with original signatures?"

"Exactly. One can never be too careful."

The door opened, and dutiful Liesel reappeared, coffee tray in hand.

"Finally," Maryanne muttered, offering an apologetic eye roll at Chase. "Set it on the side table, Liesel, and pour the coffee for Mr. Durand and me."

"Yes, Ms. Boudreaux." She completed the task with quick efficiency before skittering away.

Chase set his cup on Maryanne's desk, far more interested in reviewing the terms of the contract than drinking coffee he hadn't wanted.

"Have a raspberry cake. They're delicious." Maryanne dug into hers with gusto, licking at the mountain of thick frosting like a starving person at an all-you-can-eat buffet.

Ignoring the sweets, Chase glanced through the contract, looking for proof that the figure he'd been quoted for the work was real and not some fantasy his impoverished mind had conjured up. He flipped through the pages, scanning. *There*. In plain black ink, sure as shit. Every last penny they'd promised him.

His heart rate jacked to twice its normal speed, and

his fingers trembled, gripping the contract like it was a sacred talisman. It took him a second to recognize the signs of relief, his body's physical response at finally being liberated from years of soul-sucking stress. He released a long, quiet breath to maintain his composure.

From across the desk, Maryanne peered at the page Chase reviewed. Nodding toward the contract she said, "I trust there's no issue with the figure we discussed. It's all there, just as agreed upon."

Chase slowly nodded. "Looks fine," he said quietly. "Although I guess there's no getting around the personal appearances option?"

Maryanne pursed her lips in what appeared to pass for some sort of smile. "Now Chase, most of the compensation is of course for the art. But you did agree that you'd attend the hotel events we discussed."

"I'll do what I said I would." He sat back in his chair and placed one booted ankle atop his knee. "I just don't get why it's so important."

"Well," she said in a placating tone, as if speaking to an irritable child. That pushed her up a notch higher on Chase's "pain in the ass" scale. "These days, artists of all kind are in the spotlight. Heck, even people who bake cupcakes on TV are like A-list celebrities. Crowds always flock to the famous. And you, Chase"—she pointed a perfectly manicured finger at him—"are about to become our celebrity artist. With the fortunate combination of your bad-boy reputation, rugged good looks, and amazing art, success is guaranteed both for you and for the hotel. We know it. Pretty soon, you will, too."

Sounded like a big steaming pile of crazy to him, but Chase kept his thoughts quiet. Hell, why object? He could stand around at a couple of cocktail parties, say a few words, and sign autographs if that's what they wanted. For the amount of dough they were throwing his way, he could be the picture of accommodating. Another jolt of relief zinged through him. He could finally pay his mountain of overdue bills. Get those damn debt collectors off his ass. Hallelujah.

Picking up the contract again, he flipped through the remaining pages, assuming it was more of what they'd already discussed. But then he spotted something that hadn't come up before.

He pointed to the page. "This says I'm agreeing to terms for the installation of my art in this hotel and for *all* future hotel projects your agency undertakes." He pierced Maryanne with a stare through narrowed eyes. "We didn't discuss anything about future projects."

"Oh, I know." She brushed off his concern with a carefree laugh, but Chase was sure he heard a touch of nervousness in her voice. People said his massive size was intimidating, but he figured his obvious irritation troubled Maryanne more.

"Of course, we'd love to establish a long-term working relationship with you, Chase. You're an astounding artist, and your glasswork is going to be the crowning glory in this hotel. So why would we only be thinking short term?"

He shifted his large frame in the chair, considering. On one hand, her compliment flattered the shit out of him. He'd always hoped he'd get this kind of break. But holy damn. The hell he'd gone through to finally make it this far… If someone had told him he'd have to nearly starve, get evicted from not one but two apartments for failure to pay rent, and spend time in jail before getting his break as an artist, he wondered if he ever would've started down this path.

No, he decided. That wasn't true. There was no way he *couldn't* pursue this dream. Glasswork was his life. It might have been nice to know the shitstorm he'd have to emerge from before getting the break, though. Maybe he somehow could've prepared better for it. Still, he wasn't going to let anyone try to manhandle his career, no matter how much money they threw at him.

"Don't get me wrong, Maryanne," he answered at last. "I like the way you think. But I'm not a long-term commitment kind of guy. I won't sign a contract with that clause. I need to first see how it goes here. Then we'll talk about the future."

For just a moment, her giant red smile faltered, a small tremor on her otherwise resilient face. But from past meetings, Chase knew Maryanne Boudreaux was nothing if not glued to her impeccable image, and she recovered with the speed of a striking cobra.

"It's really not a big deal," she said, her open palms facing upward as if to demonstrate how not a big deal this all was. "I don't think we need to bother changing the contract for one little insignificant clause, now do we?"

"We do." Picking up the pen she'd shoved his way, he slashed huge Xs through the unacceptable language and next to them and scrawled his initials.

Maryanne gasped. "Chase! What are you—"

"Fixed."

He'd have this commission, but not on someone else's terms. "I struck the clauses I don't want and initialed. You do the same, and we'll be good. If not...well." He shrugged. "I guess our little signing party will have to be put on hold."

"Oh now, now." She shook her head, quick to counter his statement. "There's no need for that. Of course I'll agree to the strike-outs." She picked up a black fountain pen in front of her, the kind of thing Chase figured luxury snobs would describe as a "writing instrument," and held it between slim fingers.

"I simply can't bear the thought of not getting things started," she said sweetly, laying on thick her version of southern charm.

"Mind if I take off my jacket?"

"Of course not! I apologize for the heat. The air conditioner installation isn't quite finished yet. And you know how steamy it can be in the bayou." She sprang to her feet to take the garment from him and hang it on the polished-metal coat rack in the corner of her office. The sleek stand matched the rest of the hotel's edgy interior, a stark transformation from the genteel Whispering Bay of bygone years that had stood here before.

That hotel had once been the queen of the Louisiana bayou. But scandal, financial challenges, and an overall change in consumer demand had forced the Whispering Bay into bankruptcy. It had stood abandoned for years until financiers, seeing the potential to bring high style and luxury to the area, infused millions into the renovation. And now, as part of the overall look, they wanted permanent installations of Chase's artwork.

He picked up his pen once more. Time to make it real.

Maryanne summoned Liesel back to her office to act as signature witness while Chase took his time reading over the contract. Aside from the commitment language, it was everything they'd discussed. Flipping to the last page while quiet Liesel looked on, he signed.

"Congratulations," Maryanne said, adding her own initials and signature to both documents. "Looks like we have a deal."

She stuck out her hand toward his, and they shook.

"Now," she said, finishing her coffee and rising from her chair. "Let me show you around."

****

With the flexibility and balance of an Olympic gymnast, Autumn Rivette walked the scaffolding planks anchored near the ceiling of the White Ibis. Her chief networking engineer followed carefully behind her as she eyed the intricate wiring, snaking along the wall. It would be hidden behind a false panel once their work was complete, but first, they had a massive problem to fix.

"The connectivity isn't working at all?" She glanced back at Roberto.

"Not on the east wing. And I checked everything. *Everything*. The wires are all good, components are working. I thought it might be a firewall issue, but then—"

"You checked every wiring center?" She continued scanning the fibers while pelting Roberto with rapid fire questions.

"Of course, but—"

"All the jacks and patch panels?"

"Sure."

"Centralized control plane? IP routing tables?" Suddenly, a glint off one of the cables caught her eye.

"Whoa." She stopped in her tracks and peered closer at the spaghetti soup of wires. It appeared correct at first glance, but there was something in the twist of one of them... "Roberto, where's that optics vendor?"

"Just saw him a second ago." Her engineer peered over the side of the scaffolding. He's down there, Autumn. Wandering around the lobby."

"Probably trying to think up more ways to cheat us."

"Come again?"

No time to answer Roberto. Quicker than a fire fighter descending a pole, Autumn raced down the metal scaffolding stairs and dashed across the lobby to catch up with Elliott Sampson, her fiber optics vendor. He was pointing toward the installation of high-end information monitors and directing comments to a couple people strolling just steps ahead of him.

One was the hotel's uptight interior designer, Maryanne Whatshername. She hovered right beside a large, muscular, broad-shouldered man with a drool-worthy physique. *Hot damn.* Who the heck was the eye candy? And what was Elliot doing with him?

Cursing under her breath, Autumn sped toward the lobby's front desk to get within a few feet behind her vendor.

"Hey, Elliott." Her voice was sharp, unprofessional maybe, but whatever. She was pissed.

Elliott turned around and spotted Autumn, flashing a sparkling smile. "Oh, I'm glad I ran into—"

"I've been checking out the optics networking your crew installed yesterday." Anger vibrated through her like electrical currents in a wire.

"Everything's okay, I take it?"

"You take it wrong. Everything is pretty damn far from okay."

Out of the corner of her eye, she noticed the muscular guy had stopped walking and turned toward her, his attention probably snared by her raised voice. She glanced past Elliot and her gaze traveled up…and up. Damn, he was tall as a mountain, especially for someone like her who didn't quite clear five-foot-two. His powerful body teemed with solid muscle. He had a firm, strong jaw, as if chiseled from granite. His eyes were the polar opposite—soft, deep, sea-green with eyelashes to make a girl jealous. Same deal with his hair. Dark chestnut-brown, thick, in a rock star, longish style that notched up his rebel coolness.

He wore a black T-shirt and jeans that hugged toned legs in all the right places. A black leather jacket was slung over his forearm, and his fingers held a dark, metallic-blue motorcycle helmet with a bad-ass screeching eagle across it. *Very hot biker on a walk with the interior designer.* What's this all about? Hell if she knew.

The mountain man met Autumn's gaze with a curious expression lacking the judgment other people often threw at her. Actually, he seemed curious, kinda like he was checking to see if she needed help. Could that be it?

Nah. Didn't matter, anyway. She didn't need help from anyone.

Returning her attention to Elliot, she snapped, "I told you fiber optics, right? Throughout the entire hotel?"

The vendor's reassurance came quickly. "Of course, yes. Yes. Fiber optics throughout."

"Then why," Amber seethed, stepping closer, "am I seeing CAT 5 copper wire twisted among the fiber?"

"Copper?" He pasted on a look of thunderstruck surprise. "That can't be. I specifically told my guys to—"

"To what? Cheat us?" Her voice rose; she didn't care. Mountain Man didn't seem to care, either. Amazingly enough, the corner of his lips rose in a half smile that looked a little like admiration.

Autumn swiped aside her bangs and nailed Elliot with a razor-sharp stare. "The transmission load on the east wing is jacked because you're trying to screw us with sub-par wiring. We're paying for fiber optics, and we're getting fiber optics. Do I make myself clear?"

Elliott held up his hands. "Now, just listen, Autumn. I don't see any reason to get nasty about this."

"No? We should just take your cheating with smiles on our faces?"

The vendor turned to look at the small crowd gathered around them like he was searching for allies.

Maryanne, who'd been standing with Mountain Man, chose that moment to step forward, her lips fixed with a fake smile. "Is there trouble?"

"Nothing that concerns you." Autumn shook her head and frowned, hoping the obtrusive busybody would get the message to butt out.

She didn't. "Anything that concerns this hotel concerns me, Autumn. If there's something going on, I need to know about it."

"I'll send you a memo."

Surprisingly, Mountain Man let out a full-scale bark of laughter at that. *Interesting...*

Maryanne bristled at Autumn's remark and opened her mouth to respond.

Elliot piped back up. "How do I even know that

what you're saying is true? I can do my own inspection to verify—"

"Your inspection is as useful to me as sunscreen on a fish." Autumn stepped back, giving him space. "But go ahead; do an inspection. Just try to prove me wrong." Her words hung heavy, a yoke of a dare she'd slung around his neck.

Elliot hesitated, his mind likely spinning for a response, when a booming voice across the lobby intervened. "Anything I can help with?"

All heads turned toward the elevator bank. A short, bald man hurried forward in agitated bursts of speed, weaving through the welter of mostly construction crew congregating around Autumn. With clear impatience, his elbowed his way in, casting the idle workers a withering look. "You all have somewhere to be other than here, I assume?"

They scurried away like roaches under a light.

The man focused his attention on Autumn. "Trouble, Miss Rivette?"

Autumn set her jaw. The officious hotel manager, Wilson Wyatt, rankled like burrs under a saddle. "None that I can see."

"Are you sure? I heard raised voices." He cocked his egg-smooth head like a nervous bird, and his beady eyes looked at her with a little too much interest.

"We're all good here, Wilson."

When no one spoke up to contradict, the manager clapped his hands once and nodded. "Okay. Well, fine then. If you need me, just—"

"I won't. But ah...thanks."

When she was certain the manager, Maryanne, and the big guy were on their way, Autumn turned back to

Elliott. "You'll notice I just saved your ass from a potentially embarrassing situation," she said, keeping her voice low. "But it doesn't mean I won't hesitate to ruin your reputation if you even think about screwing over this hotel with your cheap tricks."

"Of course, I would never—"

"Save the speech. Just fix the wires."

"Sure, yeah." Elliott looked around, probably for the closest escape route.

Autumn turned away from him, sure that what she wanted would get done. As she walked back toward the scaffolding, she couldn't help but cast a glance behind her to see where Mountain Man and Maryanne were headed. He looked backward, too, and for a brief instant, their gazes met and held. Unexpectedly, he flashed her a smile. Sparkling with sexiness, the simple gesture lit up his face and softened the carved angles. His green eyes gleamed with definite interest.

Autumn's breath caught in her throat. *What the hell?* Confused by her reaction, she spun away.

She met Roberto coming down the ladder of the scaffolding and realized he must have seen her and Mountain Man doing their little eye tango. *Damnit.*

He jutted his chin in that direction. "You know him?"

"Who?"

"That guy checking you out."

Autumn rolled her eyes. "No clue what you're talking about."

Roberto laughed. "You suck at subtlety, Autumn. And you're way too smart to play dumb. You saw the guy, and he saw you." He hitched his thumbs through loops in his jeans and smirked. "Which should make things interesting."

Autumn glared at her network engineer. "Interesting how?"

"That guy's the artist they just hired. A bunch of his art's going to be installed throughout the entire hotel."

"So?"

"So a lot of the art needs an IT system to go with it. Some kind of fancy lighting designs with timers and other stuff, some of it kinda complex. Or so I'm told. The hotel manager appointed him an IT contact to take care of everything he needs."

Autumn eyed the laugh lines crinkling Roberto's face, and a sinking feeling kicked her in the gut. Still, she managed to keep her voice calm as she asked, "Who's the contact?"

"I'm looking right at her."

Chapter Two

With a burst of force that might have been a *little* over the top, Autumn shoved hard against the hotel manager's office door just as he was polishing off the last of a giant po' boy. Not bothering to apologize for her intrusion, she marched inside and stood with folded arms in front of his desk. "You need to get someone else, Wilson."

The egg-headed executive heaved an audible sigh and slowly swiveled around in his cushy office chair so he could face Autumn directly.

"First of all, Miss Rivette," he said, clearly making no effort to disguise the annoyance in his clipped voice, "you're interrupting my lunch. Second, I'm extremely busy. Everyone else in this hotel makes an appointment when they need to see me. It's how I like it. But you just barge in as if the rules don't apply."

Autumn placed both hands on Wilson's Lucite desk and leaned in. "Rules? You want to talk about rules? You're making decisions affecting the job I've been hired to do but need me to find a time that's convenient for you to discuss? Screw that. I need this situation resolved."

"As I said—"

"Fine. I made an appointment. It's right now."

She knew she was pushing her luck with the manager. Since arriving at the White Ibis six months ago after she'd been hired as their Chief Technology Officer, Autumn had tested his patience probably ten too many times. But the job was huge and the timeframe tight. In order to install all the technology the financiers wanted for the entire hotel in the time they wanted it done, politeness had to be checked at the door.

Still, it wasn't her intention to be unreasonable. As long as nobody else was.

Autumn tapped the desk. "This art guy who's here, the one I'm supposed to be the contact for?"

"Yes, yes. Chase Durand is his name." Wilson dabbed a napkin at both corners of his mouth and flicked away crumbs from his meticulously pressed pants. He looked up at Autumn. "Maryanne loves his work. We're going to feature it everywhere throughout the hotel. It gives us just the edgy look we want without it being cold or harsh."

"Sure, whatever. It'll look great. But the thing is, I—"

"You're going to be his IT contact." He set aside the papers he'd been shuffling and folded his hands on top of his desk. Twin spots of red dotted his cheeks, all the evidence she needed to understand this battle was lost. The manager had always stayed this side of prickly, but every so often, irritation spilled over into full-scale 'roid rage. When that happened, anyone facing it had no chance of getting what they wanted.

Still, Autumn could make a mule look cooperative, and her stubborn nature wasn't ready to call it quits.

"It doesn't make sense," she argued. "I've got a team of talented people who can help the guy out. Why does it have to be me? I've got a million and one things to do, Wilson, and we're opening in less than three months."

"I'm well aware of opening day. But Maryanne has insisted on you being Chase's contact."

"Why?"

For a moment, the manager hesitated, and Autumn was sure she saw a trace of uncertainty cross his face.

"We're not obligated to explain our decisions." He released a frustrated breath. "But I suppose you may as well know. Maryanne decided that appointing our top IT expert will make a big impression on the artist. She only wants the best for him."

What kind of attitude did Mountain Man carry around if he insisted on having the head of IT as his contact? Seemed like a total dick-face thing to do. But based on nothing but a two-second encounter, she didn't think he was the one insisting on her being his contact. It all had the same shit smell of Maryanne. The damn busybody had been up in her business from the day Autumn was hired.

"Anyway," Wilson continued, "you're the contact. Go see what he needs." He deliberately turned away from her and toward his computer, stabbing at his keyboard as he ignored her.

Unbelievable. Heaving an audible sigh, Autumn walked across the office toward the door.

"Autumn," Wilson's nerve-pinching voice called, "my screen's all black. I can't get this damn computer to work."

She twisted the knob and pulled the door open. "Try turning it on."

****

Autumn jammed down the push-to-talk button on

her two-way radio. "Yo, Roberto? Have you seen Chase Durand?"

Her network engineer's voice crackled back. "You talking about that big biker dude?"

"Yeah. The artist. Do you happen to know where he is?"

Autumn's stomach growled as she waited for her chief networking engineer to respond. It was pushing three, and she still hadn't eaten lunch. A case of the hungry grumpies was settling in fast.

Roberto said, "I haven't seen him since this morning. I've been wiring the e-Order system in the spa area for the past two hours."

With growing impatience, Autumn shoved the radio in its holder as she sped along the first floor hallway toward the security command center. She couldn't waste any more time looking for Chase Durand, so she'd see if she could spot him on the cameras.

The low hum of dozens of security monitors greeted her as she pushed through the door and entered the room. The monitors' light guided her way through the semi-darkness as she headed toward the main viewing area.

"Hey, Autumn," Lou Romano, former NYPD Detective and now head of White Ibis security, grunted in greeting as she took a seat beside him.

"Hey, Lou." She adjusted the chair so her feet wouldn't dangle from it. Being vertically challenged could often be a nuisance. Her gaze flicked over the monitors. "I'm looking for that new artist guy."

"Durand?"

"Yeah. You seen him?"

"No." Lou cracked a smile. "But I ain't exactly looking for him, either."

"Well, I am. Could you bring up some more views, maybe focusing on the restaurants? He could be in one of them."

Lou pushed some buttons, bringing up several different angles. "Whadya need him for, anyway?"

Her jaw clenched. Obviously, she hadn't yet shaken her annoyance. "Some of his art installations require coding or something, so he needs IT support. I'm...ah...his contact."

"You?" Lou swiveled in his chair to face her. "Didn't think the head of technology would have time for that kind of thing."

"I don't. But Maryanne said I'm his gal."

He frowned. "She makes that decision 'cause why?"

"She's a designer. His art's part of the hotel design. So she gets him what he needs."

"Did you talk to Wilson?"

"For all the good it did me." Autumn kept her eyes glued to the monitors as she searched for Chase. "He said she wants me, so it's me. Game over."

"Seems like a supreme waste of your time, not to mention the company's money."

Autumn sat back in her chair. Lou was right. She had a rare background with expertise in both hardware *and* coding. It had played a huge part in how she snagged this job. And not for nothing, she made decent money. But she earned every penny of her salary and then some through the everyday high pressure and heavy demands she dealt with. So why would anyone think it was a good idea paying her salary to be the resident artist's go-to contact when there were plenty of strong—but lower paid—members on her team who could do it just as well? Her bullshit meter spiked a notch as she filed the question away in her mind's "to be determined" drawer.

"Wait." She was pretty sure she had just spotted him in the new East/West fusion restaurant. Hard to miss someone that big. "Zoom in on the guy standing near the entrance of Rising Sun."

"The totally ripped dude with the huge guns?"

"Yeah."

A few clicks and Chase was front and center. Maryanne still hovered around him, fluttering like an anxious parent on the first day of kindergarten. What a pest. She outta leave the guy alone, let him do what he needed.

Lou was right; Chase had some guns on him. Enhanced with elaborate black-and-grey tattoos, those biceps were on the right side of amazing. He also sported quite the classic vee frame, his broad shoulders tapering down to slim and—from the look of it—rock-hard abs beneath that T-shirt. Chase wasn't carrying the helmet or leather jacket she'd seen earlier, so he must've stashed them somewhere. Maryanne's office? She frowned. Something didn't sit right with her at the thought of that but damned if she could put a finger on why.

She pushed away from the chair. "I'm going to go talk to the guy," she told Lou. "Keep him on camera until you see me enter the picture. I need to know if he goes somewhere. If he leaves the restaurant, get me on the two-way."

"No prob. I'll keep him in sight until I know you're

there."

She waved at the security chief as she made her way out. The restaurant wasn't far, but the hotel was so large that if Chase left, it could be tough tracking him down again. She hustled through the lobby and toward the east wing where Rising Sun was located, chuckling to herself. The restaurant was specifically on the east wing because of its name, but since it was strictly a dinner restaurant, the only sun patrons would be seeing was the setting one.

She swung the glass doors open and entered, spotting Chase immediately. He'd moved—with Maryanne still in tow—toward the back of the restaurant near where an indoor koi pond was planned. They seemed to be in the middle of a somewhat heated conversation; at least, it looked as if Maryanne was agitated. Chase seemed more bored than anything else.

Maryanne waved to the floor in front of her. "I was just thinking it would look so dramatic right here. Your artwork featured front and center."

Chase crossed his arms over his chest and frowned as he glanced around. "It would also block people from seeing most of the restaurant and have a negative impact on light quality and flow. I'm not putting anything here."

Chase spoke with no agitation, but the message was clear. No negotiation; no bullshit. He'd put his art where he wanted and compromise be damned. Autumn could relate.

At that moment, both Chase and Maryanne spotted Autumn standing nearby, and their conversation halted.

"Ah, I see that our CTO has arrived," the designer said, frosting on a heavy layer of enthusiasm as she batted fake eyelashes at Chase. "Only the best for our artist."

Ignoring her, Autumn turned to Chase. "Autumn Rivette. I'm your IT contact."

A slow smile, warm as honey, touched the corners of his lips as they curled upward. "Nice to meet you, Autumn. I'm Chase Durand."

His huge paw of a hand swallowed hers as they shook, the grip warm and firm. Her fingers brushed raised contours of skin on the side of his right hand. Burn marks, she guessed. Battle scars of his profession. The imperfections intrigued her, made her want to ask him questions about the stories behind them. They were interesting, just like the warmth traveling from his skin to hers and the low, gravelly sound of his voice. Though why the hell she was even thinking about that was probably the most interesting question of all.

She pulled her hand away and stuffed it in her back pocket. "I was told you have some tech needs for your art. You wanna show me what they are?"

"We're actually in the middle of something right now," Maryanne piped up.

Autumn glanced over at her. She'd forgotten Miss Busybody was still standing there.

Before Autumn had time to get annoyed, Chase intervened. "I wouldn't mind talking about the IT stuff for a few minutes, maybe giving Autumn preliminary information on what I need so she can get started."

"Oh, well. I suppose—"

"Assuming it's convenient for you, of course." He punctuated his southern charm with a wide smile, melting Maryanne like butter.

Autumn looked away so she wouldn't laugh aloud.

"Anything that works for you, works for me." The designer placed a light hand on his arm. That part Autumn didn't like at all. "Just give me a call on my cell when you're ready." She darted a look at Autumn. "You have my number."

Maryanne's heels clicked on the marble flooring as she strode toward the door, her pencil skirt making a soft swishing sound against tanned, bare legs.

Chase glanced down at Autumn. "Did you come to help me or save me?"

She looked up at him in surprise. "Why would you need saving?"

Chase looked around. "My coffee tooth is aching. Know any place where we can grab a cup?"

She nodded. "Sure. There's another restaurant called Sky High at the top of the hotel."

He raised a questioning brow. "I didn't think anything was open yet."

"It's not. But Priscilla Trannel—she goes by Pat— is the executive chef up there. She's getting the place ready for opening day. She and I are both java junkies, and she keeps a pot going for herself and me pretty much all the time."

"Lead on."

They walked side by side toward the door, their difference in height almost comically dramatic. The top of her head didn't even reach Chase's shoulder. She felt as if she were next to a gladiator. Still, there was something kinda cool about it, like being escorted by her own personal bodyguard.

Glass elevators whisked them to the top of the hotel and directly into the restaurant. The doors opened, and they entered the spacious, light-filled room. There was no one in sight.

Chase's booted feet stepped lightly behind her on the carpeted floor as they crossed the dining room toward the kitchen. Once there, Autumn poked her head through swinging double doors. "Pat? You got any coffee?"

"Always, honey-pie," a woman shouted from deep within the kitchen. "Just made a fresh pot at the place behind the bar. Help yourself."

Autumn led Chase over to the bar where they were greeted by the fragrant aroma of dark roast Arabica. She grabbed two paper cups from the stack beside the coffee maker and poured their drinks.

Handing Chase his cup, she asked, "Do you take anything in it?"

"Nope. Black will do it for me."

"Same here." Autumn nodded as she headed to a nearby table. Since the restaurant wouldn't be open for business until the hotel started booking guests, the table lacked place settings, napkins, or flowers. But even without decoration, the warm, dark wood was inviting. Autumn took a seat across from Chase and sipped her coffee, welcoming its warmth despite the heat of the day.

Chase lifted his cup toward her as if making a toast. "Well, then. Cheers."

They touched cups and drank. Chase relaxed into his chair liked he planned on being there awhile. After draining half his cup in a couple of swallows, he caught Autumn's gaze. A crooked smile touched his lips. "You look as much like a CTO as I do a guy who makes glass."

Autumn bristled as flames of annoyance swept

through her.

Before she had time to respond, Chase continued. "I like that." He nodded and smiled, as if he'd just arrived at an important decision. "I like it a lot."

Autumn shrugged, uncomfortable with his scrutiny. "You meet a lot of CTOs? So you know what we look like?"

White teeth flashed at her as he grinned, and laugh lines crinkled around his eyes. "Oh, man, finally someone who's not going to 'yes' me to death." He absently fiddled with his empty cup, turning it in his massive hands. "I think we're going to get along just fine."

His reaction surprised her. People were usually taken aback by her sometimes surly nature and ended up showing deference just to make sure she didn't get more pissed. Not that she wanted to be known as Techie She-Devil, but leading in a man's world meant she had to be tough even when she felt like a puddle.

The double doors to the kitchen swung open, and Pat barreled through, holding a loaded tray in both hands and heading toward the table where Autumn and Chase sat.

"I was hoping you'd still be here," Pat said.

As Pat set plates in front of them, Autumn looked down at what else the chef had brought. The fragrant aroma of freshly baked bread seeped out from beneath four, cloth-covered baskets. Beside them, Pat placed a crock of fresh butter and two knives.

"I'm trying out different starter breads for when guests first get seated," Pat explained. "I need a guinea pig." She looked at Chase. "Or two."

Chase rose and stuck out his hand. "Chase

Durand," he said. "It's a pleasure."

"Whoa." Pat craned her neck. "Didn't realize a mountain was going to rise above me."

"Chase is the artist whose work is being installed in the hotel," Autumn said.

"I heard about that." Pat shook hands with Chase and then looked back toward his chair. "Please, have a seat and eat some bread. I'm headed back to the kitchen, but when y'all are done sampling, let me know if we have a winner." Pat wiped her hands on her apron. Then, just before turning away, her gaze darted over at Chase before returning to Autumn. Her lips curled in a grin.

No doubt Pat'd be hunting for an explanation as to what exactly was going on. She was an amazing chef but her appetite for gossip rivaled anything she had for food. She wouldn't let this little encounter slide without demanding details. *Not that there was anything to share.* But still.

Pat had brought out four different kinds of breads. Bread was Autumn's food weakness, and the head chef knew it. If Autumn had her way, she'd polish off every last bite herself, but she supposed it would be nice to share.

"Go ahead," she said.

Chase shook his head. "My mamma raised me better than that. Ladies first."

She couldn't help the little snort. Eyeing the bread choices, she mumbled, "Don't know if I'm exactly a 'lady,' but whatever. I'm not gonna turn down bread."

The rosemary focaccia was her first choice, but she couldn't resist the warm, crusty whole-wheat rolls, either. Settling back in her chair to eat, she realized

Chase hadn't said a word in response to her last comment. As she tore off a piece of focaccia, she looked over at him.

He settled back in his chair with a curious expression of interest and amusement, and she frowned. "What?" she asked, the word spiked with a trace of annoyance.

He didn't answer immediately, instead reaching over to take bread to his plate. He slowly chewed a bite as he continued studying her, his stare darkening as it slid across her face.

A rush of heat warmed her cheeks, and her skin tingled. Confusion overtook annoyance. Why did he look at her like that? What was going through his mind? And why—much as she tried to deny it—did she kinda like the attention?

He rested his arms on the table and leaned in. A slow, lazy smile lifted one corner of his mouth as his raw masculinity drew her toward him with irresistible force. "You're more a lady," he said, "than anyone I've seen in a long, long time."

Chapter Three

The shocked look on Autumn's face nearly made Chase laugh aloud. Her mouth dropped open, her eyes went wide, and the faintest blush of pink crept up her cheeks. He'd even swear she was squirming in her chair. Her reaction didn't seem like the tough-as-nails Autumn he was getting to know, but hot damn if it didn't edge up his interest just the same.

He swept crumbs from his jeans and sat back in his chair. The occasional clang of pots and pans from the kitchen was the only sound in the room.

"What are you talking about?" Tearing off a piece of her roll, she popped it in her mouth and chewed like she was in a race. "I'm a lady like you're a gremlin."

This time he didn't hold back, barking out a bellyful of amusement like steel shot from a pistol. What a firecracker.

She continued ripping away at her bread as she pinned him with the most arresting pair of baby blues he'd ever seen, probably thinking it would make him look away. It only made him want to look more.

Without a trace of shame, his gaze traveled from her beautiful, porcelain face framed by curled tendrils pulled loose from her mass of pinned up blonde hair, down along the angle of her jaw, then dipping further still to the swell of her breasts.

A sudden image of the mythical Lady Godiva

flashed through his mind, naked atop her horse as she rode through the village, her thick hair the only shield for her lush breasts and pebbled nipples. A spear of lust shot through him as he wondered if Autumn's hair would give her the same protection if she were naked in his bed. He could easily picture her lying back, propped up against the pillows, her hair splayed across the sheets. *Holy balls.* He sucked in a sharp breath just as her tapping foot caught his attention.

Autumn had shifted to sitting sideways in her chair so he could see her small, sneakered feet on the other side of the table. One leg crossed over the other, and she lightly bounced the top foot up and down, up and down, as if a current ran through it. His thoughts wandered to what might be hiding beneath those shoes. Were her toes painted? And if so, what color? Soft pink? Fire engine red? An almost irresistible temptation to lean forward and tug at her shoestrings suddenly struck him. He wanted to hold one of those little feet in the palm of his hand and then run his tongue between her—

Arousal like flash fire zinged straight to his cock. Just in time, he bit back a groan. He had no idea where the sudden burst of lust had come from, but it sure as hell needed to stop. Now. *Get yourself under control, Durand.*

Snagging a piece of bread from the platter he started to eat, ordering his thoughts away from the far-too-sensual pint-sized computer tech and on to his art. He cleared his throat. "We should talk about the installation."

"No problem," Autumn agreed. "Just let me know what you need. I didn't get any details, only that some of your projects require IT support."

"They do. Mostly because I need simultaneous coordination of lighting on some of the larger works. The pieces go together to form a light show. Kinda similar to the dancing fountains at the Bellagio Hotel in Vegas. Know what I mean?"

For a moment so brief he almost missed it, a startled expression darkened Autumn's face. Her lips tightened, and a look almost like fear flickered in her eyes. He nearly said something, even tasted the words on his tongue.

"Yeah, I know." She pushed back from the table and shot out of her chair. "Listen, just tell me what you need, and I'll make it happen." She used the cloth napkin from the now empty breadbasket to wipe her hands before tossing it back on the table. Without another word, she turned and walked away.

What the hell? For a moment Chase just sat and stared at Autumn's departing backside. If he wasn't so gobsmacked by her behavior, he would have taken a moment to appreciate the tantalizing swell of her pert ass. As it was, he could only frown and wonder what he'd said.

Suddenly he realized that she'd forgotten to tell him how to reach her.

"Autumn," he called and rose to take off after her, his long strides making quick work of covering the distance between them.

She stopped and turned, her brows furrowed with wariness. "Yeah?"

"I guess it's probably a good idea if I know how to get in touch with you." He cracked a smile, hoping she'd lighten up.

No such luck. Her gaze dropped away from him to the floor as she nibbled at her bottom lip. "Oh, yeah. Um, of course," she mumbled, pulling her cell from her back pocket. "Give me your number. I'll text you, and then, you'll have mine."

As he rattled off the ten digits, her fingers flew over the touchpad. "Okay." She slapped the phone back in her jeans and started walking away.

"Wait." A flicker of annoyance made his voice just a little sharper than he intended. He could see this tiny gal becoming a big source of frustration. "Your number?"

"Like I said, I'll text you." She turned once more, and from her clenched jaw and the extra gear she put into her footsteps as she left, there'd be no stopping her this time.

Chase let out a puzzled sigh. If she forgot to text, he could track her down. That designer, Maryanne, seemed more than willing to get him whatever he needed. Almost too much so, but he wasn't complaining. Not yet, anyway. It was nice having someone who seemed to want to help. Unlike a certain CTO he'd just met...

Autumn slipped through the exit door, and he turned away. No, that wasn't entirely accurate. She *did* say she'd text, so it wasn't as if she were trying to ditch him or resisted giving him help. She was just intriguingly prickly about it. He grinned, remembering how she'd compared him to a gremlin. She's a feisty one, all right. He looked forward to learning exactly why.

****

The humid wind pulled and tugged at Autumn's

hair as she sped along the quiet two-lane blacktop toward home. Having the top down on her convertible tended to twist the curly blonde strands into a yarn ball of disaster, but at the moment, her hair was the last thing on her mind.

What a week. Usually, the drive home from work helped her unwind, but not today. Her shoulders tensed as her fingers gripped the wheel. Damn that Chase Durand.

For the millionth time that day, her thoughts strayed toward the hot-bodied artist, and for the millionth time, a surge of heat swept through her. Why she reacted that way toward him was one of the world's great mysteries. She should be annoyed. Seriously, what a horn dog. She'd seen his eyes going all dark back at the restaurant when his gaze flicked over her face and breasts and then down to her feet. Probably thought he was checking her out on the sly, but not much slipped past her. Typical guy, thinking only about T&A. *Except...*

She pumped the brakes to allow an ambling, brown lizard to safely cross the road. She wanted to assume Chase was just an average, mainstream guy, thinking of her as nothing more than the sum of her sex parts like so many jerks she'd dealt with in the past. Hard as she tried, though, it didn't seem to add up with him.

He was on to Maryanne for one thing. The officious, self-important vibes coming off the interior designer had bugged Autumn from day one; Chase seemed to feel the same. She had to admit, she kinda liked the way he'd sent Maryanne on her way once Autumn had showed up.

Straight ahead, light from the lamppost outside her

home burned like a beacon to welcome her back. She pulled a sharp right off the road and onto the paved driveway. Lots of people just used gravel, but when it came to her home, Autumn was picky. It had taken ages to save up to pave the drive, and even though it was only a small, two-bedroom bungalow, it was all hers.

She raised the top before shutting off the engine. The forecast called for rain, and she didn't want to come outside tomorrow to find the sports car converted to a bathtub. As she stepped on the walkway to the front door, she could see two eyes, a wet nose, and a lolling tongue peeking out at her through the window. She grinned as she pulled the keys from her purse and stuck them in the lock. As soon as she pushed open the door, an avalanche of black and brown fur came barreling toward her at full speed.

"Hey, Beau! Did you miss me?"

The Bernese Mountain Dog responded with a full-on assault of wet kisses and a swiftly wagging tail, the joy of his welcome like greeting a long-lost friend. Autumn laughed as she pet and patted her super-happy dog.

Once she'd finally untangled herself, she and Beau walked through the living room toward the back door, and she let him out into the yard. As he rollicked and sniffed, she went into the kitchen, filled his food bowl with kibble, and then stuck her head in the fridge, rooting around for dinner possibilities. A half bottle of hot sauce, a jar of strawberry jam, and milk past the expiration date glared back at her. Shit.

Once again, she'd spaced on going to the grocery store, and now, she paid the price. Her stomach growled, reminding her that the paltry turkey sandwich she'd downed at lunch had been over six hours ago. The couple slices of bread that Pat had given her and Chase to taste test weren't exactly a meal, either.

Heaving a sigh, she let the refrigerator door swing shut as she made her way down the hall. First order of business was changing into sweats and a T-shirt; then she'd figure out dinner.

Her coal-black cat, Zipdrive, turned up his purring motor as she entered her bedroom. He'd been parked in his usual spot atop her pillow; now, he stretched and yawned as she stroked his silky fur.

"Hello, handsome Zip," she cooed, smiling as he arched his back against her hand. She'd always loved animals, comforted by their unconditional devotion. The furry creatures she'd cared for as a kid had often been the only love she'd ever had. *Sure as hell didn't get anything from Nancy.*

Memories of her uncaring foster mother sent Autumn's thoughts tumbling into a black hole. Quick as lightning, she yanked them back out. She'd wasted way too many hours of her life thinking about that heartless cretin and was determined not to waste one second more.

She threw on her sweats and sat down at her desk, lifting the lid on her laptop. Zip jumped up to take his rightful place on top of her thighs. As she scratched beneath his chin, she idly wondered whether Chase liked animals. *Damn.* She shook her head and let out a snort. *I just can't seem to shake him.*

Was it because he'd called her a lady? Autumn frowned, staring at the screen. She'd resisted the compliment, but a warm buzz now flowed through her when she thought about what he'd said. For the first time that she could remember, someone had seen right through her prickly exterior and spotted her soft side. The part of herself she kept hidden from everyone. Until now.

A sick knot suddenly twisted her gut as she recalled something else Chase had said. Something that he hadn't known would unleash a shitstorm of bad memories with his casual mention of those two little words. *Las Vegas.*

Her cell buzzed on the table scattering the memories. For now. She picked it up, smiling at the text message from Pat.

I need details.

As if. Autumn's fingers tapped out a quick reply. *There aren't any.*

Seconds later, another text from Pat. *Cough it up about the artist. I won't feed you until you do.*

Artist. *Chase.* Oh damn, she was supposed to text him, too.

She sat back in her chair, chewing her bottom lip. Giving out personal information had never been her strong suit, even if it was only work. It had taken three months after she'd started at White Ibis for her to give Pat her cell even though they'd immediately clicked. Autumn had needed to decide for herself that the chef was cool, and she had taken her time doing it. Never again would she rush into trusting anyone—ever. She'd paid for it and then some more than once. And yet after only a day, she was supposed to give up the goods to Chase.

Her stomach grumbled again. Pushing thoughts of the required text to the back burner, she decided to indulge and picked up the phone to call for pizza.

Pepperoni, mushrooms, onions, extra cheese. Order placed, she got up to let Beau back inside, but the thought of that text pricked her mind like a biting mosquito. Dinner wouldn't be there for twenty more minutes. Plenty of time to take care of it.

After she let her dog in, she sat back down at her desk. She fired off a quick response to Pat, telling her she'd give her a call later. Now for the next one.

She tapped on the icon, hit the symbol to compose a new message, and pulled up Chase's name. She touched the box to begin writing, and it was if a giant eraser had swooped down and wiped her mind clean. No thoughts, no ideas—she couldn't think of a thing. The blinking cursor stared at her, taunting, the pulses a relentless reminder that she needed to type something. *Anything.* Her fingers refused to comply.

Damn it. What was the matter with her? She sent texts all the time. They were short, simple, easy ways to communicate. She loved them, actually. Fun to send, fun to receive—like a gift. But for the first time ever, she was seized with text block, unable to come up with a single word. *Why?*

Had Chase's Las Vegas reference paralyzed her? He had no way of knowing the images he'd put in her head. *Kinda similar to the dancing fountains at the Bellagio Hotel in Vegas. Know what I mean?*

She'd known what he meant all right, though wished like hell she hadn't. Vegas held nothing but a toxic fusion of bad memories sprinkled with fear. She tried reminding herself of how young she'd been, how she'd thought she'd been doing good. How she'd wanted so desperately to please. Lessons learned came at a high price.

A warm face nudged at her leg, and idly, her hand slid down to pet Beau's furry head while she considered her text to Chase. Finally she decided just to send him a greeting, nothing else. That was the whole point, right? For him to know how to reach her. She nodded to herself. Yep, this was the way to go. She pressed send just as her doorbell rang.

Beau trotted happily by her side as she rose to answer the door, and the comforting aroma of pepperoni and garlic drifted around her like a cloud of reassurance that all was right with the world. She paid the delivery kid, set the box down on her coffee table, then rooted around in the fridge to grab grated Parmesan and a diet soda.

Just as she made her way back to the table, her phone beeped and buzzed with her text tones. She froze in her tracks, knowing without seeing that the message was from Chase.

So what if it is? He's probably just acknowledging your text to him. She drifted over to the desk and picked up the phone.

Evening, Miss Rivette. Thanks for remembering the text. How's your Friday night going?

Her heart lurched in her chest. He was prying, and prying people made her uneasy. She grabbed a slice of pizza, slid it onto a plate, and flicked on the TV. Flipping through channels wasn't enough distraction, 'cause her thoughts kept returning to the text. Not answering was her usual response when people tried to insert themselves into her life. He'd get the message, all right. It was better all around if she just kept to her life, and he kept to his.

But was the man just being polite?

A gentle woof echoed beside her. She glanced down at Beau as he made googly eyes at the pizza.

"This isn't good for you, my man," she told him. "But I'll get you a treat later. It's rude not to share."

Hmm. Maybe she'd inadvertently just come up with her answer. Don't be rude. Share. They had to work together, after all. Might as well be civil. She grabbed the phone.

I'm eating pizza.

A minute ticked by, then two. His reply didn't come, and she breathed a sigh of disap—*no*. Relief. She breathed a sigh of relief.

Her phone buzzed. Relief ended.

So am I.

A flush of warmth flowed through her body like the gooey, hot cheese on her pizza. She set down her food and put a hand to her chest, slowly releasing air from her lungs. She'd always had a pragmatic approach to matters that troubled her, whether business or personal, practical or emotional. She was the type of person to consider angles, contemplate reactions. She wanted to know what made things tick, including herself. So why the curious physical response to his text?

She picked up her phone, and just reading the message again gave her a milder version of what she'd experienced a minute ago. There was something...intimate about it. As if he were there with her. Yeah, that's what it was. They were eating the same food at the same time. Virtually, having dinner together. And she was blushing like a schoolgirl.

For cripe's sake. She needed to shut this down and shut it down fast. Chase Durand was like a beetle boring into her head and messing with her mind. She had to shake him loose.

She typed: *See you Monday.*

She sent the text and silenced her phone. If only she could as easily silence her thoughts.

****

Sunshine streamed through the break room window where just outside, a chorus of chickadees, warblers, sparrows, and robins filled the air with song. *Don't know what they have to be so cheerful about on a Monday.* Autumn grumbled to herself as she waded through the flood of emails on her phone. The work never ended. It would take her half the day just to read all this stuff and then—

"Earth to Autumn."

She looked up to see a grinning Roberto snapping a finger to get her attention, his white teeth flashing against deeply tanned skin. He swiped a hand across his forehead to push aside a lock of hair, then devoured another giant bite of his sandwich while muttering something incomprehensible around the mouthful of food.

Autumn frowned. "He needs a what?"

"A Powerscope. At least, that's what he called it." Her chief networking engineer shrugged as he stuffed the remains of his sandwich in his mouth and swiped a napkin across his face. He pushed away from the table in the break room and stood up. "It's some kind of hydraulic lift. Durand says we'll need it for installing the larger pieces that go near the ceiling."

"And Facilities isn't handling because...?"

"I guess there's some kind of sequenced lighting that goes along with it. It's supposed to be operated

39

from a main control station. The lights go in time with some music or something like that. So we have to write code for it."

"This is going to take a shit-ton of time that we don't have," Autumn grumbled. "I can't believe we're just hearing about this now."

Roberto deep-sixed his sandwich wrapping into the trash and headed for the door. "So go talk to Maryanne. Or maybe Durand himself. Probably he didn't tell anyone early enough. People never think about that stuff. They just leave it up to us to figure out." He swung open the door and swished a hand through the air in a wave. "Later."

Autumn leaned forward in her chair as she sipped her coffee, her body humming with pent-up tension. The installation itself was slated to start in only a few weeks, and the code for the music programming and rotational platforms had to be completed beforehand. She could ask one of her guys to do it, but they were all buried to their ears in work. Besides, she was the best and fastest coder among them all. Her speedy coding was what had gotten her into so much trouble back in Vegas.

She finished her coffee and headed out of the break room. Time for a little chat with Mr. Artist.

It took some doing to locate Chase, but she finally found him in the main ballroom. It was a versatile space that could be opened up to span nearly fifty yards, or it could be easily sectioned off with sliding panel doors. Hanging in the middle of the space would be an enormous, glass-blown chandelier. Chase and Maryanne stood just below where the structure was being installed.

"The armature isn't strong enough. And it's too short." Chase pointed to the long metal framework hanging from the ceiling to which the individual glass pieces would be attached.

"Really?" Maryanne raised one perfectly plucked eyebrow. "I believe we brought in exactly what you stated in your requirements. It should work."

"*Should* being the operative word," Chase said. "And that's not good enough. If my requirements had been followed in the first place, we wouldn't be having this problem." He gestured to the installers, who'd been waiting around for instruction. "I need this down, guys."

"Oh, but Chase, hold on." Tremors of panic clung to Maryanne's words. "That really isn't necessary. It's exactly what you asked for; I'm quite sure."

"And I'm quite sure it isn't," Chase countered, still directing the workers. "'Cause if it were, it'd be longer and stronger." He cast Maryanne an irritated glance. "Trying to save some money on a cheaper one?"

"Of course not!" Maryanne's cheeks flushed pink. "We wouldn't think of it. You need what you need."

"Exactly." Chase must have spotted Autumn standing a few feet away, because a smile touched his lips, transforming his face from mild irritation to something almost like...delight. His green eyes fixed on her, lingering as the smile widened.

A curl of liquid heat unfurled through Autumn's belly. She broke contact and glanced toward Maryanne, suddenly embarrassed.

Maryanne's lips tightened to a hard, thin crease like a slash mark across her face. "Did you need something, Autumn? We're rather busy here as you can see."

"Actually, I can see, thanks. But I'm busy, too, and time's wasting. I need to talk to both of you."

Chase immediately abandoned his directives to the installation crew and stepped toward her, narrowing the distance between them.

"You want to talk over there?" He cocked his head toward an empty table and some folding chairs.

It would be a good place, except Autumn couldn't stomach the thought of Maryanne joining them. She'd just ask what she needed and get out of there.

Autumn shook her head. "Nah. I only have a couple of questions. Here's good."

Maryanne joined them. "What is it that you want?"

Autumn met only Chase's steady gaze. "You told me some of your art's going to be sequenced with light and music for a show, right?"

"Yep. With the project that's outside where the restaurant dining will be."

"It's a very sophisticated, elegant project," Maryanne chirped.

With epic restraint, Autumn managed not to roll her eyes. Instead, she turned her body just slightly, allowing her to face Chase more directly and shifting her back toward Maryanne.

"I need to know exactly how you envision the show," she told Chase, "because I'll have to write code for the computer to operate the light and music sequencing."

"Sure, I figured," Chase said, brows furrowed with apparent confusion, "which is why I gave Maryanne the—"

"I have the specs, Autumn." Maryanne plastered on

her signature, tight smile as she walked around to stand in front of Autumn. "I just haven't had a chance to give them to you yet."

Autumn sighed. Why the interior designer had it out for her, she had no idea, but she wasn't going to let her or anyone prevent her from doing her job.

"I need them today, Maryanne. The code takes awhile to write, then we have to test it. Call Liesel and have her get them to me if you're...you know...too busy."

The interior designer bristled, standing straighter as her eyes flashed. "I thought you were a fast coder. That's what everyone says, anyway."

"I am," Autumn assured her coolly. "Which is the only reason this project isn't already royally screwed."

Chase made a choking noise, and Autumn's gaze flicked that way. He put a fist in front of his mouth as if to cover a cough, but damned if she didn't see him holding back a wide grin.

"Tell Liesel she can call me on my cell when she has those specs," Autumn continued. "I'll be around. No matter what, I need them today."

Maryanne's lips parted like she was probably going to spew out some other BS.

Unable to take any more, Autumn turned on her heel and walked away, her strides long and purposeful to aid in her quick escape. Behind her, the click of heels tapped on the marble floor, but she didn't chance a look behind her. No point in risking saying something to Maryanne that she'd later regret.

"Autumn, hold up," a male, gravelly voice said.

Hmmm. The dampened thud of a guy's motorcycle boots followed behind her. That's not who she thought would be following. A quiver of excitement shot down her spine. She stopped and turned around.

A few quick strides of those hunky muscled legs and Chase stood two feet away. His black T-shirt was damp from the heat and clinging like a shadow to his powerful chest. As he stood before her, he stuffed his hands in his jean pockets, the casual movement causing a ripple along his mammoth biceps.

"We should talk." A light sheen of sweat coated his brow; a faint scent of leather drifted off his skin. Maybe it was from his motorcycle jacket, which he probably wore every day.

Autumn remembered how it had been casually draped over his forearm, the black leather soft and worn in. What would his jacket feel like if she were straddled behind him on his bike, wind in her hair, her cheek pressed against that buttery, black leather, her arms wrapped around that rock-hard stomach...

Cripes. She pushed aside the fantasy. What was the matter with her? Without warning, she was suddenly off in leather la-la land with its owner standing right in front of her.

"Ah..." She fumbled to recall his question, licking her suddenly dry lips. "Sure, we can talk. I need to understand exactly what you want to do with that lighting. It might take me awhile to write the code, and I—"

"Should we grab a beer?" He swiped a hand across his forehead. "It's hotter than hell in here, and I could sure use a cold one. It's close enough to happy hour, right?"

Ooooh. Autumn hesitated. "Bad Idea" radar kicked into high gear. With the way Mr. Artist made her body rev like that big ol' Harley of his, disaster seemed right around the bend. Still, with the sweltering temps outside, a cold beer sounded like heaven in a bottle. Maybe just one...

"C'mon. Follow me in that little sports car of yours. I know just the place." He seemed to take her lack of response as assent and headed toward the door.

Autumn gazed after him, the view from behind more than she could resist. Man-oh-man, the way those jeans clung to his nice tight ass... Her heartbeat thudded against her chest like a heavy metal drummer on steroids. *This wasn't good.*

Chapter Four

The whip hissed through the air, a soft whir like that of cicadas, landing with a sharp crack against Maryanne's quivering buttocks. Her lips parted as she moaned in response. "Oh yes. Another one, Master. Please. I'm begging."

"You'll do a lot more than beg before I'm done with the likes of you." Master chuckled, strutting about the room as he slapped the wooden whip handle against his palm. Maryanne waited on hands and knees on top of the bed, and as he passed in front of her, she obediently dropped her gaze to the duvet cover.

Interesting choice of color and pattern. The mauve tones match the drapes. She wondered who the interior designer was, even considered a few possibilities, before she realized with a start that she needed to pull herself together. Her "Master" had just said something, and she hadn't a clue what it was. *Focus*, she ordered herself. *You don't want him thinking you're anything but his docile, obedient slave.*

"Answer me, you worthless whore!"

Oh, right. He likes the dirty talk. She repressed a sigh. "I...my Master is far too smart, and I don't understand. As you wisely pointed out, I'm nothing but a worthless whore."

"It's all you'll ever be," he growled. "But at least you know your place." He walked around the bed to stand in front of her, thrusting his hips forward like a male revue dancer in the middle of his act. "Look at your Master."

She raised her head to gaze up at his bloated face, noting the red splotches dashed across his cheeks, a frequent occurrence whenever he drank gin. His tiny eyes, obscured by folds of puffy flesh, were further hidden behind the thick lenses of his glasses. He padded closer toward her, his leathery feet—mercifully—hidden in black socks.

"Suck."

A wave of disgust rolled over her, and for a moment, she hesitated, wishing she could hit the pause button. She'd been with him many times before and knew exactly what needed to be done to get what she wanted. Yet how long would she have to go through this? She supposed it didn't matter. For the sake of her career, she'd do anything.

She expelled a soft sigh and leaned forward, gripping his zipper with her teeth, just as he liked. With practiced skill, she smoothly slid it down, then used her hands to finish undressing him. Once he stood naked before her, she resumed her position on hands and knees and took his limp dick into her mouth, swirling her tongue around the warm flesh as it hardened.

He gasped and placed his hand against the back of her head, driving himself deeper. She relaxed her throat and took him in, rustling up a few choking noises for the sake of his ego.

As she set about her task, her mind drifted. What time was it? She needed to get back to the office pretty soon, or someone might start asking where she was. Not that she really had to answer to anyone as long as she got the job done. Still. If she had any chance of landing that multi-hotel assignment, she needed to be visible. Damn, if he would just hurry up and come...

She lifted one hand and slipped it behind him, softly caressing his buttocks while she quickened her pace on his cock. He grunted, a sure sign he was getting close. Only one thing left to do to make him pop. With one finger, she dug between his butt cheeks, ignoring the soft flabbiness of the skin. She circled his anus, giving him a signal of what she was about to do. He widened his stance, so she plunged in.

"Ah!"

She looked up to see his mouth drop open as he flung his head back. "Do it, whore. Harder!"

For Pete's sake, the whore moniker was getting old. With grim determination, she drove her finger in deeper and massaged his prostate. Seconds later, warm spurts filled her mouth while "Master" howled at the moon.

He slumped to sit at the foot of the bed, and she switched positions so she could scoot down to the edge and sit beside him. For the moment, "whore" was retired.

As he sought to calm down, his labored breaths whistled against her cheek. "Damn, woman. You're *goooood*." He grinned at her, a look of pure satisfaction shining in his eyes.

"You know it," she replied crisply, already pushing herself off the bed to gather her clothes.

He huffed in protest. "You're not leaving already?"

"Have to." Without hesitation, she slid on her stockings.

"But I was hoping you'd stay for a second round."

His voice had risen like a petulant child's. Too bad there were no parents around to shut him up.

She walked over to the bed, obligingly sitting beside him once more. "You know I'd love to linger," she purred, leaning over to teasingly swipe her tongue along his neck, "but duty calls."

He closed his eyes, putty in her hands. "My God, Maryanne. What you do to me..."

"There's more where that came from," she promised. Standing again, she finished dressing and glanced in the mirror on the wall, fluffing her hair.

"Has the financing been approved for the multi-city proposal?" She kept her voice casual but saw from her own reflection the steely determination shining in her eyes.

"Not yet." The soft click of a lighter echoed behind her, and seconds later a rising plume of smoke filled the mirror. "The contract's held up."

She turned to face him, frowning. "Why?"

"Concern over saturation in some of the markets is giving pause to a few investors." He lay naked and sprawling on the bed, his doughy flesh spread like a beach sunning walrus as he puffed on a thick cigar. Maryanne repressed a shudder and turned back around.

"I assume you're doing something to get them on board," she said, not masking the sharp edge to her tone. He wasn't getting her body for free; his influence was her payment.

"Of course, of course. I just haven't had time to—"

"Then make time. I want that deal finalized."

"I know, baby cakes. Just give me a little more leeway. There are a lot of players involved."

She knew the placating tone in his voice. It crept in

whenever he sensed her impatience—which was a lot. But it grated on her like nails on a chalkboard. Plus, his nicknames needed work. From whore to baby cakes. It made her ears nauseous.

Revulsion toward him suddenly took over, and she couldn't bear to be in the room for even another second. Grabbing her purse from the nightstand, she fished out her keys and slung the strap over her shoulder.

"If it were anyone but you looking out for me, Mason, I'd be concerned," she assured him. "But a hotshot lawyer like you is going to make sure that deal is finalized just the way we discussed. I know I don't have a thing to worry about."

She blew him a kiss from the palm of her hand as she gave him a final look of goodbye.

She imagined if he were to gaze into her eyes, he'd find them filled with ice chips, but she didn't care. Let him see her frostiness. He knew what he had to do if he ever wanted another piece of the best ass in town. Without a backward glance, she walked out the door.

****

The smooth surface of the koi pond rippled from the swish of a fish's tail as it glided just beneath the water, the orange a beautiful contrast to the lush green surroundings. Autumn took a long sip from her bottle of chilled beer and decided she really ought to get out more. This place was beautiful. Her gaze scanned the clusters of water lilies bobbing on top of the pond, the perimeter surrounded by varieties of plants and grasses swaying softly in the late afternoon breeze.

A bar set right in the middle of a Japanese garden. Of all things. It was close to the hotel, too, about twenty minutes away.

"Is this place okay?" Chase's gravelly voice rumbled as he settled in his chair.

"Yeah. I like it," she said. "Didn't know it was here."

"Now you do." He finished his beer and flashed a signal to the waitress to bring two more, then shifted in his chair to face Autumn more directly. "I come here a fair amount. It's a good place to think and get ideas."

"For your art, you mean?"

"Yeah. Nature inspires me. I like to incorporate it as much as possible into my glasswork."

The waitress arrived with two fresh beers and whisked away the empties. They drank in silence for a minute or two. Autumn was surprised that the lack of conversation didn't make her feel awkward. She'd never been a fan of small talk, which was probably why she mostly kept to herself. But the silence seemed to suit Chase just fine. Although his massive frame filled the space of the chair, he seemed comfortable as he settled back, his fingers lightly gripped around the bottle.

She studied his handsome profile as he looked into the koi pond, transfixed by the way the sunshine highlighted streaks of gold in his dark hair. She'd never noticed that before, maybe because until now, she hadn't seen him outdoors. His hair looked so soft. What would it be like to run her fingers through it, to feel the dark strands against her skin?

Autumn slammed down that way of thinking. She sure as hell didn't need to be sticking her toes into those murky waters. What would happen if she ended up getting involved with him?

The thought alone set off her "Trust No One"

alarm bells. People talked and spread rumors, especially if there was something to be gained. As a rule, Autumn ignored gossip, but not everyone played the same way. If that busybody Maryanne, for example, found out Autumn was hooked up with Chase, who knows what she might—

"Something bothering you?" He'd turned to her, eyebrows lifted with curiosity.

She sat back in her chair and shook her head. "Nah. Nothing." She took a swig of her beer, assuming he'd fill her in on why he'd asked the question, but he kept quiet. Finally, she added, "Why?"

"No reason in particular, except you started frowning a minute ago. I figure it's gotta be caused by something." One side of his mouth lifted in a grin. "I'm clever that way."

Autumn couldn't help but smile. There was something so honest and genuine about Chase. He didn't try to put on airs, and aside from a little work talk, he seemed to have no ulterior motive for asking her out for a beer other than to just sit and have a beer. Inch by slow inch, she felt herself relax.

Before she could stop herself, she said, "I was wondering. When you...when you say you're inspired by nature, are you talking about trees and plants, or do you mean wildlife, or what?"

He looked at her oddly for a moment, and discomfort seized her. Damn, had she just asked the world's lamest question? Warmth burned her cheeks. She should stick with what she knew—coding, algorithms, connectivity. She had no idea about any of this arty-farty stuff. She waved a hand. "Forget it, I just—"

"Why?" He gave an easy smile. "It's a good question; I've just never been asked it before." His gaze drifted once more to the koi pond, and he pointed a finger toward the water where several fish had gathered beneath a cluster of water lilies.

"You see those koi there?" As she nodded, he continued, "I've studied their movement dozens of times. The way they glide through the water is fascinating, how it's so effortless and beautiful. That's what I try to capture in my art, not so much an exact replica of what I see, but more a representation of how it makes me feel." He turned back with calm curiosity. "Does that answer the question?"

It answered the first question, but ten others sprang to mind. Unexpectedly, she found herself wanting more—more information, more details, more knowledge about him. Where had he learned his craft? What had intrigued him about glassmaking in the first place? What else inspired his art? Where was his studio? Would he show it to her?

Whoa. *Stop it, Autumn! Stop thinking about making this personal. You know it would be a big mistake. No, not big. Huge.* Yet for all the inner scolding, her curiosity kept growing.

"I guess I've never met an artist before." She shrugged. "So I, you know, was just curious."

His expression shifted, the previous calm replaced with heightened awareness. Setting his beer on the table between them, he leaned forward in his chair, his dark gaze flickering to her lips before lingering on her eyes. "Let me satisfy your curiosity." His voice dropped low.

The atmosphere between them was transformed, a metamorphosis from casual conversation to unspoken desire. Her gaze drifted to his sensual, full mouth, his lips slightly parted like they were about to taste something sweet. How easy to imagine that it was her mouth he was after, her lips he would taste. Slow pulses throbbed low in her core, and a patch of slick moisture dampened her panties. She released a soft breath, savoring the thought of his kiss until warning bells pealed in her mind and busted in on her mental trip to crazy town.

She leaned back in her seat. "No, I—"

"You're refusing an invitation before you even know what it is?"

True. But it couldn't be anything good, right? It was probably something she shouldn't want. "Well, I guess I…" Damn, what was he doing to her? She was fumbling over her words, all flustered like some teenager with her first serious crush.

"You said it would help you in your job to know what I'm doing, and on top of it, you expressed curiosity. Do you know how many people actually bother asking about my creative process? What I think about when I make my art?"

She shook her head.

"Hardly anyone," he said quietly, a note of hurt beneath the words. "But I'm flattered that you have, and I want to do something I think you'd enjoy."

Curiosity got the best of her. "Which is…?"

He rose from his chair and held out his hand to her. "I'd like to show you my studio."

Chapter Five

Autumn followed his motorcycle for over ten miles, the road winding through areas of dense bayou saturated with giant cypress trees. Clumps of Spanish moss draped over their branches like thousands of silver shawls. Images of the huge trees reflected in the pea-green bayou water where shore birds seeking dinner plucked at the mud. Thick humidity clogged the air as the sultry temperature stubbornly refused to back down.

A trickle of sweat slid down her temple. She brushed it away and glanced at her watch. She really should have headed back to the hotel after their impromptu happy hour. She'd told Maryanne earlier that she needed the specs for Chase's show today so she could begin writing the code, yet here she was, paying a visit to his art studio. Her common sense had abandoned its post—but shivers of excitement crept in to take its place.

At last, Chase signaled for a turn off the road, and a minute later, they pulled in front of a low, brick building. Autumn killed the engine and stepped out of her car, holding up a hand to shield her eyes from the sun as she looked around.

To her left, Chase swung his nicely toned right leg over his bike and kicked out the stand to park it. He slid a thumb beneath his helmet, undid the strap, and pulled it off his head, revealing sexily disheveled, chestnut hair just brushing the top of his shoulders.

Autumn's breath caught in her throat. She stared as if she'd ingested a paralyzing drug that made it impossible to look away. A slow burn of desire flickered low in her groin. Holy hell. Thankfully, she somehow shook off the spell and saved her dignity, tearing away her gaze before getting busted by Chase.

His boots crunched the gravel as he made his way over. "So. What do you think?"

Her brain was stuck. Thoughts refused to form because they were nailed to the intoxicating scent of leather drifting her way. *Damnit, brain. Work.* "I think it looks like a brick building," she finally managed. A half smile tugged at her lips. "I'm clever that way."

He laughed. "Between the two of us, we'll set the world on fire." Nodding toward the building, he added, "And speaking of fire, let me show you some." He led the way, pulling the door open for her to step in ahead of him.

The space was open, loft-like without dividing walls to define the areas. Low wooden tables, pock-marked and scarred from years of use, were set up front. Finished glass work of every kind from vases, bottles, and water pitchers to more decorative items like flowers and paperweights were set along the tables.

"The studio up front is for retail sales," Chase explained, weaving his way through the tables toward what looked like a huge oven. "Helps me pay for this place. I create everyday items for customers along with the bigger pieces that are installed as art."

They walked toward the back of the space where the oven was set into a brick wall. The closer they got, the higher the temperature soared. If it was hot outside, it was an inferno in the back of Chase's studio. The trickles of sweat running down Autumn's face turned into rivers. Her blouse clung to her back, unpleasantly sticking like a wet shower curtain against her skin.

"Whew," she breathed.

"That's most people's reaction." Chase grinned. "You gotta build up a tolerance to the heat if you want to be in this business. No getting around it."

"Like a chef."

"Like a chef," he agreed. "Except they don't work with two-thousand-degree heat."

Autumn's mouth dropped open. "Two *thousand* degrees?"

"Hold on. Let me show you."

Thick, stone slabs serving as doors blocked the oven's opening. Chase grasped a handle allowing him to part them and reveal an almost-blinding whiteness inside. Searing heat, hotter than anything Autumn had ever felt, poured from the opening and surrounded them like breath from the devil himself. A rushing sound of wind filled her ears.

"This is the furnace," Chase explained. "It stays at a constant temperature of two thousand degrees and keeps the glass in liquid form."

Autumn stepped closer, peering inside the furnace. Her eyes adjusted to the light, revealing a large stone vat brimming with molten glass. Beneath it, fire roared. That had been what she'd heard before, the rush of fire so strong it sounded like a hurricane.

Chase stood next to her, his close proximity shooting the temperature even higher. But this heat was internal, melting Autumn's insides the way the furnace fire melted glass. A hyper awareness of his presence took root and grew. His leather scent. His commanding height. Despite the heat a shiver raced down her spine. She imagined the ease with which he could pick her up and overpower her, do to her whatever he wished…and how the image alone quickened her pulse. She was unable to ignore it or cast it aside. Nor did she want to.

As she glanced up at Chase, their gazes locked just for a moment, until at last, he looked away.

"So," he began, his gravelly voice a few notches lower, "let me show you how it works." He walked over to where several long, steel rods were anchored to the wall on a rack like cue sticks. Selecting one of them, he held it in both hands. "This is called a punty."

She eyed it up and down, frowning. "I thought it would be hollow. For the air."

"This one's used to gather the molten glass from the furnace. If I'm making a piece where I need to blow air into it, I transfer the glass from the punty to the blowpipe." He cocked his head toward the furnace. "C'mon. I'll show you."

Together, they walked over, and Chase parted the heavy doors. Again, the roar of the fire filled the room, and shimmering waves of heat blasted forth.

Chase nodded toward the vat of glass. "It's so bright inside that it's tough to see when your punty is actually in the vat. That's why you have to use the reflection."

"What do you mean?"

With an easy, practiced move, Chase positioned the long, steel rod above the vat. "You see where I'm holding this?"

Autumn nodded.

"Now, look down at the vat. There's a faint shadow

over the glass. Do you see it?"

She didn't at first, but then Chase moved the steel rod just a bit, enough for her to finally catch the reflection. "Oh yeah," she said. "Now I do."

"It's faint, but it's there. Okay, now I'll gather some glass." He dipped the tip of the punty in the vat and in only seconds had a glob of clear glass on the end of the rod. Swiftly, he withdrew it from the furnace while turning.

"Watch yourself," he cautioned, putting distance between himself and Autumn. His strong, skillful fingers turned the steel rod as the clear glass transformed from the consistency of honey to something thicker, like tar.

Chase seated himself at a wooden chair with two metal armrests mounted on each side. He rested the long punty on top of the armrests and slowly rolled it back and forth. "This is the basis for everything we make," he explained, his sexy, sea-green eyes easily shifting back and forth between the glass and Autumn.

Her breath stuck fast, transfixed by his gaze, but she forced her focus to remain on what he was doing. "Why do you have to keep turning the rod?" she asked, throat dry.

"To keep the glass centered. Otherwise, it'll drip right off." The corner of his lip turned up in a grin. "Watch."

He stopped rolling the punty, and sure enough, the glass drooped down like a thick dollop of lava hanging off the edge of a cliff. Chase resumed rolling the device on the armrests, and the glass reformed into a ball.

"At this point, I'd begin working it with a block," he explained, "but the glass is too cool, so I need to reheat it."

Autumn stepped back, assuming Chase was headed toward the furnace.

"Not there." He nodded toward what looked like a different furnace, except this one was smaller. In front of the door was a stand the same height as the furnace doors.

"I rest my punty on this stand, which is called a yoke." He looked at her with a straight face, but she swore she saw a twinkle in his eye. "And then all I need to do is slide it into the glory hole."

"The glory...*what?*" She coughed, and she heard Chase chuckling as she choked.

"I generally get that reaction."

Autumn narrowed her gaze. "So you're making that up?"

"*Noooo.*" He shook his head. "Believe me, if it were called something else, I'd tell you. But this is the glory hole. The temperature inside is kept at around fourteen hundred degrees, and it's for reheating the glass. This is pretty much the glassmaker's best friend." He turned the punty as he reheated the glass in the glory hole before sliding it out. Then he took his seat back at the bench. "In this business, you get to be real close with your glory hole."

She swore he was saying that to get a reaction out of her, but despite the lightness in his tone, his studied expression as he worked the glass showed that he wasn't messing with her; he was just telling it like it was.

The effortless, almost delicate, movement of Chase's hands fascinated her as he gently rolled the punty across the metal armrests. He handled the steel rod with a lightness that stood in stark contrast to the large size of his hands, yet the movement was as fluid as the glass itself. All at once, her thoughts shifted, and she imagined those same large hands on her body, stroking her skin, sliding down her arms, over her breasts, across her stomach, caressing her with the same easy touch he used while working glass.

"Now I'll use the block," he said, his voice an intruder breaking into her sensual thoughts.

Willing herself to focus, she ignored the heat between her thighs and the spot of wetness dampening her panties.

Chase reached behind him to a table on which rested a bucket filled with water and what looked like a large, wooden scoop. "This is the block," he explained, pulling the scoop out of the water. "It helps me shape the glass."

He placed the rounded ball of molten glass into the scoop part of the block. Immediately, it hissed and steamed as the hot, liquid glass came in contact with the water. Chase held the block against the glass, shaping it as he liked. When he'd done what he could, he rose from the chair, reheated the glass in the glory hole, then returned to the bench, rolling and shaping.

"I keep at this process until I have the glass the way I want," he explained, "then I build by adding more glass to the end of the punty or by transferring what I have onto a blowpipe."

"And then you blow?" *Holy hell.* Autumn felt the burn on her cheeks. She glanced at Chase, who did nothing to hide his amusement.

"Yeah," he said, white teeth flashing as he grinned like a Cheshire cat, "that's when I blow." He stood up.

"You want to see?"

"I…no," she mumbled. "That's okay."

"Next time," Chase said, and Autumn was alarmed by the flush of warmth through her veins at the prospect of being with him here again. *Next time.*

"For now, let's have you at least try the punty."

Her gaze flashed up. "Me? No, no. I don't need—"

"I know you don't *need* to. But give it a try. I think you'll enjoy it."

Before she could protest, Chase retrieved a punty from the rack and handed it to her. With no choice, she took it.

It was heavier than she realized but easy enough to balance once she figured out the way to hold it.

"Grab it toward the end," Chase explained. "You want to be as far away from the heat as possible while still being able to see the punty's reflection in the molten glass."

She adjusted her hands in response.

"Looking good," Chase said, checking her hold on the punty. "Now, let's get some glass."

He walked beside her to the furnace, dwarfing her with his massive height. As he parted the oven doors, heat blasted forth, and the roar of the fire whooshed through her ears.

"Stick your punty in and gather some glass."

Autumn guided the steel rod through the doors, slowly lowering it into the vat.

"Look for the reflection," Chase reminded her. "That's when you'll know you've touched the glass."

She did as instructed, inserting just the tip into the vat, excitement chasing nerves as an unexpected desire to please her teacher took hold.

"Remember to keep turning."

In seconds, she'd gathered a dollop of glass and was turning the rod, but somehow, she wasn't doing it right. *Damn.* The glass was flopping and drooping around, not forming a smooth round ball as it had for Chase.

"I can't seem to get this glass to behave."

"Be a little quicker with your turns," Chase urged.

The glass kept giving her fits. "It doesn't like me."

"It likes you just fine," he said. "But glass is like a woman. Temperamental."

"Excuse me?"

"Relax," he said, his calm steady voice close to her ear. He'd shifted positions and stood behind her. "It's a compliment."

She was suddenly flooded with heat, not from the furnace or the glass but from Chase himself. He bent down, reaching around her waist and placing his hands on hers, guiding her in properly turning the punty.

"Like this," he said easily, his deep voice rumbling sensually in her ear. His warm breath flowed like a summer breeze as his hard body molded around hers, his strong arms an immovable snare from which she surprisingly felt no need to escape. In fact, just the opposite.

Shivery jolts of pleasure raced down her spine as her back came in contact with his steely abs and chest. She was seized with a sudden urge to sink into him, to let her head fall back and invite him to kiss her neck, to sample and taste her fevered skin.

Just in time, she caught the small moan that threatened to escape her lips. Her breath hitched in her throat, and she fumbled with the punty, nearly dropping it. Luckily, Chase was there as back-up.

"Careful," he cautioned, "or your glass will drop off. Just keep the steady motion."

His warm hands still covered hers, guiding her to turn the steel rod, over and over in slow, hypnotic movement. Beads of sweat dotted Autumn's brow. Her breathing reduced to shallow pants. The calluses on his hands brushed over her knuckles, the rough surface glaring contrast to the smoothness of hers. *How would those hands feel on her breasts*? It had been a long time—maybe even never—since a man had made her so hot and sweaty and filled with lust that she nearly begged for him to start peeling off her clothes.

"Keep turning," he urged, his voice deeper. Huskier.

Autumn closed her eyes, savoring the sensation of being in a scorching hot room with a scorching hot guy pressed up against her.

Chase shifted his stance, his pelvis aligning with her ass, and suddenly, his stiff cock pressed hard against his jeans. And…well, hel-*lo*.

Walk forward; step away from him. Her logical mind issued the order; her stubborn body refused to obey. Instead, the rebel in her roared to life, and she leaned harder against the unyielding bulge.

The sharp hiss of Chase's breath mimicked the steamy sizzle of the molten glass meeting the wet block. He faltered with the punty, and it clattered to the ground.

They stood in place, unmoving, the only sound around them the rumble of fire. Then Chase's hands settled on Autumn's shoulders. He slowly slid them along her arms, his calloused palms rough against her smooth, bare skin. When he reached her hands, his caress backtracked upward along her forearm and upper arm, branding her with the fire of his touch.

Desire sizzled along her skin where he made contact. His palms skated across her shoulders, his fingertips tracing a path along the sides of her neck, lingering as gently as air against her cheeks. As if with a will of their own, her eyes fell shut as she leaned into him.

With soft lips, he dotted a trail of kisses against her neck, hot and moist.

More. She wanted more. With a tilt of her head to grant him easier access, the invitation was issued—and accepted. Warm breath drifted against her skin as his kisses grew fevered. More urgent. With the tip of his tongue, he licked the sensitive skin around her ear and gently scraped his teeth against her earlobe. She shivered, feeling the hairs rise on the back of her neck.

A groan escaped her lips as she stroked her palms along his slick forearms. The roar of her heartbeat mingled with the thunderous whoosh of fire in the glass melting furnace.

Suddenly, Chase's grip on her shoulders tightened as he abruptly turned her around to face him.

His eyes had transformed from sea green to inky black, the dilated pupils smoldering with desire. He cupped her cheeks and tilted her face upward.

Time stopped, the moment frozen, anticipation for his kiss almost more than she could bear. Her shaking knees struggled to hold her up. A loud groan rumbled in her ears, and she realized it came from Chase just before he leaned down to capture her lips.

His kiss was hot, impatient, his tongue parting her

lips and slipping into her mouth. She rose up on her toes and kissed him back, her eager tongue meeting his in wet exploration. With both arms, she reached around his waist to pull his solid, muscled body tighter to hers. A jolt of lust shot straight to her pussy as his hard cock pressed against her abdomen.

His hands slid through the thick tangle of her pinned up hair, and the up-do came cascading down, bobby pins raining against the concrete floor as her mass of spiral blonde curls tumbled down her back.

Without breaking the kiss, he changed gears and shifted attention to the front of her blouse. As his hand slid down to cup her breast, Autumn couldn't prevent the small groan that escaped her lips. Despite having on a cotton blouse and bra, the material was no match against the scorching heat of Chase's fingers as he caressed her nipple through the fabric.

Moaning into his mouth, she pressed her breast against his hand, willing him to stroke harder. The force of her own reaction surprised her, but she held nothing back. Her free-spirited nature had sometimes gotten her into trouble, but she sure as shit wasn't worrying about that when Chase's sexy moves were blowing her mind.

Cool air rushed in as he slipped his hand beneath her blouse. His fingers burned a path as he skated them across her trembling stomach and up toward her breasts.

Unhook the bra. If only Chase could read her mind. Flashing images of being naked with him, of rolling around on a giant bed while she rocked against—

"Ooooh…" Those magical fingers of his, making delicious, shivery circles around her sensitive breasts. She squirmed against him, all but begging him to stop teasing and pay attention to *everything*.

With a quick arch of her back, her breast filling the palm of his hand, and at last she had what she wanted. Playful fingers rolled her stiff nipples, firmly tugging, causing a surge of pure lust to shoot straight to her pussy as her clit throbbed. Hungry for more, she rocked her pelvis against the hard mound between his legs.

"My God…Autumn." His gravelly voice rumbled as he kissed and sucked her lips.

In a single quick motion, he shoved her bra up, pushing the restrictive material fully out of the way so his hand was free to roam. He stroked and teased and pinched, and a flood of desire, like monsoon rain, rushed through her body. The delicious onslaught of pleasure-pain was overwhelming, making her whimper aloud. Pulses throbbed deep in her core, becoming faster, more insistent. The ache was impossible to ignore, and she was vaguely aware of her hips starting to sway.

If only we were naked. If only we were naked. The naughty mantra echoed through her mind as she panted against Chase's hot, wet kisses.

The temperature in the room soared, scorching the air. Rivulets of sweat coursed between her breasts as Chase's palm glided over her slick skin. Her hands dropped to his waist, and she eased them beneath his shirt.

Sweat coated every inch of him, his damp T-shirt clinging like plastic wrap. Working briskly to get what she wanted, her fingers peeled away the material. It felt like opening the world's most erotic gift. Every breathtaking swell of muscle was hers to explore, from washboard abs to the mountain of chest, and *oh,* *yum!...*behind him to the tight mound of his ass.

Chase dragged his mind-blowing kisses along her neck, easing down to the soft indentation at her collarbone. With the tip of his tongue, he gently probed at the hollow, and her pussy walls flooded.

Desperate as a cat in heat, she ground her hips against the hard bulge in his jeans, needing something, *anything,* to soothe the ache. She groaned as he pinched her nipple—hard. *Mmmm. Sooo* good.

With growing urgency, she shoved up his T-shirt so she could feast on his hot, sweaty skin. She kissed the laddered muscles of his abs, his salty taste clinging to her lips. As she licked his pebbled nipple and gently sucked it between her lips, he drew in a quick breath. Boldly, she slipped a wayward hand down outside his jeans to caress the irresistible swell of his delicious cock.

He groaned. "Autumn, maybe we should—"

"Hell*ooo*! Anybody home?" A female voice sang out from the front of the studio near the entrance.

With lightning fast reflexes, Autumn shoved her blouse down and jumped away from Chase. She retreated close to the glory hole with shaky knees.

He softly grumbled beneath his breath, "Fuck."

A second female voice piped up, "I don't know if anyone's here, Patty."

"Be there in a minute," Chase called out before looking over at Autumn. "You all right?"

She shrugged. "Of course."

"I'm sorry we were inter—" His gaze roamed over her curls.

Autumn narrowed her eyes. "What?"

"Nothing. It's just...Wow. I never noticed how

long your hair is. You always have it up."

"So?"

He grinned. "Autumn, it's another compliment."

He eyes dropped to the floor. "Oh."

He took a step forward and peered behind her. "My God, it's all the way down your back." With a light, airy touch, he lifted a strand between his thumb and forefinger. "And soft as silk," he murmured, tilting up her chin to look into her eyes. "So beautiful."

Her cheeks burned. Chase's open ways unsettled her. Men she knew…well, they were always so cryptic. She never knew what the hell they were thinking—and usually it turned out better that she hadn't. They kept her from confirming what lying assholes they could be.

But Chase…well, he seemed different. For one, he totally saw through Maryanne. Her attempts to win him over through phony flattery smelled exactly like the BS it was. And two, Chase just out and out said what was on his mind without trying to hide it or gloss things over. She usually didn't trust people like that. Well, not that she trusted anyone. For some reason, though, she tended to think he was being honest.

Careful, Autumn. You know what can happen when you let your guard down. The warning echoed in her mind, reminding her of past mistakes, mistakes she never wanted to repeat.

"Yeah, okay. Well, I gotta go."

He nodded, looking down at himself to make sure his clothes were straightened. "Me, too. Listen, do you want to—"

"Later." She raised a hand in a quick wave as she headed for the front door.

It had sounded like maybe he was going to extend

an invitation, ask her if they wanted to continue their sensual tongue dance somewhere more private than the middle of his art studio. And that would be a really bad idea. Best to get away as fast as possible and block out the truth…she *did* want to continue.

As she pulled the door firmly closed behind her, a strong breeze gusted, blowing back her hair, flapping against her clothes, and clearing anxious thoughts from her mind. She quickly formulated a plan, realizing that what was needed was hitting the reset button. Chase Durand with his hot body and melty kisses were chipping gouges into her self-protective guardrail. So all she had to do was to avoid the source of the problem. Steer clear of Chase, wait until the hotel opens and he leaves, and presto! Normal life returns.

She slid into the leather seat of her car and turned the ignition key. As she pulled away from Chase's studio and onto the back highway leading home, it struck her that it wasn't so much the lure of his divine body that was her main problem. No. If it was only that, she could deal with it. Her main issue was the easy and dangerous way he'd started burrowing into her thoughts and taking her down the Road of Trust. Making her forget that survival in this world meant never letting people in or paying a steep price if you do. Her foster dad knew all about that—and as a result, so did she.

She gunned the engine and picked up speed, letting the wind blow away those thoughts and reminding her of the plan. Steer clear of Chase. That's all she had to do. It would be easy.

Chapter Six

Marcel, the makeup artist, stood back and pressed a forefinger against his pursed lips and the tip of his nose. He studied Chase, scrutinizing every angle of his face through narrowed eyes.

"*Non*," he declared, a soft noise of disapproval clicking in the back of his throat. He stepped forward, dabbing a sponge across Chase's forehead with the precision of a pastry chef adding final touches to a wedding cake masterpiece.

Chase grumbled "Is this really necessary?"

"*Absolument.*" Whipping out a giant powder puff, Marcel pressed it against Chase's face to set the foundation. Chase rolled his eyes but held still, praying for strength to get through this torture.

"How fantastic!" The effusive, high-pitched praise was the calling card of a single source—Maryanne.

"Marcel, he looks perfect. I love the way you've highlighted his gorgeous eyes." She beamed at the makeup artist as together they examined Chase like patrons assessing art in a gallery.

Chase rose from his chair. "I'm outta here."

Maryanne gave a shriek of alarm. "Wait, you can't—"

"Can and will. No more screwing around, Maryanne." Chase glanced up at the wall clock. "I gave you an hour for this photo shoot. Forty-five minutes of it is gone. Do the math. If you want pictures, you'd better get a move on."

Her eyes widened in alarm. "Well, but—"

"Fourteen minutes."

She flew off like a panicked bird, yelling orders to get the set ready.

One of Chase's larger sculptures twisting with colorful, sinuous swirls of glass meant to evoke images of a beautiful woman had been strategically positioned next to a waterfall in the garden room. He would be standing next to it, the sexy artist and his sexy sculpture, the photo spread used for promoting the hotel as a sensual, romantic getaway for couples. It would be featured in an upcoming issue of *Whitepaper*, the hotel's internal magazine that would be given to every guest who stayed at the White Ibis. It would splash Chase's name around to thousands of visitors while promoting the hotel.

He'd agreed to do it as part of his contract, but that didn't mean they could take the hour-long commitment and turn it in to half a day. Truth was, he'd give them more time than an hour, but he didn't see the need to broadcast his intentions to Maryanne. Not yet, anyway.

As people raced to and fro getting everything set up, Chase's gaze drifted around the hotel as it had every day for the past week, hoping for a glimpse of Autumn. So far, nothing. Ever since they'd gone to his art studio and shared that red-hot kiss, she'd been like a ghost. He literally hadn't seen her. Not once.

For the hundredth time, his mind drifted back to that moment. He hadn't meant for it to happen, hadn't been planning on it whatsoever. He'd wanted to show her the studio, because she'd expressed an interest in his art. Honestly, he'd been flattered. It's not as if he'd never been complimented.

But Autumn's curiosity extended beyond telling him nice things. She'd actually been interested in the process of creating the art and not just in admiring the final product. It was, he imagined, like someone praising a writer for the techniques of the prose rather than just the telling of a good tale.

So yeah, he'd wanted to show her how it was done. He knew they'd be alone, and he was attracted to her. But Autumn kept a damn high wall around her, and he had no intention of breaching it. It would come down in its own good time if that's what was meant to happen.

But *oooooh baby*. He went hard just thinking about her soft, wet lips and the way she'd kissed his chest, licking his sweat like a fine wine. Her small hand had caressed his junk through his jeans in just the right way until he'd very nearly shoved her up against the wall and taken her for a long, hot ride. If only they hadn't been interrupted…

He let out a long breath. Maybe it was good that it had stopped where it had. Autumn turned him on, no doubt. From that one kiss, Chase could tell she'd set his world on fire. She had passion in her perfectly in synch with his own. He knew himself and wasn't afraid to admit that if he met the right one, he had it in him to fall hard.

But Autumn was different. Something in her past put her on guard before she even learned a person's name. Falling for her could be step one to heartbreak city. Plus, having a thing between them didn't make sense. They had jobs to do, and the timeframe was tight. Going down a path with Autumn was probably a really bad idea. Still…

"We're ready!" Maryanne's voice drilled into his ears, and he looked toward her. She waved wildly like a person stranded on an island spotting an overhead plane. "Over here!"

Chase walked to where the full crew awaited him. A large white screen had been placed behind the art sculpture, and a black "x" made with electrician's tape marked the floor.

Maryanne nodded at the spot. "That's where we need you to stand. But first, Jean Claude has to primp your hair."

"He has to *what*?" Chase didn't bother softening his tone.

"It will take but a moment, *monsieur*. 'ave a seat." A Marcel look-alike, scarecrow thin, his posture as erect as a ruler, flicked at Chase's hair with a huge, round brush.

"Maryanne, what the hell—"

"*S'il vous plaît.* Do not speak." Jean Claude frowned and pursed his lips. "I must examine your mane without interruption."

"Just putting on the final touches, Chase." Maryanne leaned forward toward his ear, no doubt on purpose, so that a gap in her blouse gave him an eyeful of her bought breasts.

"Remember," her minty breath whispered in his ear, "you're going to be a star!"

Before he had a chance to reply, a whirring noise filled the air. He steered his gaze around Maryanne to where the photographer was waiting beside a giant, humming fan.

"Don't think we need that," he said to Maryanne.

"It's plenty cool in here."

"It's not for the temperature, Chase. It's for—"

"Hold steady, *monsieur,*" Jean Claude demanded, lips tightly pressed in annoyance.

Chase darted his gaze at Maryanne, who had joined the photographer. "It's for my what?"

A cloud of aerosol filled the room as Jean Claude waved a can of hair spray with exaggerated flourishes.

"*Voilà!*" Jean Claude flung off the cape like a bull fighter in the ring. "*Absolument parfait.*"

Chase jumped to his feet. He strode to Maryanne, using his height to full advantage as he towered before her. "You got five minutes," he growled, his patience ground to dust.

"But Chase we'll need at least—"

"And someone turn off that damn fan." His gaze whipped around the room, trying to pin down an ally to help him out.

No one moved. Finally, the photographer, a whip-thin man decked out in leather pants and a white linen shirt gestured to the floor. "I'm Davey Stobbin, Mr. Durand. If you could step onto the "x" on the floor, we'll get started."

Chase cursed under his breath but did as he was asked. The sooner they got going, the sooner they'd be done. He turned to face the front where the photographer waited. As soon as he did so, the blast of wind from the fan whipped his hair around.

"Damnit, what—"

"A little more from the fan!" Davey called out, and quick as lightning, a young helper darted forth and flipped the dial to high. A gush of air blasted out, making Chase's hair blow back like he was walking in a sandstorm. His shirt and pants flapped against his skin.

"Amazing! Sexy! Just the look I want. Now stand closer to the artwork, Mr. Durand, and let's see some of those pearly whites!"

He'd give 'em pearly whites, all right. Chase let loose a string of curses beneath his breath but grudgingly did as asked, just wanting it over.

The photographer clicked away, snapping hundreds of pictures in a matter of minutes, ordering Chase to turn this way and that, exclaiming all the while how "amazing" Chase looked.

Finally, Davey put the camera down, and relieved, Chase made ready to leave. It turned out to be a false alarm.

"Get the green shirt," the photographer said, and a woman Chase hadn't noticed jumped up as if shot from a canon and hurried over.

"If you'll follow me, Mr. Durand," she said, giving his arm a gentle tug to guide him toward an area off to the side, "we'll just get you changed."

"Changed?"

"To the first of the different outfits."

He stopped cold in his tracks and turned back around. "What the hell is this, Maryanne?"

She rushed to his side, lips flared in a giant smile. "Just a costume change."

"I didn't agree—"

"You did actually." Like a magician pulling a bunny from a hat, Maryanne yanked from her oversized handbag a copy of the contract and stabbed at a line with her red-tipped nail. "It's right here," she said sweetly, batting her eyelashes, "in the 'Personal

Appearances' section."

He didn't bother looking to where she pointed. No doubt what she said was true. Score one for Maryanne. "Fine. But you're technically running over time."

"Please, just a little more—"

"I walk out in five, whether or not you're done."

The smile faltered but held. "Five minutes," she agreed with a tight nod. "Get him ready, Tiffany."

"Yes, ma'am."

Thirty seconds later, Chase was changed into a green, linen shirt speckled with tiny white dots. He looked and felt ridiculous. Jean Claude and Marcel rushed forward like warriors, their armor an assortment of hairbrushes and powder puffs. Like excited poodles, they yapped to no one in particular in a stream of frenzied French as they flicked and dabbed their tools at Chase. Tiffany flitted over and began tugging at the buttons on his shirt. Before he knew it, they were open to halfway down his chest.

He frowned. "Hey, what—"

"Finish up, people!" Davey Stobbin bellowed, unleashing a torrent of protestations from all involved.

Jean Claude spewed forth a mammoth cloud of hair spray, Marcel swished his powder, Tiffany jerked at his shirt, the fan blew everything everywhere, and just as Chase was about to tell them all to get the hell out of his sight, he glanced over toward the entryway. A lone figure stood in the doorway, mouth agape, one hand holding her side as the other swiped at tears of laughter pouring down her cheeks.

Autumn. Holy hell.

Chase rose from the chair, sending workers scurrying, and walked over to Autumn. Despite the insanity of the situation, his desire to see her kicked his pride to the back seat.

"Hey," he said softly.

She looked good. No, great. Her eyes shone with amusement, and her beautiful, pink lips couldn't stop smiling. His mind flashed back to the last time he'd seen those lips, covering his body with kisses. A bullet of lust shot straight to his cock.

"Hey, yourself," she said as her gaze flicked over his green, dotted shirt. "Don't let me interrupt."

"You're not interrupting me; you're saving me." He lowered his voice and leaned down so he could get close to her ear. "You gotta get me out of here."

It sounded like he was begging. Maybe he was. Or maybe, he just wanted to keep seeing her smile.

As he straightened, Autumn's grin grew wide once more.

"We're waiting for you, Chase!" Maryanne's voice pierced the air.

He glanced back, rolling his eyes, then faced Autumn again. "You need me for something, don't you?" he asked her. "A question on the code, maybe? Or to carry your coffee? Shine your shoes?"

Autumn looked about to answer him when the photographer approached. "We can get you out of here as quick as you want, Mr. Durand," he said, "but we do need a few more pictures." Noticing Autumn, he thrust a hand forward. "Davey Stobbin."

"Autumn Rivette."

Davey glanced at Chase. "Your girlfriend's a knock-out."

"Oh, she's not my—"

"You know..." Davey's eyes lit with excitement.

"We could use her in the shoot. She's beautiful and so tiny. And this is a promo for couples, anyway. Tempting them to book their next romantic getaway at the White Ibis. The contrast between you two would be amazing!"

"Oh, no. No way…" Autumn slowly backed from the scene like a traveler who'd just encountered a wild animal.

Davey paid no attention. Rushing back to the shooting area, he said, "Tiffany, grab that crushed velvet jacket, the one that no one can ever fit into."

Autumn cast her panicked gaze at Chase. "I'm outta here."

"No, wait. Autumn." If he had to spend a minute more alone in this ridiculous situation, he'd start smashing his own sculptures. He needed someone from the real world to save him from this insane one.

She hesitated just for a moment.

Bending forward so he could speak softly in her ear, he said in a rush, "You want someone at your beck and call twenty-four seven, you got it. A servant for life. My undying gratitude. Anything. I just—"

"I don't need any of that."

"Then tell me what you *do* need. It's yours. But for now, please…" He stepped back to see her face, wanting to show her his sincerity by looking into her eyes. "Stay."

****

He wants me to stay. Blistering heat roared through Autumn's veins. She stood as if bolted in place, emotionally torn as her logical side screamed at her to run. But another, equally insistent voice urged to her to do the very opposite. To stay.

79

A gust from the blowing fan whipped the top of Chase's shirt open, giving her a glimpse of his hard, sculpted pecs. Her mouth went dry as thoughts flicked back to Chase's art studio, to the fire, to the glass, and most of all, to that bone-melting kiss, the one she hadn't been able to get out of her mind for over a week. The kiss that had kept her awake with an ache in her core and sexy thoughts about how Chase could soothe it…thoughts she shouldn't be having.

After that kiss, she'd sworn to herself that she'd put some distance between herself and him. Let the heat cool down and common sense return. But now, the very man she'd vowed to avoid stood before her, looking into her eyes, wanting her to stay. With him. Her blood pulsed. The idea of sitting for a photo shoot was as appealing as having teeth drilled. But being with Chase…

She shrugged. Then she nodded.

His smile lit the room. "Thank you," he mouthed.

Autumn was whisked away by attentive Tiffany, who held a blue, velvet blazer draped over one arm.

"We have a private space back here where we can get you changed," Tiffany said as they reached an area just beyond the shoot setup marked off by curtains. Tiffany parted them. "It's no surprise Davey noticed you."

Amber raised a brow as she ducked through the parted curtains. "Oh?"

"Sure. Davey likes contrasts, which is why he's drawn to seeing Mr. Durand paired with someone so small. Davey also likes contrast in outfits. We'll pair this velvet blazer with the skinny jeans you're already wearing. It'll be so dope!"

Minutes later, Autumn emerged from the changing space like a chrysalis from its cocoon, transformed from everyday IT worker to someone she hardly recognized. She caught a glimpse of herself in the mirror as she walked over to where Chase waited. Dressed in a velvet blazer and peep toe pumps, with her long hair down and her face brushed with more makeup than she generally wore, she felt as if she'd undergone a metamorphosis.

At first, Chase only stared, his gaze taking her in as she approached. A low whistle escaped beneath his breath, and she couldn't deny the flush of pleasure zinging along her skin. Guys found her pretty enough, she supposed, but to have a man simply stop and stare with wide-eyed appreciation at her looks…well, that was entirely something else. Especially since the staring guy happened to be drop-dead gorgeous himself.

"Autumn?" A female voice laced with irritation doused her fun like rain at a picnic. "What are you doing here?"

Autumn looked over at Maryanne's frowning face. "I was asked."

"By whom, exactly? It certainly wasn't me." Her head whipped around the shoot area. "Who asked this girl to be here?" she shrieked, drilling the gathered group with an icy stare. "I don't think we need—"

"I asked her." Chase narrowed his gaze at the designer. "So did Davey."

Quick as lightning, Maryanne switched into flattery mode. "But Chase, you're the star of the show, the one everyone wants to see. It's really not—"

"Let's get moving," Davey yelled. "Chase, Autumn. Back over to the 'x.' Face each other.

Autumn, darlin', get that gorgeous hair behind you so we can see your pretty face. Now look up at Chase." Once satisfied, he began to shoot, maintaining a constant stream of praise as he snapped away.

Autumn's initial sense of awkwardness eased as seconds ticked by. In most of the shots, she and Chase were positioned close to one another. He smiled and kept up a steady stream of conversation, speaking softly enough so that only she could hear as the camera clicked.

"Stand behind Autumn," Davey instructed Chase, "with your hands placed lightly on her shoulders."

"You look incredible," Chase murmured as he took the position.

Warmth from his hands penetrated the velvet blazer. The last time she'd been like this with Chase, he'd stood behind her to teach her about the glass. His familiar leather smell drifted over to her now, immediately transporting her back to his studio. Memory flooded her. His crushing strength as he held her in his arms. The way his fingers trailed over her sweat slicked skin and teased her aching nipples. How she'd pressed into him, shamelessly rocking against the bulge of his cock. Her knees suddenly felt far less steady than they had a moment ago.

Almost as if he could sense her thoughts, Chase's hands slid down her arms and around her waist, gently holding her against his body. He said nothing, but the hitch of his ragged breath whistled past her ear. Her heart made an odd little flip in her chest. She wasn't the only one affected by their closeness.

"Perfect, Chase," Davey praised. "In fact, let's get some heat between you two." He snapped his fingers, and like a magical fairy, Tiffany appeared. "Position them in the 'Sultry Desire' pose, Tiff," Davey instructed. "Like that perfume ad we shot."

Tiffany rushed over and inserted herself between Autumn and Chase. "Let me just show you where to put your hands on her body by using myself as a prop," she said.

Pinprick arrows laced with annoyance and...*jealousy?* No, that couldn't be. Autumn shoved the thought aside and stepped away, but Tiffany stopped her from going far.

"Watch how I'm positioning myself. That's what we're gonna want you to do."

Without hesitation, Tiffany worked the buttons on Chase's shirt until she had them all undone, and the shirt fell open. "You'll need to lose this," she instructed, already pushing at the sleeves.

As Chase shrugged off the shirt, the last drop of moisture in Autumn's mouth evaporated as her gaze glued to his athletic perfection. She had felt that beautiful torso, had slipped her hands beneath his shirt and taken herself on a pleasure voyage, her fingertips sailing over the dips and curves of his rock-hard muscles. But until now, she hadn't actually *seen* his body. And holy smacks, what she'd been missing.

Tiffany draped one arm across the top of Chase's bare, broad shoulder. "Like this with your left arm," Tiffany said, "and with your right, place your palm against his left pec. But kind of spread your fingers a little bit—like this—so his nipple isn't fully blocked."

Autumn's gaze followed where Tiffany's fingers led, until it came to a screeching halt as she took in the stunning, black-and-grey artwork covering both of his massive biceps. Ink swirled around one in a complex tribal pattern of flames, no doubt to represent his art.

On the other was the most realistic wolf tattoo she'd ever seen. The artist's talent stopped her heart, making her feel like she stood in the cold snow right beside the magnificent animal, hearing his forlorn howl as he bayed at the full moon.

As if feeling her penetrating stare, Chase turned and met her gaze, his carved muscles rippling as he moved—pecs and lats and abs...*oh my.*

Her nipples stiffened beneath her blouse as her breath rushed from her lungs. Taking in his sculpted perfection and the flawless vee from shoulder to waist, a flash flood of lust submerged her. What would those marbled muscles feel like, pressing her down hard on a mattress? Or up against a wall? She swallowed as trickles of sweat rolled lazily between her breasts. *Damn this velvet jacket to hell.*

"Maybe we should get into place so we can get this over with?" Chase's low voice reeled her back to reality.

Autumn blinked, scattering those naughty thoughts. "Yeah. Um, okay."

"Stand here," Tiffany ordered, grabbing Autumn's wrist and positioning her in place. "Left arm draped over his shoulder, right hand on his chest."

Autumn reached up and up, trying to do what was asked, but Chase's towering height and her vertical challenge made it tough.

"What the hell is this?" Davey marched over, boot heels rapping against the marble floor. He glanced at Autumn, then turned toward Tiffany. "Really, Tiff? She looks like she's straining to reach something on the top shelf at the grocery store."

"You said 'Sultry Desire' pose, so—"

"I pay you to think. So far, you're not."

Tiffany blew out a breath of frustration. "Fine. Then how about…" She and Davey turned away to discuss what to do.

Autumn gave up trying to drape her arm over Chase's shoulder, instead standing quietly beside him as they waited for instructions. The heat from his mammoth body, his unique scent, that impossibly perfect ladder of abs right in front of her… She had to admit, they made for a damn fine way to spend the time.

"Thanks for doing this," he said, the rumble of his low voice catching her ear. "'Specially since you seem to be lovin' it exactly as little as I do."

She shrugged. "I've had worse."

"Like?"

"Got my finger slammed in a car door once."

"Ah." He nodded. "That's got its own place in hell."

A grin lifted her lips. He could relate. Nice. "Sounds like you've been there."

"I have. More than once. But you know what's worse?"

"Talk to me."

Chase's expression grew somber. "A dozen bee stings on your ass."

Before she could stop it, her loud bark of laughter ricocheted off the lobby walls. Maryanne's scowl zeroed in on her.

"Now look at the trouble you caused," Chase murmured as they both eyed the pole-stiff interior designer crossing her arms in front of her chest as she raised an irritated brow.

"Me?" Autumn feigned indignation. "You were the one who—"

"Okay, dudes, we're finally ready," Davey said, striding over. He shifted his gaze between Chase and Autumn, nodding like a bobble head doll. "There's some righteous chemistry between you two, and we're gonna capture it. I want sex. I want smolder. You hear what I'm saying? Hot enough to burn the pages in the mag. Tiff will get you into place." He spun on his heel and headed to his camera.

"So." Tiffany clapped her hands once, snapping them to attention. "Autumn needs to be topless."

"What?" Autumn's outrage crackled like gunshot. "No fucking way. I'm outta here." Shoving past Tiffany, she stalked toward the curtain to change back to her work clothes.

Davey's assistant was at her heels. "Autumn, listen."

Autumn didn't even bother looking at her. She pulled off the blazer.

"Davey doesn't want you *naked*," Tiffany wailed. "And he's not asking you to show anything."

"Last I heard, topless meant no top."

"I know, I know. But it's your amazing hair. He wants to use that to cover you up instead of the blazer. Please, Autumn."

Autumn paused. The girl's job was probably on the line if Autumn left. Not that it was her problem. Davey and the rest of them could go to hell as far as she was concerned. But Tiffany was young, trying to make a name for herself in her career. She was only following directions given to her by a guy. Autumn had been there.

She narrowed her eyes at Tiffany. "You got five seconds, or I walk. Tell me what he wants."

"You have no top, just the skinny jeans and heels. We'll give you flesh-colored pasties, no prob. But we also use your hair to cover your breasts. It's so long and those beautiful spiral curls…it would totally camouflage you except for tiny bits of skin showing through, like your arms or sides. Nothing you don't want. It'll be so sexy. Teasing, you know? And Chase will be positioned right in front of you, leaning over as if he's just about to kiss you. His lips will be hovering right near yours, and…"

Autumn didn't hear the rest, because her mind had already filled in the details. Chase. His body. His sexier-than-thou mouth almost—but not quite—kissing her.

Before even realizing it, she nodded agreement. "Fine. I'll do it."

Tiffany's shoulders slumped, and a heavy sigh whistled through her lips. "Thank God. I mean, thank *you*."

What the hell was she thinking? Autumn couldn't believe she was about to do this, but she wouldn't go back on her word. And anyway, her mind kept flashing to that promised image of Chase's mouth, lingering right near hers.

Tiffany arranged Autumn's hair so it covered her breasts. Despite questioning her sanity, when she caught her image in the full-length mirror, she had to admit that the result was…sexy. She'd never felt like that before. Her petite stature usually made her identify more with *The Wonderful Wizard of Oz* Munchkin than femme fatale, but this whole topless-but-covered thing put her in a different light.

Chase's eyes went coal-black as he whistled below his breath. "Holy. Living. Hell," he rumbled as she stood before him. "I think my pants just caught fire."

"What are you talking about?"

"From the scorching hot woman standing in front of me."

She rolled her eyes, hoping it masked the warmth creeping up her cheeks. "Aren't you Mr. Cool with the lines."

"Just calling it like I'm seeing it."

Sharp staccato raps of stiletto heels striking the marble floor drew their attention. Maryanne's eyes blazed like a possessed demon's as she pressed her lips together so tightly they were nearly swallowed by the furious scowl lining her face.

"Davey!" She glared at Autumn. "I'm not at all certain that our objective for the shoot is pornography."

Davey sauntered over, brows furrowed. "It's *art*. It's sexy. Brings customers. It'll be perfect." With deliberate force, he placed a strong arm around Maryanne's shoulder and drew her aside. "And those who matter will recognize it."

Beside her, Chase struggled not to laugh out loud.

Thankfully he was saved by Tiffany. "Okay, let me get you both in place. Chase, if you could move closer in front of Autumn, she'll be able to put her hands in the right place."

He stepped closer, the waves of heat shimmering off his body searing her skin. Again, she caught a trace of his scent, clean and masculine, a combination of shower soap and leather biker jacket.

Davey rattled off instructions. "Autumn, wrap your left arm around Chase's waist and put your hand on his back. Your right palm should be on his chest. Chase, I want your body touching Autumn's."

Oh, God. So did she. Her hand quivered as she placed it on Chase's rock-hard pec. The thunder of his heartbeat vibrated against her palm, so forcefully it seemed tangible, something she could catch and hold.

Chase leaned in, hunger smoldering in his darkened pupils. She could melt in that gaze, turn to liquid like the molten glass in his studio. Breath caught in her throat.

"Now get close enough to kiss her," Davey told Chase, "but don't quite do it. Autumn, lean back against the sculpture and look up."

As she did so, Chase leaned down, and for a hot second, she thought he was going to plant one. Her heart skipped a beat. Just as Davey had wanted, Chase's mouth was positioned just above hers, lips slightly parted. The draw to kiss him pulled hard, nearly impossible to resist. She wanted that mouth on hers. Wanted to be devoured by him. Crushed by him. Her nipples tightened and became like stone. He was so huge, shadowing her in his towering frame.

His hands rested lightly on her waist, the hardened calluses an exciting contrast against her softer skin. Insistent pulses throbbed in her core, dampening her panties. Her pussy felt heavy. Needy. And the thought of having that throbbing ache soothed by wet, leisurely, swipes of his tongue…*damn.*

She nearly groaned aloud. Seeing Chase again was very, most probably, a really bad idea. Right? Like in his studio, with the fire and the heat and his bruising kiss permanently seared in her mind. It was too distracting. Took her mind off her work and the ruthless deadline they all faced before opening day.

But still.

Although she tried not to go there, for the millionth time her mind raced back to that kiss, a savored treasure, and despite every bit of logic telling her to shut the hell up and stay away, she wanted his company. She wanted his kiss.

Throwing caution to the wind, she whispered in his ear, "Wanna grab a beer after this?"

A slow smile, warm as honey, curled his lips. "You read my mind."

Chapter Seven

Chase's cycle roared down the narrow highway as he twisted hard on the throttle. The moss-draped branches of giant cypress trees waved gently in the breeze. Snowy-white egrets circled the blue sky. The bayou scenery drew thousands of tourists to the area every year to take in the natural beauty. But the only scenery capturing his interest at the moment was the pint-sized pistol in the Mustang ahead of him.

Autumn drove like a bat out of hell, although her muscle car was no match for his hog. He kept her in sight in his rearview mirror but stayed at a respectable distance ahead.

She'd surprised the hell out of him when she suggested they get a beer after the photo shoot. Not that he hadn't been thinking the exact same thing. But Autumn was skittish. He'd wondered more than once about what kind of shit she was carrying around. Someone in the past had seriously messed with her, and it had left a mark. He clenched down on the handlebars, anger zinging through him.

Still, despite whatever happened to her, she'd been bold enough to ask him out for a beer. *Thank God.* Hovering next to her gorgeous, hot body for that photo shoot, her lips right next to his, tempting as sin…*shit.*

He let out a snort. Hopefully, no one at the shoot noticed the stiff wood between his legs while Davey snapped those pics. Damn, Autumn did something to him. That little techie turned his insides to fire with a single glance. And now, they were off to have a beer. And more? His cock twitched.

Up ahead, Autumn slowed as they approached a turnoff where a small, isolated bar was set back from the road with the swamp behind it. The lowering sun glinted off the few parked cars scattered about on a nearby patch of flat grass. Chase drew alongside where Autumn had pulled into a makeshift space, killing her engine. He glanced up at the weathered wooden sign above the door. *Swampland.*

She stepped from her car and cocked her head toward the bar. "This place okay?"

"Sure." He secured his helmet to the back of his bike with a small D-ring lock. They started walking toward the door. "How'd you ever find it to begin with?"

"Um, well." She shrugged. "I live around here, so…"

He nodded but didn't comment, sensing anything he'd say would only make her uncomfortable. She didn't easily give up the goods on her personal life.

Low lighting and wood paneling swallowed them up as they entered. They found two seats at the bar, and Autumn nodded to the long-haired, muscle head who slapped down a couple of coasters.

"'Sup, Autumn," he grunted. "Haven't seen you in awhile. That job's keeping you busy?"

"Busier than a moth in a mitten." She cocked a thumb toward Chase. "This is Chase. That's Nathan."

Chase nodded to the guy. "Good meeting you, man. Let me have a cold one. Whatever you got."

Nathan nodded. "Same as always for you, Autumn?"

"Yep. Thanks."

When he left to get their drinks, Chase shifted in his seat so he could face Autumn more directly. She'd changed back into her street clothes but hadn't bothered to put her hair up again. Its long length streamed down either side of her face and over the tops of her breasts, an instant reminder of the photo shoot.

Sweet hell, she had some of the nicest hair he'd ever seen on any woman. The way it had flowed over her nearly-naked breasts, the nipples teasingly obscured by those tiny pasties... He swallowed a groan as blood rocketed straight to his cock.

"So…" He shifted in his chair as he looked around, surveying the room. Old wood on the floors and walls, a pool table and dartboard toward the back, a few small tables in the farthest corner. "This seems like a cool watering hole."

She nodded. "It is. The people who come here are all locals. I don't think I've ever seen a single tourist, though I guess with the hotel opening, they'll eventually find their way here."

Nathan set beers in front of them. They picked them up, clinked bottles, and took a long pull.

As Chase set his back down, he said, "I'm sure you're right. The good and bad side of the tourists. They bring money to the area, but they also bring themselves."

She smiled slow and easy, and hot damn if seeing her reaction didn't spike his blood with an unexpected burn.

"You lived around here for awhile?" he asked,

redirecting the conversation.

She lifted one shoulder in a kind of half-shrug. "I guess. A few years."

"Where were you before?"

"Oh, you know…still in the same general area. But I rented a room from someone for awhile. Wanted to save up so I could buy."

Whoa. Autumn was voluntarily offering information about herself. Would she give him more? The temptation to find out was impossible to resist, although he reminded himself to proceed with caution. "So you have your own place now?"

A faint smile touched her gorgeous, tempting lips. "Yeah." She took another sip of beer. "What about you?"

Nice parry to this thrust. The usual Autumn has returned to the building. Getting the topic off of her in lightning speed.

"You've actually almost been to my place."

Her head whipped around to face him square on. "What are you talking about?"

"My studio."

"You *live* there, too?" She frowned. "And you didn't tell me because…?"

He held up his hands like a man surrendering. "I wasn't pulling a fast one on you, if that's what you're thinking."

By the way her gaze darted away for a moment, that was precisely what she'd been thinking.

"When I bought my studio," he continued, "I realized there was a second, smaller building behind the main one used primarily for storage by the guy who'd had the space before. I figured, why bother looking for an apartment or house to rent when I could just make the storage my place. So I put in electricity and plumbing, divided up the space into a couple of rooms, installed everything I needed." He shrugged and lifted his beer for another swig. "It works."

Her eyes widened as she whistled low beneath her breath. "You did that all yourself?"

Bartender Nathan set down a bowl of chips in front of them. "Couple more?"

They nodded agreement.

Chase drained his glass. "I kinda had to learn that stuff growing up. Survival, I guess you could say."

"What do you mean?" Autumn grabbed some chips, but her focus never wavered.

"My parents are what people call 'free spirits.' Probably the most unconventional mom and pop you could ever meet. They never were the type to work traditional jobs. Instead, they just sort of walked the Earth, moving around to wherever they could scrape out some kind of living."

"Taking you with them, of course."

"Me and my seven siblings."

"Seven?" She sat back in her chair, eyebrows shot up in surprise as she sipped her beer. "Holy crap."

He chuckled. "We never lacked for company."

"Where are you in order?"

"Oldest." He laughed and helped himself to the chips. "So I got to boss them all around."

Autumn slid back in her chair to re-cross her legs. It afforded him a nice view of her slim, toned thighs, apparent even through the light-blue jeans. *Damn*. His cock thickened and jammed tight against his pants.

"So that's why you know about fixing stuff up,"

she said, "because the places your roaming parents brought you all to weren't the White Ibis type."

He laughed. "More like the shantytown type."

"Seriously?" Concern etched lines across her forehead.

"Sometimes," he admitted. "But don't get the wrong idea. We were really happy."

She drank her beer slowly as if giving herself time to figure out what to say. "Money doesn't necessarily make anyone happy."

"A woman after my parents' own heart." Chase chucked.

"So these free spirit parents," Autumn continued, "did they name you Chase 'cause they were always chasing after you?"

He flashed a smile. "A good guess, but it wasn't me they were chasing. It was freedom. They believed in that more than anything. That's why it's my middle name."

"Your middle…wait, what? Your middle name is Freedom?"

"Chase Freedom Durand, at your service." He lifted his beer and cocked it toward Autumn.

****

Chase. Freedom. Durand.

Autumn shook her head as she leaned back against the bar stool. If that wasn't a name straight from the dreams of a Beatnik couple high on life, she didn't know what was.

She grinned at a mental image of two tie-dyed, T-shirt and jeans wearing twenty-somethings criss-crossing the country and reveling in their freedom—from rules, from biases, from their own inhibitions.

They did whatever they wanted, whenever they wanted to do it. Pretty amazing, as far as she was concerned. Even better—from those happy, peace-loving wanderers came Chase. A hugely talented artist, inspired by nature. Honest. Genuine. Not to mention, hot as hell. Her polar opposite in every way, a magnetic force field that kept drawing her in.

As Chase held the beer bottle to his lips, she noticed the sexy swell of his right bicep. He was built like a tank without an ounce of fat in sight. His arms were cut like granite, his tattoos drawing the eye toward those massive muscles the way a beautifully fitted dress would highlight a woman's curves.

She'd been happily enjoying that hot body next to hers from the minute they had sat down, ignoring the questioning glances from Nathan. The bartender had once asked her out, but to his credit, he had backed off as soon as she made her disinterest clear. She didn't need the complication of any sort of attachment in her life. People in general, even close ones, couldn't be trusted, so why bother? They always ended up burning her.

But then, there was Chase.

Logically, she knew she should keep her distance, but the dude was hotter than a desert sun. Her attraction to him was making her challenge her own "stay away" rule. Truth was, she didn't want to stay away. The kiss in his studio had fueled a fire in her that refused to die. In fact, just the opposite. She wanted to feed it.

The truth stared her down, and she had to own up to it. After all, her own actions were what brought her to the bar now. *She* was the one who'd initiated this. But so what? Having sex with Chase didn't mean her heart had to get involved, only her body. And right now, her body wanted him, big time. On top of her.

Inside her.

The thought tightened her nipples, making them peak beneath her T-shirt. As casually as she could, she flipped her hands beneath her hair, causing some of it to fall in front of her chest. She glanced down. Better.

She finished her second beer but held off ordering another. The effect was kicking in, mellowing her out, breaking down inhibitions. She should shut the hell up before she said something she shouldn't, but the blend of alcohol in her system, and hot guy in front of her didn't work well for keeping quiet. Chase aroused curiosity in her just as he aroused sexual interest.

She took a breath and gave her naughty thoughts a swift kick, refocusing her attention. "So, Chase Freedom Durand. What about your other seven siblings? Are their names just as inspired as yours?"

"You can decide for yourself," he replied casually. "There are five boys, three girls. In descending order of age, my brothers are Wolf, Valor Phoenix, and Zen."

What the hell? Her mouth fell open. Not a Dave or Steve or Bill in sight. Chase's name was the most "normal" of the bunch.

"And my sisters are Indigo, Jade, and Sierra." His faint smile betrayed his amusement.

She shook her head. "You have a brother named Wolf?"

"Conceived when my parents were volunteering at a rehab center for injured wildlife."

"Holy shit," she muttered. "They shared this information with you?"

His gravelly chuckle caused her insides to twist.

"There's little they *didn't* share," he said. "Like I said, free spirits." He drained the last of his beer. "I take it my upbringing was pretty different from yours?"

He'd asked the question innocently enough, but instantly, Autumn's guard shot up, her private internal security fence keeping all priers safely away. But his inquiry felt different, like he really just wanted to get to know her and not use the information for some other purpose. Maybe it would be okay to share something about herself. Nothing big, like Vegas. She wouldn't get all crazy.

"Yeah," she finally said. "Night and day different."

He said nothing, maybe waiting for her to add more.

Surprisingly, she wanted to go on. Not just because he'd shared with her, so she'd return the favor. Not at all. It was because...well...Chase seemed truly, genuinely interested. In her. Wow.

She took a breath and huffed it out, "I don't actually know who my biological parents are. They...um, well it sounds like a joke, but they actually left me wrapped in a blanket outside a fire station when I was only a few days old."

She mentally braced herself, waiting for the little, sympathetic noises people uttered that were meant to comfort but only served to put distance between herself and the sympathy giver.

But Chase just nodded and said, "Foster parents raised you?"

"Yeah."

He tossed some chips into his mouth and crunched away. "Were they cool?"

Like a trailer from a movie called *How Not to*

Raise Your Kids, Autumn's mind flashed through painful memories of—no. Not wanting to remember, her lips tightened as she shook her head. "Rick and Nancy wouldn't exactly be nominated 'Foster Parents of the Year'."

"So." Chase paused, then shrugged, like he'd come to a decision. "You pretty much got served a big ol' plate of the 'Eff-ed Up Childhood Special.' Natural parents abandoned you, foster parents were assholes."

His tone was so matter of fact that she let out a bark of laughter, her shoulders shaking with amusement. She slapped her hand down on the counter as giggles seized her. "Never had anyone put it quite like that," she finally choked out. "But you summed it up. Assholes all around."

Once Autumn's laughter died down, quiet descended between them. She fiddled with her empty bottle, her foot tapping to the country music playing on the jukebox. Quiet voices murmured farther down the bar. A TV flashed occasional light, and barbecued chicken wings scented the air.

Chase's focus stayed one hundred percent on her, and to her surprise, his scrutiny wasn't a turn-off. Maybe because it felt like honest interest instead of prying. He wanted to learn more about her, so he paid close attention. And the more attention he paid her, the more of it she wanted. The more of *him* she wanted.

It was such a shock, a one-eighty pivot from her usual "keep your distance" attitude. But Chase wasn't a usual kind of guy. He took things slow, wasn't forcing her into doing something she didn't want. New territory for sure, scary and exciting at the exact same time.

Something feather-soft and arousing pulled her

focus back to the present. Over the back of her hand and across her knuckles, Chase traced his forefinger in a slow, sensual pattern, the lazy swirls growing wider. Bolder. Her breaths quickened as her heartbeat spiked.

She slid her gaze back to Chase and heard the rush of quickened breath streaming from his lips. He skated his palm along the length of her arm in a sensual touch, cloaked in a challenge—*I'm going to keep touching you unless you stop me*.

Goosebumps dappled her skin as she shivered from his heat. With the time she'd spent daydreaming about him touching her again, no way was she stopping the real thing. She slid her arm closer to his.

His exploration continued, his hand drifting higher, caressing her upper arm, sliding across her shoulder and up into her coiled mass of hair. His fingers wrapped around a fistful of the thick strands, and he gave a sharp, pleasurable tug bringing her head back and exposing her neck to his waiting lips.

The first wet swipe of his tongue against her skin fired a blaze in every zone of her body—her breasts, her nipples, downward across her stomach, rushing like an inferno straight to her pussy. Hot, needy pulses in her core soaked her panties as ragged breaths roared in her ear. She fought the urge to spread her thighs and welcome his touch where she craved it the most.

With a frustrated growl, Chase broke the kiss. As he pulled away, he released a long breath and sat back. A sheen of sweat glistened across his brow. His chest rose and fell as a small muscle twitched at the back of his jaw.

What happened next was up to her. Chase would not push, would not force. But from the smoking-hot kiss he'd just given her, it was clear what they both wanted. Autumn's pulse jumped as she made up her mind.

She cocked her head toward the door. "Let's get outta here."

He paused for the space of a heartbeat, maybe making sure this was what she really wanted.

But she'd made up her mind. He turned her on; she did the same to him. Discussion over.

He slapped some bills on the bar. "Lead the way."

Chapter Eight

Seconds later, they were greeted with a thick gush of humid air as they walked out the door of *Swampland*. Emotion whirled in Autumn's mind like so much debris. Longing. Desire. Burning expectation. She climbed in her car and fired the engine, aware of how *alive* she felt, her body fueled by hot, pulsing anticipation coursing through her veins.

It had been way too long since she'd last had sex. Not that she hadn't had opportunity…she just hadn't felt like answering the door to those who'd come knocking. With Chase, she'd not only answered…she'd flung that door wide open.

Once in her driveway, she killed the engine. She glanced at the garage and for half a second considered asking Chase to park in there. No need for nosy neighbors to see she had company. But nah. Screw it. She had better things to think about, like the smoke show guy climbing off his cycle with whom she was about to get down and dirty.

As she stuck the key in her lock, she shot a glance at the window, where two, chocolate-brown eyes stared back at her. The lolling, pink tongue disappeared as the dog started to growl.

Damn. Beau wasn't used to strangers, and the mountain of a man standing right behind her was a giant threat. She looked back at Chase. "Um…my dog.

He's a little protec—"

Beau's staccato barking drowned her out.

Chase leaned in, shaking his head. "What?"

She raised her voice. "Stay here!"

She opened the door and dashed inside. A hundred pounds of dog immediately toppled her to the ground.

"Beau, stop." Her protests were met with frantic licking. Autumn shielded her face from the tongue and pried herself loose from beneath her dog. "C'mon, boy. Let's get you some kibble in a safe, locked up place."

She walked to the kitchen, dumped food in a bowl, and carried it to the second bedroom that functioned as her office. Puzzled by her unusual behavior but faithful as a saint, Beau dutifully followed. She set down the food.

He stared up at her.

"Eat." She pointed a finger at the bowl and backed away, knowing she had to be quick. Before the canine realized she was making a getaway, she was out and shutting the door behind her.

Trapped in the bedroom, Beau started to whine.

"Stop it!" she commanded. Her order was promptly ignored as the whines turned to howls. A stab of guilt pierced her heart, but she shoved it aside. When a scorching hot man is waiting on her doorstep, a girl's gotta do what a girl's gotta do. Beau would just have to understand.

She returned to the front door and let Chase inside. "Sorry," she said as he walked in. "I had to take care of my dog. He's not used to strangers, so…" She gestured to where Beau was held prisoner. "He'd take a piece outta your thigh until he knew you weren't a threat, so I had to put him in there."

Chase shrugged off his leather jacket and tossed it over a chair. He set his helmet on the table and turned, walking slowly toward her, looming like a shadow, ready to devour.

Her skin tingled, and her breath caught fast in her throat. Shivers of arousal arrowed straight to her pussy as it grew heavy and sweetly throbbed.

He slid a hand behind her neck and grasped a fistful of hair. His gaze never wavered from hers as he pulled at her thick locks, guiding her head back. He bent down, his thumb stroking her nape.

"Your dog's instinct is right." Warm breath blew softly across her cheeks as his lips hovered just above hers. "Because I'm most definitely a threat."

He possessed her with his mouth, his hunger so strong it rocketed through her, searing her blood as he nibbled at her lips, the welcomed pain making her groan. Steel-band arms imprisoned her, driving her against him, the delicious press of his cock firm against her stomach.

She sighed as Chase slipped his tongue inside her mouth, deepening the kiss. Standing became torture as she trembled beneath his assault. Chase's massive size, his drive, his primal reaction to her…he consumed her completely. Dizzy lust caused her head to swim. Thinking was impossible; she reacted only with instinct, refusing to deny her need.

She impatiently yanked his T-shirt from his jeans. The material caught on his belt buckle and she jerked harder, not caring when it ripped. When it was finally out, she slipped her hands beneath it, his hot skin scorching her palms.

"Mmmm." His rumble of approval vibrated against

her lips.

"Need you in my bed," she ordered, guiding her hands around his waist and over his sculpted ass. "Now."

The corner of his lip curved up as he broke the kiss and straightened. "Impatient?"

"Greedy." She took his hand, tugging at him to follow.

She sensed his grin as she pushed open the bedroom door and approached the bed.

"Stop." His sharp command rendered her motionless. "Turn around, Autumn."

She cast a backward glance. He stood behind her, several feet away. "Why?"

"I want to see you."

"But—"

"Naked. On your bed." His gaze roamed over her body; his eyes stained with lust. "Do it."

She didn't do orders, didn't answer to them. Didn't like them. Except... why was her pussy pulsing in response? Why did his command make *her* feel powerful? Like she was the one in charge? She wanted to be told what to do. By Chase.

She tilted a defiant chin toward him as a smile curled her lip. "So you want to see me, do you?"

He nodded, eyes sparkling.

"Nothing comes for free." She kicked off one sandal. "Seems only fair I get something in return." She kicked off the second one.

His gaze zeroed in on her bare feet and popsicle-pink toe polish. "I'll consider it," he said, "if you stop flapping your gums and do exactly what I want." He sat in the chair across from her bed, settling in for a show.

"Take your clothes off. Now."

Her heart stopped. So hot. Since when did she get off on being told what to do? But she wasn't going to question it now, not with a smoldering, turned-on guy sitting right in front of her, needing her naked. She lifted off her T-shirt and tossed it to the floor.

As she crossed her arms behind her back to unhook her bra, Chase shook his head. "Not yet. First your jeans."

Though his words suggested he was in charge, one look at his shallow breathing and the tent in his pants told Autumn the real story. The person running this show sure as hell wasn't Chase.

She tugged at the top button on her jeans and undid the zipper. Then tantalizingly slow, she slid them down and kicked them away, standing before him in her black, lacy bra and panties.

"Holy balls," he whispered.

His reaction made her bold. "You like?"

He nodded.

"So show me."

For half a second, he hesitated, wondering, perhaps, just how this power play had taken a turn. But then he grinned and slid lower in his chair, widening his legs, and sliding his palm over the outline of his cock.

"You see this?"

Oooh yeah. She saw it all right. Nibbling on her bottom lip, she nodded, her heartbeat slamming against her chest. "But I want more," she managed to get out.

"You'll get more." He caressed his length, gliding his palm hypnotically back and forth over that bulge, his rock-hard erection straining against the denim. "You'll get a lot more of this, Autumn. Much as you want." *Back and forth, over and over.* "But not until you're naked."

Abruptly, he scooted back up in his chair and crossed an ankle over his knee. "So get going."

She smiled, hyper aware of the heady rush of pleasure zinging through her veins at how amped up Chase was. For her.

Smoldering passion crackled the air. Autumn reached around, and with a quick flick, unhooked her bra. For a moment, she held the lacy material to her chest, flirting, teasing, drawing out his need. She liked the way his chest heaved, the breaths quick as his fiery gaze roamed her bare skin, lingering around her chest.

With the flair of an experienced stripper, she slowly drew away the material, giving him glances bit by bit of her heavy breasts and stiff nipples. When she finally tossed the bra aside, his sharp hiss filled the room.

Hooking her thumbs beneath her panties, she drew the flimsy silk down her bare legs, letting it drop at her ankles. Kicking the panties away, she stood, fully bared, a willing participant to Chase's slow scrutiny.

He stood and walked forward, dangerously overwhelming with his power and height. For one brief moment, she caught a look of raw lust in his eyes before he bent down and sucked on her lower lip.

Her mouth parted on a moan. She expected a full-on kiss, not this drawn-out tease. This seductive agony. As he tantalizingly painted her lips with the tip of his tongue, her ragged cry of impatience echoed about the room. His teasing made her head spin as she became hypersensitive to every lick, every taste. Even just the tip of his tongue fired her nerves and sent a rush of pleasure racing across her skin. Low throbs in her pussy swelled, the pulses growing stronger every second. Slick moisture wet her inner thighs as she squirmed beneath his seduction.

"Chase…. Oh, please. Please." She didn't even know what she wanted, only knew that she wanted *more*. More of him, more of his touch.

He dragged his lips down her neck, nipped at the skin. "Tell me what you need, Autumn."

"I—I don't…oh, God…"

Leisurely, he sucked his way lower down her body, his lips and tongue sliding along her throat, over her collarbone, then farther down to the swell of her breast.

Mindless with need, her back arched to bring an aching nipple toward his mouth. "Please," she begged, "take it…"

He relentlessly teased, his tongue swirling over and around the tight bud, and his teeth lightly scraping against it. In frustration she cried out and placed a hand on the top of his head, guiding him to where she needed.

"Give it to me," she ordered, hearing the desperation in her voice.

She looked down at Chase just as he gazed up at her, and she swore a ghost of a smile crossed his lips before his hot mouth—finally—latched on to her nipple. She melted.

Strong hands slipped beneath her ass, lifting her as if she were weightless. He placed her on the bed and settled beside her.

Before she lost every damn last shred of her sanity, she pushed herself away. "No." She pointed at his jeans and boots. "Get those off."

109

Luckily, Chase didn't protest as he toed off one boot and then the other before—with surprising dexterity considering his height—pulling off his socks. Now, he was all hers. Leaning toward him from her perch on the bed, she grabbed the waistband of his jeans, jerking him toward her.

Before he could utter a word, she was on him, everywhere, pulling at the button, yanking down his zipper. She pushed the denim down as far as she could before Chase took a step back to slide them fully off. All that remained were his boxers.

Her breath caught as she savored the nearly naked man before her. The dusting of dark hair on his thighs did nothing to obscure his sculpted, ripped muscles. Her gaze loitered on his six-pack abs, hard as river rock, before flicking up to his chiseled pecs.

As if Chase could feel her heated stare on his body, beads of sweat broke out on his chest, and a single, sizzling drop trickled down his stomach. Unable to resist, she pulled him forward, then leaned in and licked away the sweat.

He hissed while thrusting a hand into her hair, holding her lips in place against his stomach. Searing heat radiated from his body, consuming her as she kissed and licked his skin. With her free hand, she pushed his boxers down past his hips and the giant bulge of his erection. He stepped back, kicking away the last of what he wore and providing her with a mouth-watering, unrestricted view of every last glorious inch of him.

Her pussy clenched as she stared at his jutting length. *Big man, big cock.* A closely cropped sprinkling of dark hair circled the base. She'd hit the smokin' hot jackpot, and she wanted her payout.

"Stellar," she murmured, the calm words stark contrast to the eruption of desire seizing her insides. "Now get over here."

In two steps, he was on the bed, crushing her to the mattress. His massive body covered her, his searing hot skin setting her on fire. She writhed beneath him, grinding against the stiff cock pressing deliciously into her abdomen. Low moans rumbled against her ear as he nipped at her earlobe.

Lower and lower he slipped down her body, trailing his tongue along her neck, over her collarbone, down to the swell of her breasts. With tortuous, measured patience, he licked the sides of her breasts, down to her ribs, then back up again, his tongue circling the areola, around and around, wetting every bit of her flesh except the one place she needed it most, on her aching, swollen nipples.

With a cry of frustration, Autumn arched her back, guiding a nipple to Chase's lips. He refused the bait.

"Damn it," she growled, wrapping her arms around him to claw at his back. "Take it."

"I will," he mumbled against her skin. "When I'm ready." Then, without warning, he slipped his hand between their bodies and sank a finger into her pussy.

She cried out, speared with lust. Every last nerve in her body came achingly alive, humming with sensation, her clit and pussy pulsing against Chase's probing fingers, her hips rising up to meet every thrust and drive him harder.

She'd never had a lover like Chase, someone who ignored everything she asked for but who still knew exactly what she wanted. What she needed. He read her body like a playbook, a champion of every move, knowing precisely how to make her fly.

He ground his finger into her throbbing center before adding a second, pounding at her core, his hand positioned so that his palm tantalizingly slapped her clit. She soared, calling out his name, riding his fingers.

"More…more…" she panted.

Release hovered, seconds away. Pinpricks of dark spots danced in her vision as she squeezed her eyes shut, ragged breaths rushing from her lungs. The onslaught of pleasure blew her mind, blocking everything but her raw desire. She bucked against Chase's fingers to drive them deeper as her clit throbbed and pulsed against his palm. Track marks from her nails scored his back as she clawed at his skin.

"Come for me, Autumn," he rumbled, and then, he brutally sucked her swollen nipple between his lips.

The orgasm ripped through her body, and she screamed, fierce pulses drowning her in ecstasy. The rush continued for what seemed like forever, wave after delicious wave. She couldn't think, couldn't see, couldn't do anything but *feel,* her fingers and toes curled, blood roaring through her veins, her entire body flooded in rapturous bliss.

Finally, when the mind-blowing pulses at last began to calm, she released a long breath and wriggled out from beneath Chase as he flipped over to his back.

"Your turn," she said, still lightly panting from her racing heartbeat.

With ease, she straddled his legs, her ass resting against his thighs. Then, just as he'd done earlier to her, she bent forward and kissed him, sucking on his bottom lip before slipping her tongue into his mouth. She savored his taste, the beer, the salt from the chips, and something indescribably unique to the man himself. Memory of that first fiery kiss had burned in her mind since that day in his studio, and she'd craved it ever since. She'd wanted more of him then, and she wanted more now.

Inching down his body, she slowly licked along his solid pecs and over the rock-hard ridges of his abs. Her long hair spread over his chest as she slid lower down his body, her lips gliding over his stomach, following a path arrowing straight to his stiff cock. She paused, looking up at him.

One hand was propped beneath his head to raise it up and keep his ebony-dark gaze laser-focused on her. Beads of sweated dotted his forehead. The realization that this smart, strong, hot-as-fuck naked man was panting with hunger for *her* set off fireworks in the pit of her stomach. Her lips curved, and she raised an eyebrow at him.

"That for me?" she asked with a glance at his erection.

"Damn straight it is," he nodded, releasing a long breath. "So what are you gonna do about it?"

Instead of talking, she got busy. She bent forward and swirled her tongue around the mushroom head of his cock, licking the sensitive underside before swiping away a glistening drop of pre-cum. With the tip of her tongue she teased, gently licking the delicate ball sac before returning to the base of his cock and drawing a wet trail along the entire length.

He sucked in a breath and released it long and slow with a moan, spurring her on. She wrapped her lips around the head while using her right hand to fist his cock with long, tortuous strokes.

Keeping her grip tight, she increased her speed, pumping harder while intensifying pressure with her wet lips as they slid back and forth along his length. His low groans grew steadily louder and more ragged.

"Look at me," he panted.

Her gaze slid upward to lock with his. His ink-dark eyes exuded lust, looking at her like he wanted to consume her. Autumn's pussy clenched. And throbbed.

In a flash, Chase sat up, circled her waist with both hands, and flipped her on her back.

"Need you now," he growled, spreading her thighs. Then a shadow crossed his face, like he'd just remembered something, and instinctively, she knew what it was.

With her one remaining scrap of sanity, she reached to pull open the small drawer on her nightstand. "In there."

He peered in the drawer, and a ghost of a smile touched his lips as he pulled out a condom. Ripping open the wrapper with his teeth, he rolled it onto his cock in what had to be world-record time.

"I like a woman who's prepared," he said, slipping back between her thighs.

"I like a man who appreciates effort."

He grinned as he shifted position to be on top of her, dwarfing her with his massive size. His biceps flashed black and grey ink as he placed his arms on either side of her head, trapping her, his bulk pressing her deep into the mattress.

She was on fire. She burned everywhere, sweat rolling off her body, the sweltering air mingling with her own internal heat as Chase lifted his hips to reach between their bodies. He swirled the tip of his cock around her pussy, wetting it with her juices. She groaned in frustration and arched her hips, trying to guide him, but he held back.

"Something you want?" he asked innocently.

If he thought he could make her beg, he had another thing coming. Chase Durand had met his match.

"Nope." She shook her head and stopped her grinding hips, ignoring the pulsing need in her core. To top off her charade, she even tried squirming out from beneath him.

"Get back here, you little tease," he growled. "Talking's over."

His expression dark and seductively fierce, he used one arm to push her back beneath him and then reared up, positioning his cock at her entrance and sinking the tip of it inside her.

"Ah!" She was ready, she wanted him, but he was big. Thick. Tilting her pelvis up to accommodate his size, legs spread wide, she relaxed and blew out a breath, taking him in, inch by inch. Her eyes fluttered shut at the pleasure/pain stretch of her tight walls around his giant dick.

"More," she panted, her pussy shamelessly throbbing against the invasion.

"Look at me."

She opened her eyes to Chase's intense stare. Locking his gaze with hers, never wavering, he slowly pressed down with his hips and speared her.

"Ooooh." Her groans filled the room as she was stretched, filled, wavering between wanting to push him away to tease or pull him in deeper to feed her desire.

Fire roared through her blood. She slipped her arms beneath his and wrapped them around his waist.

"Deeper," she begged.

"Take it all," he ordered, raising his hips and slamming full force into her.

Hot. *Damn*. Never in her life had she felt more filled. Her throaty cries bounced off the walls. Greed for his amazing cock drove her to tilt her hips up to meet every one of his pounding thrusts. Holy hell, it felt so good.

Chase had inched up ever so slightly, the marginal shift in position slapping his pelvic bone against her clit. She quivered everywhere, her pussy clenching as another mind-blowing orgasm lingered just around the corner, gathering steam. Purposely, she shoved it away, hell bent on not coming before Chase did. She'd already shattered in his arms once; she wanted to see his release before she did so again.

He leaned in, his tongue licking her lips before easily sliding into her mouth. Her hands slid down the slope of his back and up again over the rounded, muscled curve of his ass, a sensual rollercoaster ride over Chase's flawless body. As if spurred on by her eager touch, he increased his pace, ramming into her needy flesh with everything he had. She took it all, desire spiraling to the stratosphere. Release hovered like a captive prisoner, desperate to break free.

When he pulled back to kiss her throat, she turned her head to the side, and her eye caught the full-length mirror on the closet door. The erotic image reflected back made her moan aloud. Her scorching hot, badass artist, dominating her with his glorious naked body, his tattooed biceps bulging as they held his weight while he thrust into her. Her entire body shook as her pussy clenched. Her orgasm was almost in reach and about to unleash hell.

She groaned again, clawing his back as she ground her hips against him. Her senses spun as she neared release, wanting it yet waiting, needing Chase to find his first. His ragged moans increased as he pistoned into her.

Suddenly, his arms slipped behind her, pulling her tight, and with a loud roar, he went still. His thick cock swelled more as his climax seized him.

Sweet, blessed relief. His release pulsed like fire against her slick inner walls. Desperate to come, she thrust hard against him, riding his wave, her clit slapping sensuously against his pubic bone. Seconds later, her eyes squeezed shut as stars filled her vision, and she shattered.

For a few moments after, neither of them moved. The heavy scent of sex lingered in the air.

At last, Chase rolled off her, and they lay side by side, chests heaving, their heavy panting cutting through the stillness. Autumn's limbs were heavy as iron, impossible to move. All she could manage was letting her head loll to the side as she glanced over at Chase. His chest slowly rose and fell as his breathing calmed.

When it appeared Chase gathered enough strength, he slid off the mattress toward the bathroom. "Gotta ditch the love glove," he joked over his shoulder.

When he returned, condom neatly flushed away, Autumn welcomed his warmth and his weight as the mattress sank beneath him. Cozying by her side, he slipped a crooked arm beneath his head to prop it up and turned to meet her gaze. "I'll say one thing's for sure."

"What's that?"

"The ending of that photo shoot was a helluva a lot better than the way it started."

Her lips twitched with a grin. "Guess I'd pretty much have to agree with that."

Chase shifted, turning fully to his side to face her. He trailed his knuckles along her arm before taking a strand of her hair between his forefinger and thumb. "I love this hair. So long. Perfect spiral curls." He held the strand against his cheek. "And soft. I've never seen anything like it."

Shyness crept in, but she resisted the urge to pull away. Funny how she could lie next to him naked without a second thought, yet a single compliment made her wary as a lonely teen.

His exploration continued with light touches skimming her jawline. "And your eyes, my god. Blue as the sky." His gaze flicked across her face with a look of surprise, like a person who's just realized something that should have been obvious all along. "You really are beautiful, Autumn."

Her face flamed. Chase's compliments were nice. Too nice. He was venturing into territory that might lead to something she didn't want to think about, much less deal with. Like feelings. Or emotions.

Luckily, she was saved by her dog's forlorn howls. Beau's tolerance for being locked away in the other bedroom had reached its limit.

Sitting up, she swung her legs over the bed and grabbed at the heap of clothes, snatching up everything that was hers and hugging the items to her body. "I'll be back."

Her abrupt departure seemed to have raised Chase's antennae. "Autumn, wait. Did I say something that bugged you?"

"Gotta get my dog," she replied over her shoulder. Her hand reached out to twist the knob on her bedroom door, and she shot out like a cannon.

The excuse to get Beau was just that—an excuse. Her dog would be fine, but if she didn't stop Chase's line of chatter, he might start feeling comfortable with asking her questions she didn't want to answer. So best to do what she always did when the heat got too intense—get the hell out of the kitchen.

Chapter Nine

The iron weights against steel bars chimed softly, their methodical clinking lending comfort as Chase went in for a fifth rep on his deltoids. His muscles already burned, the familiar pain coming to visit like an old friend. A good workout also helped get his mind off a tiny techie who'd lately been occupying way too much space in his head.

Since they'd last been together at Autumn's place a week ago, he'd scarcely seen her. A few quick glances here and there, but his effort at conversation was met with something that could only be described as reluctance at best, aversion at worst. For the life of him, he couldn't figure out why. What the hell had he said that night that had made her jumpier than bare feet on hot, summer sand?

He finished the deltoid reps and moved on to lats. It was nice that the hotel gym was finished and available for employees to use even before the hotel itself opened. Usually it was pretty full, too, although at this particular moment, he happened to be the only one there. Chase grunted as he straddled the bench and pulled down the crossbar. Guess not everyone's idea of Friday night fun was *latissimus dorsi* burn. Still, he—

The sudden sharp click of heels across the cement floor cut his thoughts like scissors through a ribbon. *Shit.* He didn't need to turn around to identify his visitor. With an irritated sigh, he released the weight and braced himself for the greeting he knew was seconds away.

"Chase! What are you doing here at this time of night?" Maryanne stepped around the bench to stand in front of him, her lips parted in a colossal, red smile. "I can't believe no one's keeping you occupied in some *other* way besides weightlifting." She waggled her brow at him in what he supposed was a naughty, knowing look.

"I've got plenty to occupy me," he said. "But we all need to exercise."

"Oh, of course. Of course." The words tumbled out as though trying to gloss over the inappropriate remark she'd made seconds ago. "I only meant that you're so popular around here, I'd think your friends would want to spend time with you."

Chase ignored her, hoping she'd take the hint and leave. No such luck.

"So, speaking of popular," she said, reigniting the red smile, "I know your art is certainly going to be. We're promoting the heck out of it pre-opening with that dynamite photo shoot. Wait until you see the magazine spread. The pictures of you are amazing!"

Chase frowned. "You've chosen them already?"

"Well…yes." She hesitated for a damn good reason.

He was guaranteed prior approval on all photos before publication. If the spread was completed, Maryanne was in breach of his contract.

"It's just, ah…it's just a mock-up," she stammered, twisting her ring around and around one finger as she swiveled her head for anywhere to look besides at him.

Chase sighed, turning his back on her as he resumed his lat work. Pulling down the bar, he let out a deep breath and said over the clink of the metal, "Well, that's great then. Show it to me Monday."

"Monday? Oh, well…sure."

Though he couldn't see her face, Chase was certain if he turned around, he'd see panic flaring in her raccoon eyes.

"If it's just a mock-up, then nothing's gone to the printer, right?" He let the bar up, then pulled it back down. "So, like you said, I can't wait to see the proofs."

"Of course." Her heels clicked the ground as she advanced around the bench to stand in front of him again. "My schedule's jammed all day Monday, but for you, I'll make time." A row of big, even teeth peeked through her parted lips. "Anything for our favorite artist!"

"If you don't have time, just leave the proofs for me on your desk," he said, letting the bar go and standing up from the bench, towering over her. "That'd suit me just fine."

"Oh, no. No!" She conjured up a giggle. "Of course, I want to show them to you myself, Chase. Two o'clock?"

"Fine." He stepped around her and picked up a pair of seventy-pound dumbbells to begin bicep curls. "See you then."

"Oh, ah. Okay." At least she was perceptive enough to know when she'd been dismissed. "Monday at two. My office." She gave him a tight nod and twisted on her heel, marching away like an obedient soldier.

Chase watched her go, wondering what she'd have

to do to drum up those proofs. Because he sure as shit could guess there weren't any.

****

"Stop the printing and get me some fucking proofs!" Maryanne jabbed the end call button on her phone after she'd woken up Liesel to scream instructions at her assistant, then let out an ear-shattering shriek as she stormed around her office.

Damn it all to hell, why did Chase have to insist on seeing those proofs? The layout was all set, the photos chosen. Now she was going to incur enormous additional printing costs for putting the job on hold, and all because Chase would surely want to include irritating little computer know-it-all, Autumn, in the final spread. *Shit*.

She glanced at the wall clock. Nearly eleven on a Friday night. She really ought to be home by now, trying to get some sleep. Such a busy weekend ahead. She needed to review vendor contracts, authorize payments, and go through a pile of pillow fabric samples—all before Monday.

Plus, there was that party she'd been invited to for Saturday night and—*crap*. Her annoyance meter spiked as she remembered her promise to Mason for a quickie tomorrow afternoon. She was supposed to bring those butt plugs, too, which she hadn't even gotten around to buying.

Her mind ticked off everything she needed to do tomorrow. A stop at the Love Boutique hadn't factored in. Mason was just going to have to do without. He had an enormous penchant for backdoor playtime, but he also wasn't picky. Frankly, he'd probably get off if she stuffed a carrot up his ass.

She sighed and picked up her purse, heading for the door. But...wait. Why was she even considering going to Mason's tomorrow? As of today he *still* hadn't shown her the approved multi-city deal for those other hotels. The deal that would guarantee her spot as head designer on every single one of them. And that, after all, was the sole reason he got to dip his flabby little wick in her divine honey pot. That pudgy prick wouldn't have a chance in hell with her if not for the deal. For that mega prize, she'd fuck Mason and more. Much more.

She let her mind drift for a moment, drawing up images of her in that esteemed top position, awash in power and cash. She could design those hotels any way she wanted, put her stamp on them all, and let the world see her exquisite taste. Naturally, Chase's art would be prominently featured. The man had more talent in his little finger than any artist she'd seen in her entire career. He was also the sexiest badass she'd ever laid eyes on, making her loins howl with a single smoldering glance. His towering frame and those exquisite muscles...

Her pussy contracted with delightful little throbs as she imagined how divine Chase must be in bed. A man that huge ought to have quite the pleasant package parked between his thighs. She ran her tongue over her lips, imagining how it must be to slide them along Chase's marble hard chest, then down, and down, taking his cock...

Damn that irritating Autumn Rivette and the apparent interest Chase had developed in her. She frowned before immediately smoothing out her features, a gesture she'd done a thousand times.

Wouldn't do to be getting all wrinkled like an old prune. It would be tough to use her looks and body to get what she wanted if she started resembling a desperate grammy.

Maryanne let out a frustrated sigh. There was no way that little IT hussy was going to be messing up everything she'd put in place for herself. She needed Chase for her rise to the top. Any designer worth her salt was responsible for launching the career of an unknown artist. It was crucial in order to solidify her rightful place among the best designers this country had ever seen.

She nodded to herself. Chase's art would get her there all right, but he was much more appealing to the female patrons if he remained unattached. Rich bitch art patrons with silly fantasies of snagging Chase as a love toy... thinking they'd have a chance as long as he stayed single. The more they dreamed, the more money they'd spend on staying at hotels featuring Chase's art, and she would rise like cream to the top of the designer heap. Hell, she could start bringing in celebrity clients!

No way would she allow that damn Autumn Rivette to screw things up by getting involved with Chase and weighing in on his decisions. No. Fucking. Way.

She thrust her jaw forward, determination lashing through her blood. She'd do whatever she needed to make sure Autumn wasn't a problem for Chase—and most importantly, for her. She smiled, awash in a sense of calm now that she'd made her decision. She hadn't gotten to where she was today by passively sitting back and hoping for the best, and no way in hell would she start doing it now, not with designer super stardom just around the corner.

Maryanne glanced at her watch. Nearly midnight. She'd better get the hell home and grab some rest. She didn't need a lot sleep, and there was so much to do. But if she planned things right, she'd have just enough time to get those butt plugs after all.

****

Autumn's teeth clamped down to hold the pen flashlight steady in her mouth as she aimed it at the Toslink audio cables for the pool area. Loose strands of hair, freed from the messy pile atop her head, clung like wet straw to the sides of her face. Beads of sweat trickled between her breasts. Her nose itched, and her feet were killing her.

She'd been on this site for the past four hours with no food, no water, no AC. The wiring guys were supposed to have had it hooked up and tested by now, but rumor had it they were purposely slowing work down, because that cheap ass Wilson, the hotel manager, was playing hard ball with payments. Autumn did her best to ignore the gossip and keep her mind focused solely on what she and her IT crew needed to do to get their work done. Besides, it helped her to avoid thinking about a certain artist...

And just like that, she was thinking of him again. *Damnit.*

Over and over and over, images of their time together spooled through her mind like scenes from a movie. Guiltily, she indulged in each and every moment, trying like hell not to admit to herself how much she'd liked it. And lusted for more.

She'd purposely avoided Chase since they'd slept together, thinking it would help stop the constant thoughts of him from burrowing beneath her skin. An "outta sight, outta mind" approach that had ended up being as useful as a trap door on a canoe. She absolutely could not shake thoughts of him.

The tightening of her nipples beneath her thin T-shirt was a perfect example. She tried ignoring the reaction, but it was like trying not to breathe. It happened every time she remembered Chase's mouth sucking on her breasts. Or his hands skimming over her body, knowing just where to touch her, where to make her feel good. Small pulses like tiny heartbeats quickened in her core as she refreshed the image of Chase skillfully licking her pussy and tonguing her clit. For sure, he'd known what he was doing down there.

The light wobbled, and she tightened her lips, saving the flashlight just in time from fumbling out of her mouth and clanking down on the scaffold plank where she stood. But then, the screwdriver slipped from her grasp, her sweaty palms unable to maintain a firm hold. She let out a resigned sigh just as her stomach rumbled. Time for a break.

With ease, she leapt down from the scaffolding and let herself out of the airless back room. As she pushed open the door leading into the main pool area, she couldn't help but admire the layout and design.

The pool was intended to be the largest one in any Louisiana hotel, and its design was created to resemble the bayou. The elaborate tile work included scenes of bald cypress trees and other native plants, along with alligators, muskrats, osprey, herons, and snakes.

Autumn mentally shuddered at the last one. Rivard Research, only a few miles away, was home to over two hundred king cobras. Kelly Grassle, a girl Autumn knew from Les's restaurant where they both occasionally hung out, worked as a research tech over there. Autumn had to give Kelly credit—she'd never be able to conquer her fear of snakes to do something like that.

Her grumbling stomach reminded her that she'd had nothing to eat, so she whisked out of the pool area and headed to Pat's kitchen. She hadn't seen her friend in several days but knew she'd be cooking up something good. When it came to creating recipes, Pat was relentless, sometimes trying a single one thirty or more times before she was satisfied. Autumn had often been the lucky recipient of her friend's cast-offs.

As expected, the enticing smell of cooking wafted through the empty restaurant as soon as Autumn pushed her way through the double doors leading to the kitchen.

"Pat?"

"Over here, hun."

Autumn followed the sound of the chef's voice and found her over in the pastry area, up to her arms in flour.

"Hey!" Pat's always upbeat greeting was made even more amusing by her appearance. The tip of her nose was powdered white, a smudge of dough dabbed her chin.

Autumn grinned. "You plan on baking yourself to see how that turns out?"

"Aren't you the funny one?" Pat's attempt at annoyance was ruined when she wiped a floured arm over her forehead, leaving behind an additional streak of dough.

"The hungry one is what I am." Autumn looked

around, sniffing the air. "C'mon, take a break and feed me. I'm smelling something awesome."

Pat grabbed plastic wrap and covered a bowl with it before popping it in the large, commercial walk-in refrigerator just behind her. "You can't be faulted for your timing, that's for sure," she said as she stepped out of the fridge. "My sticky ribs should be just about ready, and I need to chill my pastry dough." She nodded toward a large, stainless steel table and several tall stools. "Have a seat, guinea pig. I'll be right back."

Autumn went where indicated as Pat grabbed a towel and lifted out a large pan from the oven. An enticing combination of spices, ketchup, onions, ginger, and honey shot Autumn's hunger to the moon.

"Holy hell, Pat. I'm fixin' to start gnawing this table if you don't get those ribs over here." She looked over to where her friend was plating lunch.

"Hold your horses." Pat spooned rich, steaming mashed potatoes alongside the ribs. Grabbing a plate in each hand, she made her way to the table. "Genius can't be rushed, you know."

With the knife Pat handed her, Autumn cut into the tender rib meat and forked up a mouthful. She chewed slowly, her taste buds exploding over the tantalizing combination of slow-cooked southern ribs coated with Pat's sweet/spicy decadent glaze. She closed her eyes and smiled.

"Man oh man, what you do to food." She finished her bite and nodded to her friend. "Don't change a thing. This is perfection on a plate."

"Glad you like." Pat took her own bite, nodding as she chewed. "Yep," she said firmly, like she'd just come to an important decision. "This one is it. This is the recipe I'm using."

"I need more," Autumn announced, sliding off the chair.

But before she could take a single step forward, Pat held up a hand. "Not so fast, my little friend. Spill the details on what's going on with you and Mountain Man."

"There's nothing to—"

"Chef Pat wasn't born yesterday, Sweet Pea. A pig has a better chance of flying to the moon than you do of convincing me there are no details."

Autumn's hand clenched the fork tighter as rib meat settled like glue in her stomach. The kitchen had morphed from cozy refuge to scary interrogation room. All she needed was a naked light bulb swinging over her head.

"I've seen you two together," Pat continued. "And I saw the proofs from that hot photo shoot. If that man's not smitten, then I don't know my own name."

"No way." Autumn swiftly shook her head, her defenses spiking. "He's not smitten, it's just…ah…"

"Yeaaah?" Pat leaned forward, a conspiratorial gleam in her eye. "It's just what?" When Autumn failed to answer right away, her friend tightened the screws. "If you don't give me at least a forkful of dirt, you're not getting another forkful of my chow."

"Well, hell." Autumn groaned. "I never took you for someone who played dirty."

"Hey, it's the only bargaining chip I got." Pat laughed.

The twinkle in her friend's eye assured Autumn that Pat really was only pulling her leg. In the few months since they'd been friends, they'd grown pretty close, or at least as close as Autumn ever allowed. That was saying something. But she'd never felt comfortable talking about herself and adding Chase to the mix…that made it doubly tough.

Yet curiously, a part of her wanted to talk, to share a little girl gossip. So weird. She'd never, ever had that impulse before. Of course, she'd never actually had a close female friend before, either.

"Well," Autumn began, trying to figure out what exactly to say. "Um, so I don't know about your lame 'smitten' business, but he and I…" She shrugged, a little horrified to realize her cheeks were growing warm.

Pat's eyes bugged out of her head and her mouth fell open. "You did the *deed*?" She slapped her thigh, laughing to herself. "Holy smacks, Autumn. That's awesome."

"Hey, I didn't say—"

"And hot damn. What a catch, too."

Inwardly, Autumn groaned. She hadn't meant to spill the entire can of beans, only to give Pat a sampling of what she and Chase had done. But Pat had drawn her own conclusions, and nothing Autumn could say at this point would do any good.

"So." Pat leaned in, lips curved in a wicked grin. "How was he?"

"Knock it off." Autumn made a cutting motion across her neck as she pushed herself off the chair and headed for the ribs tray. "You're not getting specific details."

"Why the hell not?"

"'Cause I said so." Autumn walked back to the table with her loaded plate, ignoring her friend's needling as she dug into the ribs.

Despite the uncomfortable topic, her appetite hadn't vanished. After a couple of minutes, she declared herself stuffed and licked sauce off her fingers. She eyed her friend, who was giving her a look of barely restrained patience as she waited for Autumn to finish.

"Just give me a little bit, Autumn. One tiny detail might save your food privileges from being revoked."

Autumn rolled her eyes. Yet despite playing the part of fake-annoyed friend, she had to admit it was fun having someone so interested in her life. What a crazy new experience.

"Fine," she relented. "Here's your detail. He's…he's an awesome kisser."

"Oooh! I knew it!"

"Excuse me?"

Pat laughed. "Oh, please. Don't be getting your feathers ruffled at lil' ol' me, Autumn. I don't actually *know*, for gosh sakes. But just looking at him, at that mouth of his, those lips…*mmm*. A girl can just tell he'd know how to use 'em."

He sure does. Warm tingles skittered across her nerves. She let out a long breath and shifted in her chair.

"I gotta go." She grabbed her phone from where she'd set it on the table, stuffing it in her back pocket.

"Oh, c'mon, Autumn. What's your hurry? I'm working on dessert."

"Nah, that's all right. You know I don't have much of a sweet tooth."

"Not even for chocolate lava bomb? Decadent ganache oozing out of a divinely inspired sponge cake?"

Normally that would have been sufficient temptation to make Autumn stay. But suddenly, her appetite had nothing at all to do with food.

****

Autumn expelled a frustrated sigh. The new Asian-fusion restaurant was empty. Ditto the main entrance lobby, the spa, both dance clubs, and the casino area. *Damn it*. No sign of Chase anywhere. Well, it was Saturday, after all. Maybe he wasn't working.

Obviously, she could find him more easily than running around the hotel like a mouse in a maze. Texting him would probably do the trick. For a couple of indecisive seconds, she nibbled her lower lip before annoyance smacked her upside the head, and she pulled out her phone. *For cripe's sake, Autumn. You want something, go get it.*

She stabbed at the text buttons and hit send before second-guessing herself. *Where are you?*

She remained standing in the middle of the empty restaurant, staring at her phone like she could will an answer out of it by beaming brain waves at the screen. Nothing. Ignoring the spear of disappointment in her gut, she told herself it was a bad idea, anyway, looking for Chase in the middle of the day on Saturday. Just because she had nothing better to do than come to work on the weekend didn't mean he felt the same. He was probably busy, maybe blowing some glass, or eating lunch, or getting a pedicure. She rolled her eyes. Sure, that's what he was doing. *Admit it. You're afraid he's with someone. A* female *someone*. Okay, fine. It's true; she was thinking about that. So? She should probably just—

Three dots appeared on her phone screen. He was writing back.

I'm at the hotel, in the President's Suite, looking over an installation. What's up?

Her heart actually flipped, rolling in her chest like a happy little puppy. *Get a damn grip.* She tapped the keyboard.

I'm at the hotel, too. Was just wondering what you're doing.

You need me? I can meet you somewhere.

Need him? Well, yeah. You could say that. She thought of suggesting a beer, but what was the point? She didn't want a drink. She wanted *him.*

No need. I'll come to you. See you in a few.

She hit send and slipped the phone in her back pocket. An excited quiver zinged through her body, flashing through her arms, down her legs, sending butterflies dancing in her belly. She left the restaurant and rushed toward the lobby elevators. As she rounded a corner, she had a near head-on collision with another person equally in a hurry—Maryanne.

"Watch it!" the designer shrieked as she spun on her heel to avoid crashing straight into Autumn. A snappy red handbag flew off her shoulder and skittered across the marble floor, scattering its contents.

"Cock-sucking *shit,"* Maryanne yelled, racing around to retrieve the strewn items like a kid grabbing candy from a busted piñata.

Autumn bent to help her, noticing a plastic bag from the Love Boutique several feet away among the scattered items.

Maryanne shooed her aside. "I'm fine," she bristled, stuffing a lipstick in her purse. She looked up, and her irritation turned five-alarm hostile. "What the hell!" Her eyes flared. "Anyone ever tell you to watch where you're going?"

Autumn frowned. She was in no mood right now for the designer's shit. Not that she was any other time, either. "Right back at you, Maryanne," she said evenly. "Don't get yourself run over. Wouldn't look good to be busting your nails or getting a hair out of place."

Maryanne rose from her crouched position and narrowed her gaze. "Nor would it look good to have 'fired from the White Ibis' listed on your resume."

Autumn raised an eyebrow. "I agree. Good thing my employment has nothing to do with you."

"Just because I'm not your boss doesn't mean I don't have influence around here, Autumn. Do yourself a favor and remember that."

Autumn rolled her eyes, sick of this verbal cat fight. She had way more interesting things to think about besides the nauseating head designer.

"Thanks, Maryanne. I appreciate the words of advice," she said in a silky-smooth tone, punctuating her alleged gratitude with a big smile. "Allow me to return the favor." She nodded toward a sofa where the white, plastic bag emblazoned with the silhouette of a nude woman peeked out. "Don't forget your bag from the Love Boutique."

Maryanne's eyes turned wide as saucers and her face flamed deep tomato red. Autumn chuckled as she walked away. It was childish, but she couldn't help it.

Chapter Ten

"In here," Chase called out in response to the light knock on the door of the Presidential Suite. He took a step back and studied the piece of his artwork that had been mounted to a wall in the spacious room. *No.* He shook his head. *All wrong.*

Light steps on the carpet alerted him that Autumn had arrived. He turned around.

"Hey," he said as she approached. His gaze swept over the grey skinny jeans that perfectly hugged her ass. *Holy hell.* He resisted the urge to whistle. Just barely.

Curiosity about why she was here swirled in his mind, but he kept cool and said nothing, not wanting to come on too strong. Though Autumn had taken up permanent residence in his thoughts since they'd slept together, he was unsure if she felt the same. Mystery overlaid with caution surrounded her. She had revealed few personal details about herself, which made him want to probe for that much more.

He walked to the room's bar area he'd had the foresight to stock. Slim glass beer bottles poked up through the ice in the bucket. He grabbed one for himself and raised a questioning eyebrow at Autumn.

"Join me?" he asked casually, twisting off the top.

She nodded and gave him a grin. "You're well prepared."

He twisted the top off of hers as well and handed it

over. "Cheers," he said as they clinked their bottles together and took a long drink.

"I had some stuff to do in here that I knew would take time," he said, setting his bottle down on a nearby side table. "So I figured why not. Anyway, it's Saturday. Good day for a cold beer or three."

"No argument there."

They stood in silence as Chase let his gaze drift as casually as possible over Autumn's tight little body. Hot damn, but she looked amazing. She pulled off the jeans and T-shirt look better than any woman he'd ever met. And that mess of curly blonde hair piled up on her head... What he wouldn't give to slowly start pulling out whatever contraption she had in there, holding it up. He could watch it fall down her back, over her shoulders... Even better if she had no clothes on while he was doing it.

He dragged his gaze away as he grew hard. *Shit.* He didn't want to look like some desperate horn dog every time she stood next to him. Scrambling for something to distract his wayward thoughts, he nodded to the sculpture he'd been studying when she'd arrived.

"What do you think of that?" he asked, sipping his beer. He wiped his forearm across his mouth and added, "I don't mean so much the sculpture itself, but where it's placed on the wall. Do you think it works?"

She blinked and took a step backward, distancing herself. Her eyes held a shadowed look, like she wanted to hide from him whatever thoughts she might have about the sculpture. Warmth flushed over him and he frowned. *Maybe she hates it. Or maybe it's the questions I'd asked.*

For sure, Autumn had smarts. Anyone could see it.

But her familiar world was binary numbers and lines of computer code. Art and design took her out of her comfort zone and put her on edge. He felt like smacking his palm against his forehead. What a prick.

"Don't worry about hurting my feelings." He chuckled, adopting a casual tone to put her at ease. "There's no right or wrong answer."

She nodded, and he took that to mean his hunch was dead on. She looked at the wall for a minute or two as she sipped her beer. Then she shrugged and turned to him.

"I like the sculpture just fine," she said. "Actually, a lot. And I'm not just blowing smoke up your jeans. But where it's hanging..." She took another sip of her beer like it gave her a swallow of courage. "Well, it doesn't work. The piece is too small for the big wall it's on. It looks...I dunno. Kinda lost."

Bingo. His feeling exactly. Maryanne had completely missed the mark on this one, and smart, sexy Autumn had immediately picked up on it. While she studied the sculpture, he glanced at her profile, drawn to the dusting of freckles on her nose. The sudden urge to trace his finger along her jawline and kiss that cute, little nose became impossible to resist. He set down his beer and walked over to her.

With the backs of his fingers, he reached out and skimmed them along her bare arm from shoulder to elbow and back up again. Her tanned skin stippled as goosebumps raised the fine hairs on her forearm.

But she didn't turn away. Didn't resist. Instead, she leaned into his touch, allowing him to turn his hand over and trace his full palm across her soft skin on her arm. With his other hand, he turned her toward him, so their bodies faced one another.

She looked up at him, her wide-open, blue eyes telling him without a doubt that she wanted his attention. He brushed aside her bangs to see every detail on her face. Then he slipped his fingers into her mass of hair and did what he'd imagined only moments ago. He plucked out a few pins and watched the curls tumble down.

Grasping a fistful of her thick mane, he tilted her head back and leaned down to kiss her. She welcomed him with a breathy moan, running her tongue over his lips before inviting him to explore the warm, moist depths of her mouth. The blood revved straight to his cock, and his deep growl echoed in his ears. With his hand still wrapped in her hair, he guided her back toward the bed until her thighs hit the mattress and she was forced to stop.

He straightened, breaking the kiss. Impatience and lust roared. The tiny, tempting package standing before him could cause a man to lose his sanity. With a leisurely eye, his gaze traveled over her flushed face, her swollen lips, down to where her stiffened nipples poked against her T-shirt. *So. Fucking. Hot.*

Infused with an urge to rip off her clothes so he could see those fantastic breasts and suck those hard nipples, he released a long breath and slipped his hands beneath her shirt, pulling it up and over her head before tossing it to the floor. Then he reached around and unhooked her bra, flinging it to the floor. A bead of sweat slowly trickled its way down her cleavage. A spear of lust turned his dick stone-hard.

"Touch your nipples," he said, and when she hesitated, he added, "Now."

Autumn sucked in a breath. Never in her life had she been more turned on. Chase's sharp command, his touch of impatience, the way his gaze scorched its way over her exposed breast... The desire to please him and obey his order should shock her, but it didn't...because she was the one in control. She was the one who could obey him—or not. The choice was entirely up to her.

Her gaze flicked over him. His body was tense as a coiled spring. Ragged breaths gusted from his lips. The musky scent of his arousal hung thick and heavy. And it was all because of his desire for her. If that wasn't the hottest thought this side of the Mississippi, she didn't know what was.

She smiled, and with thumb and forefinger, pinched her nipples. A jolt of raw desire pulsed in her core, growing stronger and more insistent with each passing second. Moisture built and spotted her panties. She cupped her breasts and slid her palms along the smooth, sensitive skin, moaning as desire soared. Her knees shook.

Chase stepped forward, and with an easy flick of his fingers, undid the top button of her jeans and pulled down the zipper. Then, he grasped a handful of material on either side of her hips and jerked it down.

He commanded, "Sit on the edge of the bed."

Gratefully, she obeyed.

"Lay back and lift your ass." As she slid down, he added, "Keep your hands on your breasts. Play with them. It's so hot. I want to know what you like, what turns you on. Show me."

Again with the commands. But just as before, her panties were soaked, her nipples painfully hard. Desire soared. Locking onto Chase's gaze, Autumn raised her hand to her lips, opened her mouth and, with slow deliberation, licked her fingers. Then, she again touched her nipples, pinching and tugging, groaning aloud. She did what Chase wanted—no, what he demanded—and loved every second of it. His stiff erection bulged beneath his jeans as he watched her. Clearly, so did he.

With clear impatience, he shoved her panties down her legs and threw them aside. She sat up, her entire body shaking with excitement as he knelt in front of her. For sure, she wanted front row seating to see this show.

Without hesitation, he put a hand beneath each calf and lifted her legs over his shoulders. Chase turned his head, and hot wetness coated the inside of her thigh as he slowly kissed and licked the sensitive skin. Raw lust flooded her as every nerve ending in her body flamed under his touch. He traced his tongue higher, and higher, stopping a hair's breadth from her pussy.

"Spread your legs."

No need to ask twice. Autumn's thoughts swirled in a delicious, erotic haze. The backs of her thighs slid off his shoulders and down his huge, muscled arms. She spread her legs wide, hiding nothing from his appreciative gaze. She lay back on the bed, languidly pinching her nipples as the first stroke of his wet tongue swept over her pussy lips.

She cried out, shamelessly opening her thighs as far as she could, encouraging him. Again and again, he flicked his tongue lightly over her clit, teasing until she thought she'd go mad. Her heartbeat slammed in her chest; blood roared in her ears. She arched against him, panting. "More. *Harder.*"

He pulled away.

"No, damn you!"

She swore she felt his grin against her pussy. "What do you want, Autumn?"

"I want...ahhhh." His tongue swirled around her clit as he plunged a finger into her tight heat.

"More," she whispered. "I want more."

"Like this?" Two fingers. He thrust hard, and his thumb replaced his tongue as it grazed teasingly over her clit.

"Yes." Her hands dropped to her sides, and her fingers grabbed handfuls of the bed cover in a tight death grip. "Don't you fucking stop," she growled.

Thankfully, Chase didn't give her shit about dictating orders. He was tuned to her body, reading her signals like a map. He knew exactly what she wanted and just how she wanted it.

He added a third finger and increased the pace, slapping against her. Again, he dove in with his tongue, working her clit. Fire roared in her veins as desire consumed her, pouring from every last cell in her body. She writhed against Chase's hand and mouth, grinding like a dancer. Release shimmered just out of sight.

She brought one hand to her nipple, pinching tight, desire shooting through her with the speed of fire chasing gasoline. She drove her pussy against Chase's hand, harder, higher, her clit swelling against his swirling tongue. The musky scent of sex filled the air, mingling with her groans. The orgasm loomed, almost there. Close. She reached for it, her body tight as wire, the pulses consuming her.

With one hand she pressed the back of Chase's head harder against her core, needing that one last, final thrust of his fingers while his wet lips sucked her swollen clit. She held her legs wide apart and ground against him, release barreling toward her like a freight train, and then she screamed in ecstasy as her orgasm exploded.

When the stars finally cleared from her vision and her breathing slowed, she sat up, staring at Chase. "How the hell are you always getting me naked while you keep every stitch of clothes on?"

"I'm not complaining."

"Well, I am." She reached out an arm and tugged at his T-shirt. "I need you naked. *Now*."

From his crouched position, he rose like a mountain and stood in front of her. She looked up, meeting his gorgeous, green eyes, liking the way his penetrating stare never flicked away from her. His massive chest rose and fell as he slipped his hands beneath his T-shirt to pull it off and throw it aside, his pecs rippling, the muscles contracting like a flawless machine.

Even if she saw him naked a million times, she'd never grow sick of seeing that fucking perfect body. As he bent forward, working to pull off his jeans, it was all she could do not to let her mouth fall open and simply gape at him with the awe of a star-struck fan, mesmerized by the sight.

At last, his naked, sculpted perfection was hers to devour. She licked her lips and slid from the bed onto her knees. His half-erect cock hung heavy between his legs. She reached out to cup his balls while with her fingertips lightly skimmed the length of his arousal, the skin warm and velvet soft. Above her, Chase gave a soft moan as his cock stiffened.

She leaned in, suffused by his heat. Her tongue slid

slowly along his length before she drew the tip into her mouth. A faint, musky scent clung to his skin. It excited her, this earthy, Chase scent, so uniquely him. If she smelled it, he was with her.

Gently, she played with his balls as she sucked him. His moans grew along with his erection. Inch by inch she slid him into her mouth, using her tongue to wet the warm, smooth skin of his cock. His deep moans were her prize, assurance that she pleased him. With her hand, she stroked the base of his cock as she swirled her tongue around the head.

"Yesss..." He thrust his hips upward, meeting her strokes "More, baby. Give me more."

She relaxed her throat, wanting to take in as much of him as she could and bring him the mind-blowing pleasure he'd just given her. Chase wound strong fingers in her hair as he guided her mouth onto his cock.

She looked up. His face was awash with pleasure, eyes dark, deep groans rumbling from his parted lips. His palm cupped the back of her head, holding it steady as he pumped against her mouth.

She slipped one hand around his waist, her hand caressing the curve of his sculpted ass. Hard muscles flexed beneath her touch as Chase rocked against her. Need for him soared. She took what he gave, her slick mouth and tongue drawing him in deep.

All at once, he pulled out from her oral tease and bent, slipping a hand beneath each of her arms to bring her to her feet.

"Hey! I want that back," she protested, her hand reaching for his cock. "What are you—"

He put his hand against her mouth, silencing her.

"You'll see." With a few quick steps, he walked back to the pile of clothes and reached into the pocket of his jeans, palming a condom pack.

The man comes prepared. Although her green-eyed monster peeked his head up as she hoped Chase's foresight was for her alone.

As he turned back toward her, he flashed an easy grin. "I was hoping I might see you." He ripped off the foil and rolled the condom onto his stiff dick.

Her green-eyed monster took a hike. She returned the grin. "And now that you have…?"

Before she realized what he was doing, he'd slid his hand beneath her ass and lifted her easily. "Put your legs around my waist."

The instant she complied, he kissed her, devouring her with his mouth as he carried her across the room. He pressed her against the wall, her hair serving as soft padding. Without breaking the kiss, he shifted her position and impaled her on his stiff cock.

"Ah," she cried as she was filled, stretched, her wet walls taking him easily.

He held a hand beneath each of her thighs, angling her in place against the wall as he pounded hard. She wrapped both arms around his massive shoulders and held herself against him, her breasts mashing into his chest as they rocked.

Skin slapped skin, the sharp blows mingling with rising groans. Sweat coated their heated bodies like oil. Chase held her tight, grinding her against him, pumping fast and hard. His gusty moans whistled against her ear.

Desire roared through veins. Release hovered so close, she could almost catch it. Her pussy clenched around Chase's pounding cock, her groans rising in pitch as she was deliciously filled. The hard press of his fingers dug into her thighs where he held her, a stark, delicious reminder that she was trapped, his to do with as he wanted, and more than willing to please.

Trails of sweat poured down their bodies. She kept one arm circled around his neck, but she pulled back from him so she could slip her other hand between their slick bodies and tug on her stiffened nipples. Mindless lust surrounded her like a cloud of fog.

A line of pleasure fed directly from her breasts to her pussy, driving the pulses in her core harder and faster. The more Chase gave her, the more she craved. Loud groans ricocheted like bullets off the walls. Their bodies dripped with the musky scent of sex. With every thrust, Chase's pubic bone slapped her clit hard. Her mouth dropped open as she panted against him, flooded with desire. Her pussy clenched as she reached for release, thrusting again and again, the climax building, racing toward her. Another thrust, again, and then a sob tore from her lungs as desire exploded.

She clung tightly to Chase as the pulses consumed her, pleasure flooding every pore, every cell of her body. Seconds later, Chase stilled, mashing her against him. From deep within his throat, he let out a groan as he found release.

When the pounding thumps of his heartbeat lessened and his breathing returned to normal, he relaxed his grip and set her gently on the floor. She took two steps and promptly collapsed into a nearby arm chair, leaning over the side to grab her bra and panties from the discarded pile of clothes. To her appreciative delight, Chase didn't bother with clothes as he headed over to the bar area, his magnificent, tight ass flexing while he walked.

She slipped on her under garments as Chase pulled two cold, wet bottles from the ice bucket. He twisted off the tops, returned, and handed her one. His gaze drifted over to the clothes scattered across the floor. Setting down his beer, he found his boxers and pulled them on before sinking into the armchair across from hers.

They drank without speaking, the soft hum of the air conditioner the single source of noise around them. Sated, Autumn felt like she could fall asleep right in that chair. Sweaty sex and a cold beer chaser made for a sleepy combo.

"So what'd you actually come here for, anyway?" Chase's deep voice shook away her drowsiness.

"Oh, ah…" Shit, how was she supposed to answer? Should she come up with some excuse?

Autumn's gaze flitted over to where Chase lounged with the half-lidded eyes and sexy lips of a contended man. She'd wanted pulse-pounding sex with him, and that's exactly what she'd gotten. No reason to lie with some lame-ass, made-up story, right? Besides, she felt like his head wouldn't swell if she told him the truth. Well, not too bad, anyway.

"I wanted you."

He kept quiet, except…was that a damn smirk? "So." He drained the bottle and set it down with a soft clink. "Did you get what you were after?"

She rolled her eyes. Definitely a smirk. How could she possibly have thought his head wouldn't swell? But yet with Chase, it seemed okay. Sure, he had puffed up a little with male pride, but she almost felt as if his question was genuine. Like he actually wanted to make sure he'd satisfied her. Was that possible?

"For now."

He let out a soft chuckle. "Just for now?" He folded his arms across his chest and eyed her up and down, his gaze as unhurried as a lazy river. "Well then, I guess I've got some work in my future. It's no good if my Tiny Techie isn't satisfied. Who knows what she'll do if that happens?"

"Tiny Techie?" She raised what she hoped was a stern eyebrow at him, never admitting in a million years the thrill his pet name gave her.

"Well, you *are* pretty small. As well as pretty damn amazing with that IT stuff. So if the name fits..." He shrugged, a lopsided grin lifting one corner of his mouth.

"No problem, Mountain Man. I get it."

His chuckle turned to genuine laughter as he got up to fetch her another beer.

She held up a hand. "Thanks, but I can't. I actually have to get back to work."

He sat back down, frowning. "It's Saturday, you know."

"True. But it's also only a couple months away from opening."

Chase reached over on the table for his phone. After glancing at it, he looked up at Autumn. "I'll make you a deal. It's almost seven, and I'm starving. Let me take you to the best pizza place for dinner. If you still feel like working when we're done, I'll personally bring you back here safe and sound. On the other hand, if you find yourself feeling unsatisfied...well, I'll help you out with that, too." He wagged a knowing eyebrow at her.

That did it. The hottest dude she'd ever seen was

flirting with her. Why resist? There'd be plenty of time for work later, but right now, it was time to play.

She gave him a nod. "Lead on, Mountain Man."

Chapter Eleven

Hot wind whooshed against Autumn with every passing mile, blowing her hair out from beneath her helmet. Her arms circled Chase's waist as he tore along the empty road, the rumble of the cycle vibrating against her ass. He'd followed her back to her bungalow so she could drop off her car, insisting it would be easier to reach the place he had in mind via his cycle.

He wouldn't tell her exactly where they were going, but as the road narrowed to little more than a dirt strip as it edged the swampy bayou, she had to admit that even her sports car might have been challenged to make it through here.

Finally, they pulled up to a small stand in the middle of nowhere with a few sets of chairs and tables grouped around it. As Chase parked, Autumn noticed that behind the stand was a food truck. She'd bet Pat would kill to know about this if the pizza lived up to Chase's bragging.

He killed the engine and slid off the cycle, holding out a hand to help her. They pulled off their helmets and stood beside the bike.

Chase nodded in the direction of the stand. "Welcome to Juan's."

Autumn eyed the wooden structure with its faded, cracked paint and slight lean to one side. It had the look of a northern abandoned ice cream stand in the dead of winter. "This is a pizza joint?"

He cocked a grin at her and nodded toward the stand. "Listen and learn, oh Doubting One."

They approached the empty stand and Chase called out Juan's name.

Seconds later a tanned, brown eyed, unexpectedly handsome man emerged from the side door of the truck. Catching sight of Chase, a smile lit his features. *"¡Hola, amigo! ¿Cómo estás?"*

Without missing a beat, Chase replied, *"¡Estoy genial! ¿Cómo estás tú?"*

"Estoy bien." Juan approached the stand, a questioning look on his attractive face as he glanced at Autumn.

"This is my friend, Autumn," Chase told him. "Autumn, meet the best Mexican pizza maker in the country, Juan Flores."

Juan extended a hand, and Autumn was surprised both by the warmth and strength of his grip.

"Nice to meet you, Autumn," Juan said, his smooth voice sharp in contrast to Chase's rumbles.

Introductions made, Juan turned to Chase. "You've come hungry, I hope?"

Chase nodded. "Starving. At least, I am."

"Same here," Autumn confirmed, her stomach growling as if on cue.

"You want your usual?" Juan asked Chase.

"Usual but double it."

Juan laughed. "You got it. Take a seat, and I'll bring out a couple of cold ones."

He disappeared back into the truck as Chase and Autumn sat at a nearby table. The sun was low in the sky and partly blocked by the majestic, bald cypress trees lining the bayou. The high-pitched chirps of warblers and the "who cooks for you" distinctive call of barred owls filled the air.

The door of the food truck clinked open as Juan stepped out with a cup of beer in each hand. "Indio Cerveza," he announced as he set the drinks in front of them. "I just got this in a week ago. Let me know what you think." Then, he turned and disappeared back into the truck.

Autumn and Chase lifted their cups and tilted them toward one another. The chilly, amber beer flowed smoothly down Autumn's throat as she took a sip. "I think I'm in love," she said, setting her cup on the table.

"I'm known for that effect on women." Chase shrugged. "Although this is a little earlier than usual. What can I say?"

"Ha ha," Autumn replied, struggling to contain a smile. "I was talking about the beer. It's amazing."

"It is," Chase agreed. "Juan loves introducing different beers to his customers. I'm sure it's partly why folks keep coming back." He looked around. "Don't be fooled by the fact that it's so quiet here now. The late-night crowd swarms this place. Good luck getting a table in a couple of hours."

"You and Juan know each other a long time?"

"Yep," Chase nodded. "I was one of his earliest customers, back before he even had his food truck. We've...well, let's say we've helped each other out."

From the hesitation in his voice, it sounded like there was more to the story, but Autumn wasn't sure if she should probe. She didn't like people nosing around in her business, but he'd brought it up... "Care to elaborate?"

"It's not all that exciting but sure." He shifted in his chair to face her more directly, setting his arms on the table to lean in closer, as if confiding a secret.

"I told you my parents were essentially nomads," he began. "Content to wander the country like tumbleweed and going wherever the wind took 'em. At one point, we ended up in southern Texas, close to the Mexican border. It's where I picked up some Spanish." Chase's right leg rapidly bounced up and down as he spoke. Was he nervous?

Autumn steered her gaze back to his face. Nothing telling, although it seemed like a shadow had darkened his eyes. Or maybe that was just the light fading beneath the setting sun?

He continued. "Mom and pop were working in a restaurant, and my sibs used to go over there after school for dinner. I'd already graduated and had a part-time job there, too, washing dishes. The restaurant was across the street from an empty lot that used to be a gas station before it was torn down." He paused for a drink of beer. "Eventually, I started noticing a guy setting up a little stand every day over in the lot and selling food. It was Juan."

"He didn't work in the restaurant?"

Chase shook his head. "No. He'd tried to get a job, but the owner refused to hire him. Rumor was the dude had a problem with Mexicans. But Juan was a talented chef and wasn't about to be scared off by a narrow-minded bigot. He just made food in his trailer at home and sold it to people at the stand in the lot. Even got a permit so it was totally legit. Pretty soon, people started realizing Juan's food was miles better than the restaurant's, and their money started going his way. Obviously, the owner didn't like that much."

Anger burned a path through Autumn's blood. "Especially an owner with a racist problem."

"You got that right. He tried talking tough to chase Juan away, but he had no grounds. Juan had a permit and wasn't on the owner's property."

Chase paused to take a long sip of his beer, then wiped a hand across his mouth. "One day, it seemed like the owner decided to extend the olive branch, apologizing and saying as long as Juan didn't sell on his property, there'd be no problem. He'd even said Juan could use his restroom if he wanted."

"A goodwill gesture?"

Chase emitted a humorless bark of laughter. "Something like that. Things went okay for a week or so. Then one day, Juan came in to use the restroom. I happened to be in there at the time, standing at the sink, washing my hands. Juan walked in and we started shooting the shit. We, ah—" Chase's eyes narrowed as a muscle jumped in the back of his clenched jaw. His face turned dark as a cloud, like buried anger was clawing its way to the surface.

Autumn shivered. She wrapped her arms around herself. "Chase?"

He swallowed. "While we were talking, two assholes were outside, trashing Juan's stand." His gravelly voice was tainted with frost.

Now she understood his internal battle. "You think you're to blame. If you and Juan hadn't been talking in the john, the timeframe those jerks had for wasting his property would have been smaller. Maybe they wouldn't have been able to do as much damage."

He acknowledged her with a tight nod. "Stands to reason."

It wasn't his fault, but anything she'd say to try to change his mind would roll off him like water from a duck's back. She'd been in his shoes. Experience was a smart teacher.

"So what happened?"

"Juan and I walked outside and saw what was going on. We ran over and we…ah, stopped them."

By that small hesitation, she sensed what Chase meant. "I'm guessing you did some pretty good damage?"

He clenched his fists, and his knee bounced faster. He gave her a tight nod. "It was like a beast was let out of a cage. I was so furious I couldn't even see straight. I don't remember everything that happened. Someone called the cops, and next thing I knew, my ass was tossed in jail."

"*What*?"

"It was a setup. The owner wanted to let Juan use the restroom so his goons could trash his stand. Took awhile for that to get proved, and my parents were actually the key for doing so."

Autumn took a drink from her beer, buying time, not wanting Chase to guess how his story affected her. How it hit so close to home. She'd talked to no one, *no one* about her own experience. It had always seemed like an easy choice. In the blink of an eye, people judged, deciding that only worthless losers spend time in jail. If you have a rap sheet, you must be one of them. So she kept secrets to herself.

Yet here was Chase, talking about his time in the slammer with very little prompting and absolutely no shame. Of course, he was a guy. Things were different for them. Right?

She gulped another mouthful of beer, the cool liquid calming her as it slid down her throat. Could Chase actually be someone who checked his judgment at the door, who would understand someone with a record?

She filed away that thought and prompted Chase to keep talking. "Yeah? What'd your parents do?"

"They'd overheard some stuff from the restaurant owner. Their statements eventually sprung me free, but it took over a month before everything was straightened out. In the meantime, I cooled my heels in the slammer."

Her jaw hit the floor. "That's a bunch of BS!"

Chase let out a breath. "Apparently, those two guys were kinda hurt. One of them had a broken jaw."

"Jerk-off deserved it. He was trashing private property. He's the one who shoulda been locked up, not you." She shook her head. "No damn good deed goes unpunished."

Chase's eyes were warm, thankful, but also tinged with something like curiosity. "Sounds like you know something about that." His voice lowered although they were still alone.

Her cheeks warmed. *Holy hell, nothing gets by him easily.* Her flustered brain stammered around for an appropriate response.

Juan came out of the truck with a piping hot pie that emitted spicy aromas straight from the Food Gods. "The Juan special," he announced with a smile, setting down two plates and the giant tray in front of them. Steam rose from the pizza, where gooey melted cheese tantalizingly mingled with spicy pepperoni, basil leaves, crimini mushrooms, rich tomato sauce, and layers of seasoned crawfish.

"Enjoy, *amigos*."

"This looks insane," Autumn said, her mouth watering.

"And tastes even better." Chase slid a large slice onto her plate before serving himself.

"Hot damn," she muttered between bites. "Heaven on a plate."

Chase nodded. "Crazy, right? A Mexican chef who'd make an Italian mama weep."

They devoured their first slice, and as Chase served them again, Autumn prompted him to finish his story.

"That's pretty much all there is," he said. "Juan didn't get any time, because I was the one who'd actually hurt the guys. But while I was locked up, he visited me every day. He and I have been friends ever since. I'm the one who encouraged him to move to this area. He was burned out on Texas, anyway, and since I was coming here, I told him he should, too. It's been a good decision for both of us."

"How long ago was that, anyway?"

Chase set down his pizza and looked into the distance, his eyes narrowed. "Well," he said slowly. "Lemme think. I was eighteen at the time and I'm thirty-two now, so…wow. Fourteen years. Crazy how time flies."

Autumn nodded agreement but said nothing, her mouth too full of pizza to talk.

Chase shifted in his chair, his eyebrows raised as if a question had just occurred to him. "Can I ask you something?"

Instantly wary, she set down her slice. She folded her arms across her chest, her protective shield for when things turned personal. "You can ask whatever you want," she said quietly. "Doesn't mean I'm going to answer."

Chase let out a soft chuckle. "I'm not looking for deep dark secrets, Autumn. But fair enough. I'll ask; you answer. If you want to."

Her mind shifted back to their conversation of a few minutes ago. Chase had just shared some pretty intense stuff of his own. Seemed only fair to reciprocate. She slowly released a breath. *For Pete's sake, lighten up. You just had amazing sex with the dude. A little pillow talk after is the usual thing, even if it's over pizza without a pillow in sight.*

"Yeah, okay," she said. "Sure. What's the question?"

"I was only wondering when your birthday is. Seeing as I confessed my age, seems fair you should, too."

She nibbled her bottom lip while considering how to respond. Chase probably thought it was a simple enough question. He wasn't trying to bring up nasty topics or pry into her business. How could he know he'd asked something she couldn't easily answer? Then again, he already knew about the fire station. He might as well know the rest.

"You didn't actually tell me when your birthday is," she pointed out. "Only how old you are."

"August first. Now you."

She shrugged. "Fine. Well…remember I told you about how I was found?"

"Yeah."

"The woman who gave birth to me left no papers. Just wrapped me in a blanket with a bottle and dumped me at the fire station." She paused, forcing aside the bitterness in her voice. "So it means I don't know the exact day I was born."

"Hot damn, that's so cool."

Whatever reaction she might have expected from Chase, it sure as hell wasn't the big toothy grin he flashed.

"*Cool*?" Will this guy ever stop surprising the hell out of her? "Are you kidding me? Everyone knows when their birthday is. How is *not* knowing cool?"

His rumbling chuckle was punctuated with a quick shake of his head. "You're missing the point. Everyone who knows when their birthday is has no say in it. But how many actually get to pick out their own birthday? Pretty much no one, that's who. Except you." He drained the last of his beer. "That's what's cool."

She relaxed in her seat. He sure had a different way of looking at things, of making points no one else ever had—or ever cared enough to bother making.

Chase finished off his slice as he asked, "So what day did you pick?"

"The fire fighters at the station took me to a nearby hospital, and the doctor estimated I was anywhere between a week and a month old. Hard to tell, 'cause I guess I was undernourished and severely dehydrated." She pushed aside the hurt that always came with that thought. "I split the difference and use the day two weeks before I was found."

"Which is?"

"January first. It seemed right. New year, new age."

He nodded agreement. "Makes sense. So how old are you?"

"Twenty-six."

"Twenty-six? Huh." He smiled. "That's right about what I figured. Although I actually pegged you for more like twenty-five."

She raised an eyebrow. "What's that mean? You calling me old?"

"I wouldn't say that." His eyes sparkled in that way they did when he teased her. "But a whole year older than I thought…well, let's just say you hide it well."

"Oh, yeah?" She tossed her crust on the pizza tray and grabbed a third slice. "Thanks, grandad. I appreciate the compliment."

"*Grandad*?" He frowned, and his eyes narrowed. "Better watch that mouth of yours, whippersnapper, before you get yourself in trouble." He leaned forward, his voice low and husky. "'Cause then I just might have to spank you."

As if his big, tanned hand had already laid one on her, Autumn's bottom tingled and a rush of warmth pulsed in her core.

"Go ahead, gramps," she goaded him. "But try not to throw your back out in the process."

One side of his mouth curled up in a smile, but Autumn also noticed the quickening of his breathing as he transformed from amused to aroused. Acknowledging his obvious desire, she said in a low voice, "I'm thinking it's time for my punishment."

He threw some bills on the table and shot out of his chair like a rocket. He grasped her elbow and hauled her up, steering her toward his bike. "Damn straight, naughty girl."

Chapter Twelve

Chase drew a finger along the high-gloss photo proof, right at the slender curve of Autumn's waist, tracing the indentation where it narrowed before flaring out to her sexy little hips. He loved how her hair spilled down her back, those insanely long curls brushing the upper part of her ass.

From the photo, she looked up at him, glossed lips parted, the blush on her cheeks suggesting arousal, a woman in need of release. And the way her hands rested on his bare chest like she was claiming him made it clear he was the only man she wanted for the job.

His cock pressed painfully against his jeans. With a quick flick of his hand below the table, he adjusted himself to a marginally more comfortable position. Of course, the only true comfort he'd get would be from tracking down Autumn and burying himself in her amazing, hot body. He withheld a groan and focused. First things first, get the hell out of this meeting as fast as possible.

"This one," he said, stabbing his finger on the photo as he looked up at Maryanne. "This is the promo shot I want you to use."

The head designer conveyed both disgust and delight at the exact same moment. A deep trench creased the space between her eyebrows, while her fire-red lips curved upward in a rictus of maniacal glee.

"It's a marvelous picture of you, Chase," she gushed. "Just marvelous. But—"

"No 'buts.' This is the only one I'm authorizing."

"Oh, of course. Of course!" She giggled nervously, like he'd just told an off-color joke. "The only thing I wanted to point out is simply a reminder that the art we're featuring throughout the hotel is *your* art. Not anyone else's. I wouldn't want our guests getting confused about who the artist is. If there's more than one person in the photo, well…" She gave him a helpless, almost embarrassed shrug, as if presenting a delicate but thorny problem to which there was only one solution—hers. Chase ignored her veiled effort to cut Autumn out of the shot.

"My contract says I have final approval on the cover photo. This is the one we're using. Period. If you want other pictures for the inside spread that accompanies the article, you can use…" His gaze swept over the array of photos scattered around the table in front of him before plucking out four of his favorites, all of which included Autumn.

He set the pile in front of Maryanne. "These are all approved. That's it. These four, plus the one I picked for the cover, are the only ones you can use."

"Excellent choices. I love them. So will everyone else. I can't wait to see the final spread." She scooped up the approved prints and shoved them into an oversized bag. "I'll get these over to production immediately. We're painfully passed deadline, so I'll put a rush on it. Thank you for all your help, Chase."

He ignored the false eyelashes she fluttered his way. "You wouldn't have missed the deadline if you'd honored my contract in the first place."

His quiet voice of authority halted her fawning nonsense, making her words spill to the ground like so much water from a burst balloon. For half a second, her face crumpled, disappointment darkening her normally composed persona. He wondered why she seemed so intent on cutting Autumn out of the photos. Maryanne hadn't ever come on to him—which would have been a damn disaster all on its own—so why did she act almost like a jealous girlfriend getting ruffled over another woman?

Quick as lightning, Maryanne recovered her poise and hid whatever feelings she had beneath a veneer of adept hospitality professional. "You're absolutely right, of course. And believe me, it'll never happen again. I shouldn't have relied on…" Her last words were mumbled beneath her breath.

"Relied on…?"

She held out both hands, palms up, a "what are you gonna do?" gesture of annoyance. "Oh nothing, really, Chase. It's just…I made the mistake of relying on some uneducated advice instead of sticking with my own gut feeling, which is what I generally do. And I suppose Wilson didn't really know what he—"

"It doesn't seem unreasonable to get the hotel manager's opinion on the photo spread. He runs the place, after all." Chase stood, tired of Maryanne's nonsense. "To be honest, I don't know why *you're* involved. I thought you were in more of the picking-out-sofa-patterns job rather than PR Lady."

Once more, Maryanne's composure slipped, and this time, she didn't slap it back into place as she rose from her chair. "I'm far beyond selecting sofa patterns, Chase. I'm the head designer of this hotel. I know exactly what to do to bring in the type of high-end clientele the investors want, and that includes my being involved in publicity.

"Frankly, I'm part of every single decision made here, and I plan to keep it that way. The place would fall apart without me, and so will the future deals if hotel execs don't get their shit together." Twin spots of red bloomed across her cheeks.

But the second the words left her mouth, she looked stunned, as if realizing she'd disclosed more than she should have. Had let some cats out of the proverbial bag. She clapped a hand over her mouth, her cherry red nails blending in with her flushed face.

"Future deals?" Chase frowned. He shifted so he stood right in front of her and deliberately crossed his arms in front of his chest.

Maryanne retreated a half step, smoothed a hand over her hair, and flashed a warm, apologetic grin. "It's nothing, nothing. I'm so sorry. The pre-opening stress seems to be getting to me."

"Do I need to remind you of the contract I signed?"

"Of course not. I—"

"Everything we've discussed, relating to me and to my art, is for this hotel and this hotel only. Don't forget that."

She grabbed her purse before placing a gentle hand on Chase's arm. His skin twitched with revulsion, but he didn't shrug it away. She probably thought this new approach would go over better than her previous outburst.

"I actually have been meaning to talk with you," she said, plastering charm on top of her softened tone. "It involves your art and a potentially *huge* opportunity.

Something that would make what we're doing here look like child's play. I'm so excited about it, but I can't say anything yet." She giggled, her eyelashes fluttering once more. "So for the moment, I'll just leave you with this little teaser. I promise to say more just as soon as I can."

With a last little squeeze of her hand on his arm, she headed for the door of the conference room in which they'd been meeting.

"See you later!" she sang out, twisting the door handle. But at the threshold, she paused, like a last-minute thought had just popped in her head. "And by the way, when I can tell you more, it certainly shouldn't be in a dreary conference room. Nothing less than dinner will do. I insist." She tossed her head, flipping her hair behind her back as she flounced out the door.

Chase stood fixed in place as he watched her go. Devious, opportunistic, greedy, and a liar. Four words that described her to a T. Something fishy was going on with Maryanne. He felt it in his gut. For the moment, he let it go as there wasn't anything to do about it right now. But it didn't mean he was going to forget it.

His gaze shifted back to the conference table. Maryanne had taken only the five photos Chase had approved for use in the magazine, leaving plenty of others behind. And one in particular…

Stepping back to the conference table, he leaned in for a closer look. It was nearly identical to the one he'd just been looking at before. A topless Autumn was posed in front of him, her small hands placed on his chest, her gaze locked with his as she looked up at him.

But this shot had one sexy advantage over the ones he'd approved. She must have shifted slightly, or maybe it was that damn fan the director had insisted on. Her long curls didn't fully cover her gorgeous, pert breasts, and the swell on one side of her breast peeked out from beneath the blonde strands.

Chase groaned as blood rushed to his cock. *Talk about petrified wood.* With a sweep of his arm, he drew the remaining photos into a pile and shoved them into a folder Maryanne had left behind. Time to seek out the source of his discomfort. He whipped his phone from his pocket and stabbed a hurried text to Autumn.

Need to see you. Now. Emergency. Tell me where you are.

He grinned, wondering what she'd think. He doubted she'd be fooled. If there was an actual emergency, he sure as shit wouldn't just rely on texting to reach her.

Seconds later, he got his reply.

Sounds serious. Better let me take a look. I'm in the server room.

Sweet merciful molasses, she knew what he was after. Even better, sounded like she was happy to give him what he needed.

Be right there. Don't go anywhere, and make sure you're alone. Confidential situation.

Before he could put his phone back in his pocket, it buzzed right back.

Coast is clear. Show me what you need.

****

Autumn grinned as she slipped the phone in her back pocket and finished tying down a bundle of mainframe power cords in the server room. Chase was horny; no doubt about it. "Emergency," her ass. The man seriously just needed to get laid.

But she couldn't deny that the idea of him thinking about her, getting turned on and then demanding that he come find her was…well, it was flattering. And massively hot. Her nipples pressed painfully against her bra, and demanding pulses beat between her legs. She shivered, and not from the blasting AC cooling off the IT hardware.

The door swung open. Chase stood in the frame, his enormous chest heaving. The room shrank when he stepped inside. With the back of one foot, he kicked the door shut. His gaze searched the room before settling on a metal, fold-up chair in the corner. With one hand, he grabbed it and shoved it beneath the doorknob. Locking everyone out. Trapping her inside.

Hunger for her poured out through his quick, shallow breaths, and Autumn's blood surged, roaring in her eardrums. Chase ambled toward her, his leisurely footstep like those of a stalking, ravenous wolf who knew his prey was trapped. He reached out, palms cupping her face as he brought her forward. She looked up as she rose on her toes, straining to reach him before he bent down and pulled her in for a long, hard kiss.

His hands roamed everywhere, caressing her face, sliding down her back and over the slope of her ass. She barely suppressed a groan as Chase yanked the cami out from her jeans and replaced the thin material with his hand. Coarse calluses slid over her skin, and his fingers dug into her flesh as he drew her against him.

He broke the kiss, stepping back to eye the button on her jeans. His ragged panting loudly whistled past her ears above the hum of the server as he grabbed the waist of her jeans. With a quick flick of his thumb and middle finger, he popped the button and dragged down the zipper.

The parted material revealed a peek of sheer black lace. His gaze shifted to hers, eyes glittering dangerously in the dim light. "Nice," he said, nodding at the panties. "Show me more."

Autumn cocked her jaw. "See for yourself," she challenged.

Before she could blink, he was crouched in front of her, and her jeans were around her ankles. With no effort to be gentle, he lifted her foot and pulled off her sneaker and sock, tossing them to the corner.

He looked up and cocked an eyebrow at her. "Nice pedi, Techie. I like the red."

"I—"

His tongue slid along the sensitive bottom of her foot, swirled between her toes, before he slowly drew her big toe between his warm, moist lips.

"Ah!" She sucked in a sharp breath. Tingles raced up her leg directly to her core, a sizzling path of fire in its wake. Cool air hit her foot when Chase took his mouth away, but heat rushed back in once more as he yanked the jeans off her left leg before doing the same to her right. Next came her black lace bra. Then, he pulled her matching lace panties down her legs before standing to tower above her.

Heat shimmered off her skin while beads of sweat dotted her chest and the swell of her breasts. She stepped forward, sliding into Chase's embrace as she shoved her hands beneath his shirt. He finished the work for her, lifting off his shirt and tossing it in the corner with her sneaks.

She let out a frustrated cry as she fumbled with the belt, unable to release it. "Get it off," she ordered.

His lips twitched in a grin. "Hold on, tiger."

In one slick movement, he tugged the belt free and undid his jeans. Autumn helped him shove them down, not noticing whether or not he even took them off. She was on him like a vampire in desperate need of a fix, licking, kissing, nipping at his heated skin. His chest muscles flexed beneath her lips. She slid her arms around his waist, skating her hands over the curve of his back and down his perfect ass. Her fingers dug into the muscles, pulling him closer to her as she continued to lick and kiss her way along his chest and down the rungs of his ab muscles.

Musky scent surrounded her as she headed south. She shifted her hands to fist his marble-hard cock, stroking it, teasing him before she slowly slid her tongue along his length.

"Ahh…" Deep, throaty groans rumbled above her.

She varied her strokes while playing her tongue against his pulsing length, swirling around the head and tip as she licked away the bead of moisture that had formed. Chase's fingers threaded into her hair to guide her mouth onto his cock. She opened her throat, taking him deep. The salty taste of him coated her tongue, the flavor intimate and unique, all his own. She caressed his balls while the other hand gripped the base of his cock to stroke him as she sucked.

Suddenly, he hauled her to her feet. "Turn around."

Her heartbeat jumped, excitement pelting through her. She spun, grabbing hold of an empty shelving unit. Her fingers slid between the chrome bars of the shelf, clutching tight.

"Spread your legs," he demanded, his warm breath tickling the hairs on the back of her neck. "Show me how ready you are for me."

Oooh, bossy Chase has come out to play. Her moan echoed loudly in the small room as she obeyed his order.

"More." Menace coated his gravelly voice, adding to her thrill.

But before she had time to comply, her ass burned with a sharp sting. "Ah!"

The crack of his palm against her butt cheek held the power of a drug. She wanted more, *needed* more, craving the seductive burn like an addict. Her nipples tightened to rock hard pebbles. She spread her legs wider, so willing to obey. Her hips swayed as she shook her ass, showing him what she wanted.

Crack!

She failed to stifle a groan before he landed another spank, and another. The blows came fast and hot. Too much. Not enough. Her clit pulsed. Leaning in to stick her ass out farther, inviting—no, *begging* for more spanks—she closed her eyes and held tight to the shelf as hot moisture ran down her thighs.

A thick finger, then two, slid easily inside her pussy. He pumped them into her wet heat as he continued to spank her.

"So damn wet," he murmured.

He landed two more slaps before his fingers slid free. The quick tear of a foil wrapper quieted her protests for more.

The head of his cock teased her opening, circling. Probing. He slid only the head of his cock just inside her pussy, then stilled. She frowned and pushed back. He retreated.

What the hell? She bit back a frustrated cry.

"Give it to me," she ordered.

"And then…?"

"And then…then…" Her brain was oatmeal. She couldn't think. "C'mon, Chase," she pleaded, beyond caring about the desperation in her voice.

"I need to hear what you want me to do, Autumn," he rumbled. "Tell me."

"I want you to fuck me!" she gasped.

"How?"

"Hard. Fast. Deep." She wiggled her ass, desperate for his cock. "And now, damn it. Fuck me *now*."

He slammed into her, his full length buried to the hilt as his balls slapped her pussy. Blood roared through her veins. She was so filled, his cock mercilessly slamming into her. Her fingers gripped the steel bars as she shifted her hips to meet every one of his thrusts.

Never before had she wanted him like this, so needy, so desperate. The sharp slaps of skin against skin, the musky scent of sex filling the room, his salty taste when she went down on him, and now this—this supreme ecstasy of their connection, of how he dominated yet served her needs. It was like nothing she'd ever had. She was dizzy, floating, swirling in a torrent of desire. Her eyes fluttered shut as her pussy clenched and throbbed, release already only seconds away.

His hand caressed her face, sliding along her cheek and jaw line. He slipped his middle finger between her lips, and she tasted her own salty juices.

Another sharp blow landed on her ass.

She swallowed a cry, but she couldn't hold off any longer. Her legs shook, her heartbeat slamming like a jackhammer.

As if sensing she was about to come, Chase's hand closed over her mouth to quiet her cries. His other hand slid into her mass of hair, pulling her head back. She was trapped, unable to move, completely under his control, and she loved every second of it. He pounded relentlessly, skin slapping skin, filling her completely.

Two more thrusts and she reeled over the edge of the cliff. The orgasm consumed her, possessing every nerve as she was flooded with pleasure. She gripped the storage rack like holding on for life while her core pulsed and throbbed around his hard cock. Seconds later, Chase let out a strangled groan as he stilled and found his own release.

Long, ragged breaths filled the small space. Chase wrapped her in his arms as they stood in place while their breathing slowed. She closed her eyes, indulging in the moment of tenderness. Weird how it didn't feel scary or wrong or like she should be running away. Being in Chase's arms…well. It just felt right.

Cold air whooshed in when Chase pulled away. With a weary tilt of her head, Autumn glanced behind her. Chase caught her eye and reached down to get their clothes, handing hers over. They dressed quickly and silently before leaning heavily against the wall to catch their breath.

Autumn shoved back loose strands of her hair that had come undone and looked over at Chase. He stood beside her, sporting a loopy grin.

"Someone's happy," she said.

"More like my mind is blown." He released a long breath and shook his head. "Wow. Autumn. That was amazing. *You're* amazing."

She tried and failed to suppress a smile. "I aim to

please." She hesitated before adding, "Sir."

"And a quick learner, too." He cast her a grin but a slight shadow darkened his eyes. "You're okay with that, right?"

"With?"

"Well, with…" He paused as if searching for the right words. "With me being a dominant, I guess. In the bedroom."

"Or closet."

"Ha. Well, yeah. There, too."

Autumn expelled a final deep breath before walking over to her discarded sneakers and slipping them on. *Was* she okay with it? Surprisingly—shockingly—she was. 'Cause with him, she felt safe. And she realized with a jolt, she trusted him. *Holy shit.* How did that happen?

"If I wasn't, I'd let you know, and we'd be having none of it. But…" She shrugged. "Turns out I like it."

Chase nodded. "Cool." He pulled on his boots. "So, I guess I should get outta here. Don't want to get you in trouble. Or me for that matter."

"You couldn't get in trouble if you tried."

He paused in the middle of pulling the chair out from beneath the door handle. "What do you mean?"

She gave him an exaggerated eye roll. "Oh, c'mon Mountain Man. Maryanne gushes over you like a teenage girl at a boy band concert. There's nothing you can do to put her in a douchey mood. Me on the other hand…"

He frowned, anger flashing across his face. "What do you mean? Did something happen?"

"Nah." She waved away his concern. "Nothing like that. She's just got me stuck in her craw. I can't figure why."

He looked for a second like he was going to protest against what she said but then appeared to think the better of it.

He shook his head. "You're right. She was supposed to show me the proofs from that photo shoot a week ago. Finally got around to it today. Turns out, she'd tried to go ahead without my say-so beforehand. None of the photos she picked out included you."

"Why am I not shocked."

"Don't worry, I straightened her out. Get ready to see your mug on the cover of *Whitepaper*."

She groaned. "Bet she loved that. Not."

"I don't give a shit." He slipped his phone into his back pocket and went to twist the doorknob open, but something stopped him. He froze and slowly swerved back around. "You know, twice now she's mentioned something about future deals to me."

"Future deals? What's that mean?"

"I'm not sure. But my gut tells me something not quite right is going on with her."

Autumn nodded. Her suspicion radar had been spiking since the minute she'd laid eyes on the pushy designer. "Same here. Something is rotten in Denmark with that chick."

He cocked a raised eyebrow. "Well, I'll be forsoothed," Chase drawled in his rumbly voice. "Tiny Techie knows her Shakespeare."

"Everyone knows that expression, Mountain Man." She waved off the compliment even though her insides blushed like a tomato.

"Not true," he said, adamantly shaking his head. His gaze swept the length of her. "Damn, woman, you keep surprising the hell outta me." He cupped her cheeks, drawing her forward for a hard kiss.

"Forget work. I'm starving," he said when he finally let her go. "Let's eat."

Autumn let out a breath, calming her racing pulse. She glanced at her watch, surprised to see it was nearly six. No wonder her stomach was growling. But there was a small problem. "I gotta feed Beau."

"I'll go with you."

"Yeah?"

"Sure," he said with a nod. "Every time I'm at your place that pooch of yours gets to know me a little more. We actually had a recent bro-to-bro talk."

"A bro-to-bro talk?" She raised an eyebrow. "With my dog?"

"It's a guy thing. You wouldn't understand. But Beau and I are making progress and I wanna keep it going so he eventually ditches the urge to bite my face off."

"He actually does like you," Autumn confirmed, remembering how Beau had licked Chase's hand the last time he was over.

"So let me feed the dog at your place, then I'll feed you over at mine. I'm cooking."

"You cook?"

"Bet your sweet ass I do," he said with a leer, his hungry gaze skating across her body. "I do mean sweet." He whistled, low. "Very sweet. And I'll be needing more."

Chapter Thirteen

"To the White Ibis!" A chorus of cheers joined clinking crystal champagne glasses as the Louisiana elite toasted the pending hotel opening, now only a week away.

Maryanne forced her glossed lips into a toothy smile. Like everyone else, she fawned over the supposed stellar work hotel manager Wilson Wyatt had done, even though she knew his fat ass wouldn't be earning nearly the praise he was getting if it weren't for her. She was the one who'd really pulled off the minor miracle of meeting the tight deadline. Some manager he was.

Good thing she wasn't shy about steamrolling right over him to ensure the timeframe was met. For now, Wilson could have his little moment in the sun. Her own reward would come once that multi-property deal was inked, putting her in charge of overseeing over a dozen luxury hotels instead of just this one.

The black-tie affair had brought in some of the oldest and wealthiest money in the state. Blue bloods to the core, they were treated to the first formal dinner the hotel would host before its official opening. It gave them a taste of the high-end indulgences the White Ibis would offer, ensuring their patronage and endorsement of the hotel to their well-heeled friends.

Her elderly seating companion on the right leaned

over as the salad course was served. "This is splendid," she said with a wide smile, spearing a slice of glazed pear.

Maryanne nodded as her fork idly circled her plate. The head chef—Pat, she believed her name was—more than earned her reputation.

But Maryanne was far too wound up to think about food. There was so much to do. If she could figure a way to bust out of this dinner, she'd have been gone hours ago. Instead, she had to waste time playing nicey-nice to these loaded bores.

"I can't wait to see the art show," the woman continued. "I hear Chase Durand is quite the talent." Her eyes sparkled just like the diamond-studded headband planted in her jet-black mane. The high sheen clearly indicated a professional dye job.

"He is," Maryanne assured her.

"A friend told me Mr. Durand's show is simply over-the-top, with all kinds of astounding technology behind the lighting and movement of the objects in time to music."

"It's astounding all right," Maryanne agreed, her responses on autopilot as her attention drifted to Mason. He had that big meeting today and had promised her he'd be finalizing the deal. Measured by the excitement already brewing over Chase's art, she *had* to make sure she got him on board as well.

"…his girlfriend, although it's a shame in a way." Jet-black hair sighed wistfully.

Maryanne snapped to attention as if someone had cracked a whip beside her ear. "I'm sorry, what did you say? Something about a girlfriend?"

A devilish sparkle lit her companion's eyes. "It's

always rather decadent to imagine him unattached, isn't it? Like maybe the rest of us mortals might actually have a chance. But seems like he's off the market as I assume that gorgeous, petite blonde is his girlfriend." Her shoulders lifted in a resigned shrug. "The good ones are always taken."

Maryanne's heart raced like she'd been goosed with a cattle prod. If this old tart was gushing over Chase and hoping he was flying solo, imagine how the wealthy socialites who actually might have a chance with him would feel? If they thought Chase was off the market, his appeal would drop. Just as she'd assumed.

It was imperative for her to assure these windbags that Chase was definitely unattached. "Chase is absolutely a bachelor," she said firmly. "Quite unattached. I know that for a fact."

"You do?" The woman frowned, but a hopeful glimmer lit those aging eyes. "And how would you know that for sure, if you don't mind my asking."

Maryanne leaned in toward her companion and patted the back of the woman's liver-spotted hand.

"I'm never one to betray secrets," she said in a conspiratorial voice, "but let me just say that Mr. Durand is a *very* dear friend, and he confides in me more than anyone else. And well, he just hasn't found the right woman yet...though his eyes are wide open for when she comes along." She punctuated her fake gossip with a wink, sending the old crone into a fit of blushing giggles.

"Oh, my goodness. Such a talented, handsome man and yet no woman by his side."

"He just hasn't found the right one," Maryanne reiterated, cocking a brow at the woman before taking a last forkful of miso-glazed salmon. She'd had enough. Time to get back to work.

She released an audible gasp as she looked at her slender wristwatch. "Oh my! Is that the time?"

"Nearly half past eight," her companion confirmed, but Maryanne was already pushing back her chair.

"Please forgive me," she said, glancing at her phone to validate her bogus excuse. "I just received a text about a pressing issue I must resolve before nine. So sorry to be off!"

Without waiting for the woman to reply, she grabbed her night bag and whipped her wrap over her shoulder. Weaving through the welter of tables like a surfer on a wave, she made her way to the exit and slipped through the back door, silently as a thief.

****

Chase's good buddy, herpetologist Dr. Jackson Rivard, shoved at his glasses from where they'd slipped down the bridge of his nose and peered closer at the monitor. "This is unusual," he muttered. "These two mated four days ago. Now, they're back for more. What the hell…"

Chase's gaze tracked to the same corner of the giant monitor where Jackson was watching an amorous pair of king cobras doing the horizontal mambo. Looked like hot times in snake town to him, but Jackson's frown told a different story. His buddy glanced over the additional twenty monitors that were mounted around the walls of the control room.

"Unless they're marked incorrectly, and this is a different pair from who I thought I was looking at." He shook his head and a wry smile lifted one corner of his lips as he turned toward Chase. "When you've got over two hundred king cobras to track, mistakes can happen. New interns sometimes mix them up."

"Two *hundred*?"

"I'm actually down a couple dozen from the usual population."

Chase chuckled and clapped Jackson on the back. "You're awesome, man. The work you do looking for the cure to MS through the cobra venom...I tip my hat."

Jackson nodded in thanks, but the tight stress lines around his mouth revealed just how heavy the weight of his work affected him. Again, his gaze glanced over the monitors before he finally shook his head.

"I'm not gonna find what I'm looking for. Not now, anyway." He tossed his notepad on a desk and cocked a head toward the door. "C'mon, let's get outta here. We could both use a break."

Minutes later, they were racing down a two-lane highway toward Les's. The popular Cajun restaurant was normally packed, although at three in the afternoon they found seats at the bar. The bartender brought cold beers and a bowl of chips. They cocked the longnecks toward each other in a silent cheer and drained half their bottles.

"Man, that tastes great," Jackson said, drawing a hand across his brow. "It's a hot one out there today."

"Murder," Chase replied. "Especially working without AC."

"What the hell? Aren't you about to open?"

Chase nodded and crunched on a handful of chips. "In three days. It was working fine but stopped yesterday afternoon, and the problem hasn't been fixed yet." He couldn't hold back a wry grin. "Needless to say, the head honchos in charge are losing their shit."

Jackson flashed a satisfied smirk. He wasn't exactly filled with sympathy for corporate goons.

They sat in silence for a few moments before Chase said, "Let me ask you something, man. You know a gal by the name of Autumn Rivette?"

"Rivette?" Jackson put a finger to his lips as he thought about it. "The name is familiar," he said slowly, "although I'm not sure—" Suddenly, he snapped his fingers. "Now I know. She's one of Kelly's friends."

"Kelly?"

"A research tech working at the center. She was kind of a problem awhile back, and I didn't know if I was going to keep her around. But she's got brains and is stubborn as a dog with a bone." He finished his beer and held up two fingers to signal another round. "She and Autumn are pals."

"Oh, yeah?" Chase hadn't heard Autumn mention Kelly's name. Then again, there was a lot he didn't know about Autumn.

"She used to come around more, but I haven't seen her in awhile," Jackson continued.

"She heads up IT for the White Ibis."

"Doesn't surprise me. Now that I remember, she's a genius at that tech shit. Fixed a bunch of computer stuff around my lab."

The bartender brought over their fresh beers and Jackson took a long pull.

"Anyway," he said, wiping a hand across his mouth. "Why do you ask? You and she got a thing?"

Chase answered with a grin.

"Cool, man." Jackson raised his bottle in a salute. "Good for you."

Chase sat back in his chair. Good for him was right. Autumn could torture a man with those amazing baby-blues, ruthless determination and no BS attitude. He whistled beneath his breath.

"I don't know where it's going," he admitted. "But..." he shrugged. "I like her."

"Starting to get under your skin?"

More like under my heart.

Wait, what? He jerked like someone startled by a loud noise. Where the hell had that come from? Surprising as it was, he didn't immediately reject the thought. He and Autumn were definitely having a "thing," as Jackson put it. Chase wasn't sure what would happen or even what it really meant. But the Tiny Techie and her 'tude were starting to make a permanent mark on him, staining his heart like a tattoo.

The outside door swung open and a striking, raven-haired woman sauntered in. Chase and Jackson swiveled on their stools to watch her. Her confident swagger suggested familiarity at Les's, that she'd been there a time or three before.

As she walked up to the bar, her gaze latched on to Jackson's. "Hey," she said, nodding.

"Just the person we were talking about." Jackson waved her closer. "Kelly, there's someone I want you to meet."

She approached them and gave Chase the same short nod. "'Sup?"

"Cool to meet you, Kelly. What're you drinking?" Chase signaled the bartender.

Kelly pointed a slim finger toward the assorted whiskeys. "Black Sky. Rocks. Thanks, man."

"I think you know Chase's girlfriend," Jackson

said after Chase gave Kelly's order.

For half a second, Chase almost corrected the scientist but then decided he kinda liked the way "girlfriend" sounded.

"Yeah?" Kelly's gaze shot toward Chase. "Who ya seeing?"

"Autumn Rivette. Jackson said you know her?" The bartender dropped off the drink, and Chase held it out.

Kelly took the whiskey and downed half of it in a single swallow, then nodded as she set the glass between them on the bar. "She's a friend, yeah. Scary smart with technology stuff. Why you asking?"

"She and I work over at the White Ibis," he explained. "And Jackson mentioned that you two are friends."

"Autumn's cool," she said to Chase. "She and I get each other because of our backgrounds, you know? Both of us had shit to deal with when we were kids. It shapes who you are." She narrowed her gaze. "She told you about her childhood?"

"Yeah," Chase acknowledged. "The bad foster family. She told me about it."

"'Bad' is the biggest understatement on the planet," Kelly said with a frown. "Lazy, worthless users is more like it. Especially her 'dad,' Rick. What an asshole that guy was." She crunched an ice cube between her white teeth. "All that trouble he got Autumn into. That whole Vegas situation. It's some messed-up shit. But I'm sure you know all that."

Asshole dad? Worthless users? Chase *didn't* know all that, but hot anger burned his blood now that he did. His fingers curled into fists at the grim picture Kelly had painted of Autumn's shitty childhood. Lucky for asshole Rick that he wasn't standing in front of Chase right this second.

Kelly waved a hand toward a group of people at a table across the room and set her empty glass on the bar. "I'm outta here. Friends are waiting. Later." Without a backward glance, she headed across the room.

Jackson watched her and grinned. "I know her attitude might seem abrasive," he said, "but trust me when I tell you she's a thousand times better than she used to be."

They swiveled their chairs back toward the bar. "A thousand times better?" Chase grinned. "I don't even want to know what she was like before."

Jackson chuckled. "I told you, man. Good help is hard to find. When you find a good woman, you hold onto her."

Chase nodded as he sipped his beer, an image of a petite, feisty woman he'd be pleased to hold on to staking permanent ground in his mind.

****

Autumn frowned as her gaze flew over thousands of lines of code on the screen. Where the hell was the problem? Something was definitely misconfigured. But what? "Did Evan look through this?"

"Twice." Autumn's primary programmer, Keith Sanchez, sat at a terminal right beside her and reviewed the same code. "He said everything he wrote is exactly what the specs called for."

"Then something's gotta be wrong in the specs," she muttered.

Chase's largest artistic display, the one stationed in

the huge outdoor seating area beside the koi pond, wasn't working. He'd created a delicate, twisting piece composed of thousands of intricate glass tubes that fit together to form an ibis in flight. The glass wings of the bird flapped up and down while the whole sculpture turned on a dais. It also lit up, with the colors changing every twenty seconds. It had required intense engineering to get it working, and the amount of code behind it was crazy. But something wasn't right, because it wasn't working.

For the past three hours, she and Keith had been glued to their laptops as they searched for the problem. With grand opening two days away, pressure had rocketed up the wrong side of insane.

She brushed sweat from her brow as she scanned the code. Something was messed up….programmed incorrectly. Or—

"Hold on," she told Keith. "Go back to that previous page."

Keith brought up what they'd just been reviewing. "I don't see anything wrong."

"'Cause there isn't." Her eyes flew over the code, reviewing it again. *There*.

"Look at that," she said, pointing to a line halfway down the page. "You see where it jumps from here to here."

"Yeah."

"What's written is correct. But a command code for the wings to go down is missing. It's there for them to go up, but not down. So the bird can't fly."

Keith's eyes flashed with excitement. "Oh, I see what you mean! Yeah, that's it. It's gotta be." His fingers flew over the keyboard, inputting the missing code. After Autumn reviewed it, they were ready for a test run.

"Fire it up," she said tersely to two of the other techs standing by.

Streams of colored lights flowed through the glass tubes of the bird. The dais started turning, and the head of the ibis slowly swung around to face Autumn and Keith. In a movement as smooth and graceful as the bird itself, the glass wings lowered before lifting up and up, filling the room with color and light.

Autumn expelled a long sigh of relief. "Good work," she said to Keith.

"You're the one who discovered the problem," he pointed out. "Guess that's why you're the big boss."

"Or little boss," a voice rumbled behind them. "As the case may be."

Unable to suppress a grin, Autumn turned toward the doorway filled by Chase's massive frame. He was dressed as usual in a grey T-shirt, jeans, but for some reason today, he looked even more mind-blowingly amazing than usual. The obvious spark of desire in his eyes mesmerized her, making her heartbeat pound inside her chest. *Holy crap. I'm acting like I'm in some kinda romance novel.*

"Looks great," Chase said, nodding toward the sculpture. "Works exactly as I wanted." He nodded in turn to both Autumn and Keith. "Thanks to you both."

Autumn shrugged as heat raced across her skin. Compliments were circuit breakers tripping her brain and shutting down her ability to think.

She cast her gaze to the floor. "It's nothing," she finally mumbled before looking up again at Chase. He was so…wait. She looked more closely. His usual smile was there, but so was something else—a tightness around his lips she hadn't noticed before. What was going on?

Chase seemed to realize she'd picked up his vibe. "Could I talk to you in private for a minute?" "Yeah, sure." She got up and nodded toward the doorway. "Let's go inside to the restaurant. No one's there now."

They walked without talking, Autumn's nerves fraying like cheap fabric. Something was etched in Chase's expression that she couldn't quite figure. Had something happened? Was he worried? Were they breaking up? Of course, they'd have to actually be a couple in the first place in order for them to *not* be a couple. And they weren't really a couple…were they? Her stomach twisted as thoughts gathered steam, racing through multitudes of unpleasant scenarios.

Without asking him where he wanted to sit, Autumn chose a table in the corner, partially obscured by a lack of lighting in that section of the restaurant.

"What's up?" She didn't bother softening her tone. In the few seconds it had taken them to walk to the table, she'd already begun imagining the worst. She wiped sweaty palms across her jeans and rested a hip against the side of the table, too wound-up to sit.

With a quick glance around to ensure they were alone, Chase pulled her into his arms and lowered his head, his mouth crashing down hard on hers.

All the tattered nerves from moments ago melted as scorching lust sizzled through her body, a path racing straight from her mouth to her core. Rising on her toes, she wrapped her arms around his neck to bring herself closer and deeper into his kiss. She slipped her tongue between his lips, tasting him. Groaning, his strong fingers squeezed her ass.

Ragged breaths escaped her as Chase nibbled the sensitive skin at her throat. Desire hovered at the edge of sanity, threatening to erase all common sense and compel her to start whipping off her clothes and flinging them across the room. *Probably a bad idea in the middle of the restaurant.* With iron-strength will, she eased herself from his grasp.

Chase locked his gaze with hers, his eyes dark as creosote. His deep, heaving breaths continued undiminished, evidence of how crazy fast they could rev each other up. Twin turbo engines firing like rockets whenever they touched.

She expelled a long breath herself and smoothed her hair as she took a seat. "What was that for?"

Chase shrugged as he sat. "Just felt like it." His gaze slid down the length of her. "You're a tough one to resist."

"Then don't try."

A corner of his lip rose. "You've been warned."

She grinned at his low, teasing response.

Chase set his left ankle on his opposite knee and eased back in his chair. "So, you know the big party's coming up, right? Opening day?"

Autumn nodded. She and her team had worked their asses off, but they were ready. "Your stuff's good to go," she assured him. "That coding bug with the ibis is fixed now, and everything else tested out perfect."

He held up a hand as if to block her words. "I have no doubt it's perfect," he said. "I'm not after that."

"Yeah?" She raised a questioning brow. "So what *are* you after?"

"I want to take you to the party."

She sat back in her chair, frowning. "Take me? But I'm already going. I assumed you were, too, since it's right here in the hotel."

His eyes took on a gleam as he let out a soft chuckle. "Sometimes I think that mass of hair blocks your brain, Autumn. I'm talking about us going to the party together." He waited a beat, then added, "As a couple."

She swallowed. *Oh.* A mild sensation of panic welled up, but then calm rushed in. So what if people knew they were a couple? There was no reason to keep it under wraps. They had broken no rules. Neither one of them reported to the other or had influence on pay or promotions. There was nothing to bring the HR police down on their heads. So why not let their relationship—or whatever it was—be out there?

Thrusting out her chin defiantly, she couldn't help but challenge, "A couple? So, you thinking you're like my boyfriend or something?"

Chase didn't flinch as he reached forward, and his hand swallowed her fingers in his giant palm. His thumb lightly stroked the back of her hand, up, down, back and forth, the caress as soothing as rain.

"Yeah. I'm thinking I am."

She didn't immediately respond, captivated by the simple intimacy of him holding her hand and declaring without hesitation that he was, in fact, her boyfriend. Such an easy step for him to take, such a mountain for her to climb. Yet here they were, an honest-to-God couple. He was all hers. Holy shit.

"You got a problem with that, Techie? 'Cause if you do, I might have to spank you."

Molten lust slid through her veins at his seductive

tease. Just the thought of his hand cracking hotly across her backside had her ass burning and her pussy starting to throb. "I don't have a problem with it, Mountain Man, but you might have to spank me anyway. Just to be sure."

He waggled his eyebrows at her as a grin split his lips. "I'll be over after work."

"Don't be late."

Chapter Fourteen

As Chase stepped into the dining room for the opening night party with Autumn by his side, the hotel guests and staff clapped with the enthusiasm of star-struck fans.

Chase stopped dead in his tracks, uncomfortable with the overwhelming attention. He'd always been more of a behind-the-scenes guy, content with having his art get the accolades. He gripped Autumn's hand, thankful for the small but powerful reassurance of normalcy within her warm grasp.

"Chase!" Wilson Wyatt stepped out from the crowd with his arm stretched forward. The hotel manager shook Chase's hand and then turned to the room waving to quiet the noise.

"Folks," he said as the cheering eased, "let me formally introduce Chase Durand. You all know he's our resident artist, and the creative genius behind every one of the stunning glass displays throughout the hotel. His art is already gaining outside attention, and Chase is going to be a huge draw for our guests. The White Ibis will be known as a luxury hotel for its comfortable rooms, first-rate amenities, incomparable staff, and unique artwork. By coming here, our guests will get the full Chase Durand experience. We're lucky to have him, so please join me in making Chase feel at home."

The crowd erupted into thunderous applause, more

effusive than the last.

Man, what an unbelievable turnaround compared to where I'd once been in life. The routine eviction notices, stacks of overdue bills, the relentless calls from smarmy collection agents. He squeezed Autumn's hand once more. His Tiny Techie was a much better companion, and hot damn was he ever glad to have her with him now.

He thanked everyone and quelled the applause as quickly as possible, steering Autumn through the jam-packed room. They pressed their way up to the bar. "Beer?"

To no surprise, she gave him a vigorous nod. Even at a formal party, Autumn was Autumn. A smart, sexy, down-to-Earth girl who swore like a sailor and drank beer at a fancy shindig.

They clinked their bottles together as Chase surveyed the room. "I think every person who works in this hotel is here."

"It *is* the grand opening party, after all," Autumn pointed out. "It's tough to turn down free food and booze."

A waiter carrying a silver tray of appetizers appeared. "Pesto-infused orange roe bruschetta with roasted pine nuts?"

Chase frowned, taking a wary step back. "I don't even know what language you're speaking, my man. Thanks, but no thanks. I'll stick to cocktail wieners."

Autumn's chuckle rose beside him as the waiter shuffled off. "Cocktail wieners?"

Chase took another drink of his beer. "What? Did you want that pesto-whatever doohickey?"

"Nope, I'll pass." A wicked gleam lit her eye. "I

like to know exactly what I'm putting in my mouth."

Holy hell. His cock stirred.

Only two hours earlier, they'd been at his place tangled up in covers—and each other. Autumn had gone down on him, expertly teasing as she drew his cock into her hot, wet mouth until he'd begged for mercy. He'd plunged his hand into her hair, those golden curls like silk as he wrapped his fingers around the strands and guided her pace. Her tongue had teased the sensitive spot right beneath the tip as she relaxed her throat and then took him deep. Man-oh-man-oh-man, did she ever know how to set him on fire.

He let out a breath and willed his dick to deflate. Somehow, boner and formal party didn't quite go together.

Help arrived in the form of taut red lips curved skyward as Maryanne greeted him with frenzied enthusiasm. "I was wondering where you were. The party started an hour ago." She fluttered false lashes. "Our esteemed guests have been waiting."

"They seem fine to me," he said mildly, his mind racing for an excuse to get away. "Anyway, I was…busy." He glanced at Autumn with a smile.

When his gaze returned to Maryanne, her curved lips had flatlined and all her former enthusiasm drained away. He had no doubt that the hair up her butt was a hundred percent related to Autumn.

"Well," Maryanne said briskly, "you're here now. Why don't you come with me, and I'll introduce you around." She made to grab his arm, doing everything she possibly could to ignore Autumn.

"Maryanne, I'm—"

"Yoo-hoo!" Autumn waved a hand inches from

Maryanne's face. "I know I'm small, so you probably didn't see me, right? But I'm actually here, too." She leveled a cold-dagger stare at the interior designer.

Maryanne tossed a frosty smile right back. "I'm aware of that, Autumn. But the star of the show is actually Chase, not you. So if you'll excuse us—"

Damn, swallowing burning coals would be easier than melting the ice between these two. But Chase had to intervene before World War Three erupted at the White Ibis.

"I'll be along in a bit, Maryanne," he said, trying to detox the situation. "As you said yourself, we've just arrived."

"Chase, your contract states—"

"And I'll honor it. Just give me a minute." When she didn't immediately leave, he added, "Alone."

"Fine." Maryanne thrust her jaw forward. "Find me when you're ready. And don't be long." With a final, piercing glance at Autumn, she walked away, heels like pistol shot clicking in her wake.

"Nothing like a warm welcome to get the party started." Chase looked down at Autumn. She was quiet and composed, much as she'd been before the strained encounter with the head designer. But he could sense nervous tension, like a live wire, humming just beneath Autumn's calm exterior. "You okay?"

She didn't answer for so long he thought she wasn't going to. But then she expelled a soft breath as if blowing out the last of her anger. "Yep."

"I...ah. I'm supposed to say something," he said. "Thank everyone for their help with my art, that kind of thing. A lot of concessions were made to the hotel's preliminary plans in order to accommodate the installments."

"Installments they wanted."

"I know," he agreed, shrugging. "Still."

"So go." She tried drawing her hand from his, but he held on.

"No. I meant what I said, Autumn. We're here as a couple. I'm not pretending l came alone."

****

Autumn's heartbeat picked up a fast, two-step pace as Chase hauled her toward the front room where the band was set up. He really was serious. They were kind of a couple. Or something. He wanted it out there, wanted everyone to know. Clammy sweat coated her palms, and again, she tried tugging her hand free, but he was having none of it.

"Come on," he said, ignoring her escape effort by tightening his grip as he stepped onto the stage, hauling Autumn with him.

"I'll make this quick," he said into one of the microphones once the noise had quieted, "but I do want to say a few words." Chase's dark gaze swept the room. "Y'all treated me like a rock star when I walked in the room a few minutes ago. And I'll be honest, it felt awesome." He held up his beer bottle toward the crowd. "But it's you guys who need to be saluted. Without everything each and every one of you has done to get this hotel ready for opening, my art would be nothing but glass on a wall without anyone to see it."

He paused, looking out at the crowd. "Thank you doesn't seem like enough of a thing to say, not for everything you've done. So I thought maybe I could tell you a little something about myself, so you'd really understand how much this means to me."

He gripped Autumn's hand tighter as if drawing strength from her touch. Her heartbeat thudded and she squeezed back, assuring him she was by his side.

"I know most of you don't know me personally," he began. "Probably what you were told is that some art guy's having his shit installed in the hotel, and you need to go out of your way to make sure it looks good. Which probably doesn't amount to a hill o' beans. You got other things to do besides deal with some unknown dude's art project. Your normal jobs, for example."

Nodding heads bobbed around the room, and pride swelled Autumn's heart at the easy way Chase connected with the audience.

"Thing is, though," he continued, "I'm not some weird artist who insists on bathing in pasteurized pickle juice or taking his pet lobster for a walk. I'm just a normal guy. At one point before I got my break, I was living in a rented room over by Tallulah. The stove didn't work. Neither did the AC. But hey, I had a bathroom. Well, a toilet, anyway."

Scattered chuckles pinged around the room, and several heads nodded in understanding. People related to what Chase said, and Autumn got that. But until this moment, Chase hadn't spoken much about his background. She knew about his family, but not anything he was talking about now. Her heart ached, thinking about him living in crap conditions. No one should have to do that.

"So when a guy like me gets a chance to change that situation," Chase continued, "I'm sure as hell not gonna be stupid and take my good fortune for granted. I don't forget where I come from, and I don't forget who's helped me along the way."

He held up the beer bottle he still had in his free hand and tilted it toward the crowd. "Here's to you guys, and to the fan-fucking-tastic job y'all did in getting this hotel to look amazing, and for my art to look like it belongs here. Thank you."

The crowd raised their glasses and bottles right back at him, a raucous clinking in a unified toast to a job well done.

Autumn thought that was it and she could finally escape the spotlight of the stage. But Chase held up his hand for quiet.

"Just one more thing," he said, glancing at Autumn.

Her stomach dropped. He was going to single her out. She wanted to make a run for it, but Chase's grip stayed vice-like, firmly trapping her.

"I do some funky things with my art, and it requires a lot of fancy computer help with coding and installation. No way would any of it have worked without the IT team, headed up by the gorgeous gal by my side, Autumn Rivette. What she and her team did was nothing short of a damn miracle. I don't get any of it; I just know it was a ton of work."

Heat flooded her cheeks. The first instinct was to run. Get away. Escape the praise and the spotlight.

But then Chase looked down at her, a grin touching one side of his sensual mouth, and the desire to flee vanished, leaving unexpected happiness in its wake. Chase was *proud* of her, and he wanted this crowd to know it. She swallowed against a rising lump in her throat.

Then before she realized it, he was lifting her arm. "So give this gal and her talented group of guys a good

197

ol' fashioned, Southern thank you. To the Tech Geeks!"

"Tech Geeks!" the crowd hollered back, swilling their drinks with hearty enthusiasm.

From the corner of her eye, she spotted her group of guys laughing and smacking each other with high fives. Pride like a tidal wave swelled throughout her body. She felt like a mother when her kids had done good.

Chase grinned at her before turning from the microphone to lead her down the few steps and off the stage. Raucous applause accompanied them, the outburst of vigorous clapping as sharp as a sudden hailstorm.

People thanked them with wide smiles and claps on the back as they wove their way through the crowd toward the far end of the room. Chase nodded toward a passing waiter as he held up his empty bottle.

As they waited for a fresh round, Chase leaned to press his face into her hair, close to her ear. The warmth of his breath whispered across her cheek. "Thank you, babe. I know you didn't want to be in the spotlight, but there's no way I could keep quiet about everything you've done for me."

Her heart fluttered, bouncing against her ribcage like stones skipping water. *Babe*. A boyfriend/girlfriend word if there ever was one. Heat rushed her cheeks.

She shrugged, not sure what to say, her mind obsessively focused on the single term of endearment over anything else he said. He still held her hand, too, stubbornly refusing to keep their relationship secret.

She let out a breath and nibbled her bottom lip as it spread to a grin. They were official. "You're….ah— You're welcome. Babe."

The waiter arrived, planting a beer in each of their hands before melting back into the crowd. For a moment, they were tucked in a private cocoon, sheltered from the majority of people by their location in the back. Her mind flashed back to the moment up on stage when her heart swelled from his warm praise of her work. Of *her*. With unexpected bravado, she shrugged off her usual introverted nature and opened her mouth to tell him so, when like a cloud of steam, the moment evaporated.

"Chase." Maryanne's signature red-lipped, wide beam was ominously gone, replaced by a thin, tight gash.

He turned at the sound of his name, darkness shadowing his face when he realized who'd said it. "You need me, I assume?"

"You assume right." Without shame, the designer wedged herself between him and Autumn. "There are people I need you to meet," she continued, "and they've been waiting for quite some time. This way, please." Maryanne held out her arm in the direction she wanted Chase to go.

He ignored her directive and glanced down at Autumn. "I won't be long," he said in a clear, firm voice. "Where do you want to meet up?"

If Maryanne were a cartoon character, visible smoke would be spurting from her ears.

Autumn looked away, hiding a wicked grin. "I'll be around," she said. "I'm gonna look for my guys and see how they're doing."

"Okay. If I can't find you, I'll text you." He planted a quick, hard kiss on her mouth before allowing Maryanne to usher him along.

The designer glared at Autumn before tossing her head and turning her back, heels clicking as she marched away.

Freakin' weirdo. Autumn didn't know why Maryanne had it out for her, but the designer could cause enough trouble to make life unpleasant at work. It'd probably be smart not to poke the bear.

****

Autumn propped herself up against her pillows and looked down at Chase, the mild soreness between her legs a pleasant reminder of the past several hours. Piles of discarded clothing and a heap of rumpled blankets were tossed to the floor, leaving only a thin sheet covering the awesomeness that was also known as Chase's naked body in her bed. He rolled to his side with a deep, rumbly sigh as his head lolled against the pillow. He blinked slowly, like a man bone-weary after days of hard labor.

"Get your smokin' hot ass over here," he croaked.

Autumn complied, scooching down to nestle herself in the crook of his arm. Heat coated with a thin sheen of sweat radiated from his skin.

"My God, that was insane." He expelled a long stream of breath and glanced down at her. "How is it someone so small can plum wear me out?"

She grinned at his weary expression. "What are you sayin', Mountain Man? Not up for another round?"

"You're gonna regret those words, Techie. Just give me a few, and you'll see. 'Up' is where I'll be, and down is where you'll be going."

She laughed. "Big words."

"Big cock."

She trailed her hand down his stomach to where his

200

flaccid length rested against his thigh. Even soft, she had to admit it was impressive.

"We'll see," she teased. "'In a few.'"

Chase tightened his arm around her and kissed the top of her head. "Damn, I think the birds are gonna start chirping in a minute."

Autumn glanced at the clock. Nearly four. Crud. Where had the night gone?

"Not just yet," she said. "Give 'em another hour."

"Thank God it's Saturday," Chase mumbled, and by the heaviness of his breath, he'd be dozing off soon.

Fatigue tugged her eyelids as well, but just as she felt herself drifting off, an image of Maryanne startled her awake.

Chase must have sensed something, or maybe she'd moved. Regardless, he grew alert. "Something wrong?"

She shook her head. "Nothin'."

Clearly, he didn't believe her. He shifted position, propping himself up against the pillows so he could see her more easily. "Maryanne," he pronounced with the weightiness of a doctor giving a grim diagnosis.

"We don't need to repeat this conversation." She nervously nibbled at her bottom lip. "I just wish I knew why she's such a witch to me."

"I have a guess."

"Yeah?"

"Sure. She's jealous."

Autumn pulled away to put distance between herself and Chase. "Jealous? What makes you think that? Did she say something?"

For the first time since she'd become involved with Chase, her own knot of jealousy reared its ugly head.

"Nope. Not in specific words, anyway. But she acts like I'm her trained monkey, leading me around on a leash for the wealthy hotel patrons. And she told me last night that the older ladies—Louisiana High Society—liked seeing me 'available.' It makes me more appealing to them."

"*What?*" Autumn sat up, pulling the sheet to cover her breasts. "What the hell does that mean?"

"Pipe down, Techie. It means nothing."

Autumn scooted off the bed and threw on one of Chase's discarded T-shirts. She clenched her jaw, annoyance churning hot and sour in her stomach.

"Are you supposed to, like, date those high society ladies or something? Show them a good time?" Heat coursed over her cheeks. Unexpectedly, a sting of tears pricked her eyes. *What the fuck?* Furiously, she blinked them away.

"Autumn." Chase patted a spot on the mattress, indicating she should join him.

But stubborn as a mule, she folded her arms across her chest and refused to budge.

He sighed but to his credit, he didn't push. "You have no reason to be jealous."

"Who says I'm—"

"As long as you want this…this thing we have between us." He shrugged, ignoring her protest. "Well, then. I'm yours."

"Mine?"

"Yeah. Look, babe. I don't exactly know what we've got going on here, or where it'll lead. All I know is that I have a damn good time with you. You're hot as hell, smart as hell, and there's no one I like being with more than you." His eyes, so dark, were coated with warmth. And sincerity. And he'd called her babe again.

Shit. She was gaping like an idiot. Her mouth clapped shut.

"C'mere." Chase patted the spot beside him again.

This time, she went. His massive arms enveloped her, warm as a blanket and just as safe. She snuggled against him and closed her eyes, breathing him in.

They stayed quiet for awhile, their soft breaths the room's only sound. Autumn's eyelids grew heavy as sleep grabbed hold.

"So, are we cool?"

She smiled against him. "For sure."

"Good."

Seconds later, his steady breathing told her he'd drifted off. But though the need for sleep stayed strong, she wasn't quite ready. Memories of the night and especially Chase's speech flitted through her mind. She hadn't realized before how much they had in common. The way he'd always talked about his past and those bohemian parents of his made it sound like he'd grown up in a Sixties love fest. But his words tonight told her something different.

I was living in a rented room over by Tallulah. The stove didn't work. Neither did the AC. But hey, I had a bathroom. Well, a toilet, anyway.

Tallulah, in Madison Parish, was one of the poorest cities in Louisiana. It was some tough living up there. A girl from her high school had spent time in the area and used to talk none-too-kindly about growing up "without a pot to piss in or a window to throw it out of." Chase's description of his life there hadn't sounded much better.

He rolled to his side, his giant left arm spooning her against him in a steel embrace. She smiled in the dark as the trail of curly hair on his abdomen tickled her bottom. It was shocking to realize how comfortable she'd become with him in such a short amount of time. Hell, even Zip and Beau nowadays were practically treating Chase like an old friend. Thing was, though, it usually took her months and months to even begin trusting anyone. So why Chase?

Mentally, she ticked off some possible reasons. He was kind. Good in bed. He dug her...

It was all true, but none of it explained why she'd let her guard down and trusted him. Completely. Hell, they'd ramped up the trust level even further after a recent talk when they agreed that since they were exclusive, they could ditch the condoms, which just made things extra—

She sucked in a breath. Her body froze. Maybe... *Oh, God, this isn't happening, is it?* Maybe the reason Chase had crumbled the concrete-solid walls around her was because...was because she lo—

No. Shit, no, no, no. No! *No way, no how. She was so not ready for that.*

She mentally buried the thought, shoveling dirt on top of it like a grave digger racing to finish his shift. Her agitation caused her to roll in bed and disturb Chase.

He looked down at her, sleepy eyes blinking in the waning moonlight. "Wassa matter?" He pulled her tighter against him.

She tensed, scared of the feelings for him that were barreling straight toward her like a Mack truck. But it felt so good, so *right* being next to him. The trust between them was something she'd never had before. And rather than wanting it to stop, she wanted it to grow. She wanted more trust. Deeper trust. But she also knew it was a two-way street. Chase had fessed up to some stuff about his past that she guessed didn't exactly fill him with pride. Payback time.

She let out a breath and eased away from the safety and warmth of his big arms. The chill of its absence hit her immediately, but being sheltered in Chase's embrace took away her focus, distracting her from what she needed to say.

She turned back around. His gaze fixed on her with questions in those sea green depths, no doubt wondering why she'd moved. Outside the window there wasn't a sound. No crickets, no birds, no cars. Nothing. The few remaining moments where the world slept brought a sanctified stillness to the night.

Autumn pulled the sheet around her torso and propped herself against a mound of pillows piled against his scrolled iron headboard. She looked down at Chase's rugged face, smiling at the bed head he had going on.

"So." She clenched and opened her fists, drawing in a fortifying breath of air. "Could you fix us up a pot of coffee? I have some things to tell you."

Chapter Fifteen

Steam hissed from the top of the espresso maker while it brewed up the Americano Chase knew Autumn liked. As the machine churned out the final shots of dark brew into their cups, he glanced behind him to where Autumn lay propped on pillows in his bed.

She looked like an actress ready to take the stage in her own one-woman show. Her fingers gripped the sheet as she held it above her breasts like a shield, bracing herself to tell him something. A knot of anxiety twisted Chase's gut. She'd never looked so serious before.

What was going on? Had she planned to up and do something stupid, like say she'd decided it wasn't working between them and she was gonna skip town? His jaw tensed. If she even tried leaving, they'd be having words.

He handed her a steaming cup of coffee and took his place back beside her on the bed.

"You've been telling some stuff about yourself to me," Autumn began quietly. "Stuff that was probably tough to deal with. And talk about."

He nodded. True, but his life was what it was. Nothing to be ashamed of. Still, it harbored pain, and bringing up certain things picked at the wound.

"So, I figure it's my turn." She nibbled at the bottom right-hand corner of her lip, a habit she turned to whenever something difficult came up.

"You know you don't have to, Autumn."

"I know. But…I want to."

He nodded.

"So…" She cleared her throat. "Not sure if you remember or not, but one time you mentioned something about the Bellagio Fountains in Las Vegas."

He nodded. "And you shut down like a busted generator."

She gave him a faint grin. "That's a good way to put it."

"I've wondered what the story is," he admitted. "But it's none of my damn business, least not 'til you're ready to tell me."

"I'm ready."

"Then I'm all ears."

Her fingers twisted in the sheets, wrapping them like a boxer taping his hands before a fight. "Well, I told you about my foster parents, right?"

"The assholes? Sure."

Her slight chuckle eased his tension a little.

"Nancy, I don't want to talk about. But Rick…he was mostly just pure asshole, but every once in awhile, he could be okay. It was 'cause of him, in fact, why I got into computers. He brought one home one day when I was around eight years old and just let me play with it. Whatever I wanted to do. He didn't have a clue how to use it, so he didn't care."

Chase frowned. "Computers are expensive. So he just put out that kind of cash for a computer and let a kid pound away on it?"

"I didn't say he paid for it," Autumn said quietly.

"Ah."

"Anyway," she continued, "I took to it like a duck to water. Got really good, really fast, and even started teaching myself basic coding."

"Fucking amazing."

"Thanks." She sipped her coffee while holding the warm cup between her palms. "What I really liked were the chat rooms. Getting to know coders and other people like me interested in technology. It made me feel like I wasn't alone." She shrugged. "I spent hours there."

"It was your escape." *From a life of shit*, he wanted to add.

She nodded and set the cup aside. "After spending a lot of time in the chat rooms, it didn't take long before I found my way to the hackers." She paused as if bracing for what he would say.

But he kept his lip zipped and waited for her to go on. Sooner or later, it would sink into that pretty head of hers that whenever she was with him, she was in a No Judgment Zone.

"So, um. As it turned out, I liked hacking. It came easy and trying to break into places was like a game. Solving a puzzle. I didn't really understand that the internet wasn't just a big playground for kids. There's some seriously dark shit lurking out there, stuff no eleven-year-old should know about, much less access. But no one was stopping me. In fact, when Rick saw what I could do, his scheming brain also realized he could make money off it. So when I was thirteen, he took me to Las Vegas."

Chase frowned. "To do what?"

"To…ahh…." She looked down, shaking her head. "There were people he owed money to. Bad people.

And he couldn't pay them back. But he figured there was another way to settle the score. He could work off the debt by giving those guys something worth more than the money he owed."

"Information."

"Yep. So he set up meetings with them in hotel rooms, shitty places far off the Strip. Not exactly where the tourists go."

"And took you with him?" At her tight nod, toxic anger churned in his stomach. The slow simmer burned hotter and faster the more Autumn talked about her shitbag foster father. And that guy was supposedly the better parent. What did that say about her foster mother?

"All I had to do was hack into hotel databases and pull up contact information for any name they gave me."

"What did the guys he owed money to do with the intel?"

"Who knows. I was a kid; they never told me anything. Probably better like that, anyway."

His fingers curled into fists, wanting to plant them hard into Rick's scheming face. Knock his head off his shoulders. Pound him into dirt. Rage pumped through his body, but he held it back so that Autumn kept talking. "Fucking unbelievable. A guy pimping out his daughter to settle his debts."

"His thirteen-year-old daughter."

"Jesus. No wonder Vegas has a bad association for you."

She reached for her coffee. "They were scary looking dudes; I'll tell you that. They carried Glocks in their pockets like we carry phones. But at first, I thought the whole thing was just a fun game, you know? It was cool when I could get what they wanted. Rick was so pumped. Whenever I hacked into databases and pulled up what he needed, he'd buy me stuff. Soda, candy, ice cream."

"Everything a kid wants."

"Yeah." Autumn nodded. "It was cool. But even better than that was…um…" Her voice caught, and she stopped, staring down at her lap. Her hands balled into fists, still twisting that sheet, over and over. She swallowed several times and he could see her furrowed brow. A few ragged breaths escaped her lips and…*hell*.

Chase peered closer. Was she crying? In that moment, she looked smaller, more vulnerable than he'd ever seen her, almost like her thirteen-year-old Vegas self. He ached to pull her into his arms and tell her everything was going to be okay. That the bad Vegas time was over.

But instinctively, he knew it wasn't what she needed. He'd bet the farm this was the first time Autumn had told anyone about what had happened. Bringing up old shit always caused a swirl of deep emotions to come along for the ride. She needed time to adjust to the pain.

After a minute, she seemed to have things under control. She cleared her throat. "Even better was knowing that I was making him happy. He'd smile and laugh and…um. He would hug me. You know, like a normal father."

"And you'd do anything for that love."

"Yeah." Her voice was nearly a whisper. "I would."

"How'd it end?" Chase asked.

She stayed quiet for another minute, the faraway look in her eyes reflecting some shit Chase didn't like seeing. Like fear.

"Well, as I said, at first it was okay. The info I pulled was worth a fortune. The asshole thugs got what they wanted, and Rick was happy. There were even parties in the hotel room to celebrate, complete with drugs and hookers."

"My God." The anger in him roared. If Autumn's foster father was here now, there'd be nothing stopping Chase from beating the dirtbag to a pulp.

At the same time, he wanted to draw Autumn toward him, comfort her in his embrace and block out all the tough shit she'd had thrown at her. But when he looked at his gorgeous Tiny Techie, he didn't see a fragile flower. He saw a woman with iron strength. A woman who'd been through the ringer and had come out swinging. Autumn didn't need to be protected; she needed to be applauded.

"Giving them the shit they wanted was like feeding heroine to an addict. All it did was make them want more. Eventually, they started asking for information I didn't know how to get. Not back then anyway.

"One day, they asked for info on certain guests staying at the Bellagio. I tried hacking into their system and couldn't break it. The security was too sophisticated for me at that point." She let out a deep breath and he felt his own body tense, bracing for impact.

"The assholes Rick owed money said the debt wasn't paid until I could get this one final bit of intel. But I just couldn't, no matter what I tried. The scums started making threats against Rick. And against me.

Started saying stuff about a night with a thirteen-year-old virgin maybe settling the score, but they'd have to do it first and then they'd let Rick know. I wasn't a hundred percent sure what they were talking about, but I sensed it was something bad."

A muscle jumped in the back of his jaw where he clenched it shut. *Fucking shit.* "What happened?"

"We got the hell out of Vegas," Autumn said simply. "Took off in the middle of the night and never looked back. We returned to Texas where we were living at the time. Rick told Nancy to get her shit; we were leaving. Within an hour, we had suitcases packed and took off for Louisiana. No forwarding address, no phone number, nothing. Our new life started here."

Although questions spun in his mind like tornado debris, he couldn't figure out how to form them into actual words. There was so much to say that he couldn't say a thing. So Chase did what he'd wanted to before. He drew Autumn into his arms.

Thankfully, she allowed herself to be comforted. Protected. She probably didn't feel she needed it. His feisty girl knew how to take care of herself. But maybe, his urge to protect Autumn was more for him than it was for her. He was the oldest brother, the one who always looked out for others. Whether Autumn needed it or not, he wanted to do the same for her.

They stayed quiet in the room for several minutes as the sun rose and streams of light filtered through the curtains. Outside, an excited chorus of birds made sure the world was waking up. Autumn relaxed against him, her breathing slow and steady. He wondered if she'd fallen asleep.

"I never told anyone that before," she said, her

quiet voice breaking the silence.

"Yeah." He kissed the top of her head. "I figured."

She moved just fractionally, enough so those blue eyes could look straight up at him. "Why?"

"'Cause you're not really one to spill the beans on your personal life. That much I know about you for sure."

"Well, I just—"

"Self-preservation. I get it, Autumn."

She released a low breath. "You seem to get a lot about me."

"I've been paying attention. I do that with people I—" He snapped his mouth shut. This might be too much. Autumn had just opened a long-buried wound. He didn't want to pour salt on it. And yet…why was he so sure that revealing his feelings would do damage? Maybe it would actually help.

Ah, hell. No time like the present to find out. They'd been talking Vegas, after all. Maybe it was time to gamble.

"I do that with people I care about," he said quietly. "And I care about you, Techie."

The expected tensing of her body didn't happen. Nor did she scoot her cute ass off the bed and run for the hills. Instead, a soft smile lit her eyes and cast itself onto her gorgeous lips.

"Likewise, Mountain Man," she replied. "I…um…I care about you, too."

A rush of pleasure as potent as any drug warmed his blood.

"Well." He could hear happiness in his own damn voice, but words escaped him. At that moment, he could only *feel*—the thump of his heart, the soft warmth of Autumn pressed against him as he held her. So he said simply, "That's cool."

She gave a soft chuckle. "Yeah. It's cool."

Chapter Sixteen

The White Ibis' reception area buzzed with the frenzy of a Mardi Gras parade. As Chase strolled through the lobby, he heard excited bits of conversation that further ramped up the chaotic mix.

"Magnificent! The renovations, the upgrades. The astonishing artwork. I can't believe this is the same hotel." The wealthy socialite who'd delivered the praise craned her perfectly coiffed, blonde head toward the lobby ceiling where his intricate hummingbird installation greeted arriving guests.

He couldn't help the thrill of satisfaction putting a spring in his step. It had taken him months to craft every single one of the multi-colored little birds and the flowers into which they dipped their fragile, glass beaks. But the end result had been worth it. The sheer size of the piece soared the entire length and width of the ceiling. When the sun poured through the windows as it did now, it reflected off the glass and cast a rainbow of prisms onto the white marble floor.

Hordes of guests were appreciating the result. The hotel had been booked to capacity since opening day over two weeks ago, and business showed no sign of slowing. Reviews of the White Ibis in industry trade magazines and traveler review sites were nothing short of stupendous, and word spread fast. The hotel was a jaw-dropping success.

If only his sunny day weren't about to turn cloudy. A spear of annoyance lanced his good mood as he arrived in the executive area where Maryanne's office was located. Dealing with her snippy attitude masked in a big, red smile grew tiresome. He sighed as he approached her closed door, shrugging off his leather jacket as he took a seat and waited to be summoned.

Seconds later, the door opened and Liesel, Maryanne's perpetually perky assistant, greeted him with a bright smile. "Hello, Mr. Durand. Ms. Boudreaux is ready for you."

"Thanks." He rose and followed her into the lion's den.

True to form, Maryanne sat ensconced behind her massive desk, looking as if she'd been beamed there straight from the beauty shop. Her hair was slicked back and pulled fiercely into a tight, eye-pulling bun. Her painted nails reflected the same deep red she favored on her lips, and her tailored suit expertly fit her pencil-thin frame. Coffee service awaited on a nearby table.

As he approached, Maryanne rose and held out a hand like a queen greeting a loyal subject. Well, he sure as hell wasn't kissing the ring. Instead, he grasped her fingers lightly and shook her hand.

"Wonderful to see you as always, Chase," she said in a throaty voice, indicating with a nod that they would take seats at the table.

He tossed his jacket on the chair next to Maryanne's desk.

"Coffee?" Maryanne asked, not bothering to wait for his response as she poured.

He ignored the steaming cup she handed him. The

sooner they were finished with this little tête-à-tête, the better. "What did you want to see me about?"

Her smile faltered briefly, perhaps taken aback by his brusque manner. But Maryanne's attitude toward Autumn had only gotten more acerbic as days went by, and Chase was sick of the designer's sanctimonious behavior toward someone he cared about. It took all his effort just to maintain civility toward her, never mind niceties.

She sipped at her coffee as if composing herself for what she had to say. "Well, as you know," she began, smile firmly back in place, "reviews of the hotel have been nothing short of extraordinary. The same goes for your artwork. The buzz is incredible. People calling the reservations desk are actually asking about it. We're booked solid, and interest is skyrocketing. People absolutely love the hotel. The feel of it, the style, the energy. And your art is a huge part of the exact look and sophistication we were going for."

"That's cool," he said, already anticipating the fun of telling Autumn. His artwork wouldn't be half of what it was without her technical brilliance.

"So," she continued, flicking imaginary lint off her skirt, "you know I've mentioned the possibility of future hotels to you."

"I remember."

"Splendid. The time has now come for us to begin solidifying our arrangement. The investors behind the White Ibis have their eye on other properties, and we want you to be a part of the investment."

He frowned. "Part of it how?"

"Your artwork. It's a draw into the White Ibis, and these bumpkins down here aren't even art lovers.

Imagine how much more receptive sophisticated guests are going to be. Their appreciation will go through the roof!" She giggled and flashed him a wink as if they conspired on a big secret.

But rather than feed her nonsense, Chase narrowed his eyes and frowned. "I have kin here, Maryanne," he said quietly. "And plenty of friends. Smart, sophisticated people who I don't guess would be too happy about your characterization of them as 'bumpkins.'"

It would be too much to hope she'd have the grace to blush, but a sense of satisfaction soothed Chase's annoyance as Maryanne squirmed in her chair.

But her unease slid away as composure quickly took hold. "Apologies. It was a silly little nickname, nothing more." Her wrist fluttered nonchalantly through the air. "Anyhow, back to business."

After a quick sip of coffee, she set aside the cup and leaned forward in her seat. "Like I was saying, the investors behind the White Ibis are putting together a multi-property deal for upscale hotels in several states across the country. This is going to be huge, Chase. *Huge.* And you need to be a part of it."

He sat back, stunned, heartbeat jackhammering. This opportunity could put his career on the map for years. He'd get to choose whatever project he wanted, whatever art he felt inspired to create. His prices would go up. As would his demand. Holy shit.

"You can't buy exposure like this," Maryanne pointed out. "Any artist would kill for it."

"So why me? Why not feature a different artist in each location? Seems like that would keep the interest up."

"Oh, Chase."

Her placating tone chafed like coarse underwear scraping his balls. He clenched his jaw.

"There's no other artist out there who creates the pieces you do. They're unique. Different. We want your artistic theme repeated in all our luxury properties. It's part of establishing the brand. Chase Durand art in a hotel means style, sophistication, and luxury." She plucked a mini raspberry cake from a plate beside the coffee pot and broke off a corner. "That's why it must be you."

"I don't think of myself as a theme, Maryanne. Or a brand."

"You need to. Branding is what it's all about. You've got to establish who you are and what your art stands for."

"I know very well who I am. And my artwork stands on its own." He heard the bite of annoyance in his voice.

From the way she held up her hands in a placating gesture, she'd heard it, too. "Of course, of course," she said soothingly. "You create your art a certain way in your unique style. But without even realizing, you're already branding yourself. And what I'm saying is that we're capturing that brand and reflecting it in the hotels. Your art will come to mean luxury."

He ran a hand through his hair. "I don't know that I want it to."

"Oh, really?" She leaned back in her chair but pinned him with her icy gaze, a curious half smile on her red lips. "Not even for five million dollars?"

He sat rock-solid in his chair as if sudden paralysis had seized every muscle, every bone, every last damn chromosome. All he could do was focus on his breathing as his scrambled brain attempted to understand what she'd just said. Five million dollars? Five *million* dollars?! What the…five million? He tried like hell, but the information just wouldn't compute.

"What, ah—" He cleared his throat and started over. "What do you mean?"

"You'd get that upfront for the work you'd do in the hotels. Then there's a backend component as well tied in with the exclusive showings we'd feature from time to time in one of the hotel galleries. There's also strong enthusiasm from the investors to have dedicated stores within some of the hotels selling smaller original pieces of your work, or possibly selling replicas made by a third party—of course, with your approval. We'd probably begin with the property in Miami. There's an appreciative—not to mention wealthy—base of enthusiasts there. Art Basel and all. You'd obviously receive a percentage of every sale."

His own unsteady breathing gusted in his ears. His heart thudded like a drummer on steroids. Exclusive showings. Dedicated stores. Five *million* dollars. This was some crazy, fucking unimaginable shit. This didn't happen to guys like him. Southern boy with a prison record, his education non-existent after high school. He'd lived in squalor, struggled as an artist. Dumb luck on the sale of a single piece had finally gotten him some actual money, enough for the down payment on his studio. Even after that, he'd had to stay ultra-careful with finances. But now this. Pauper to prince.

He shook his head in disbelief. "What's the catch?"

"Catch?" Maryanne sipped her coffee, eyeing him over the brim of the cup. "Everything I'm offering is real."

His legs twitched. Sitting stuffed in Maryanne's tiny guest chair was too much. He stood, feeling exactly like the Mountain Man Autumn always called him. His large frame towered over Maryanne.

"I wasn't born yesterday," he said, his voice icy as he drilled her with his gaze, "and I know you're too slick just to offer me all this without wanting something in return. So lose the coy attitude and spill it. I agree to nothing without knowing about the strings attached to this deal. And sure as shit, I know you've got strings."

He had to give her credit; she didn't flinch while he glowered. Composure intact, Maryanne pulled a slim folder from a drawer. Her smile remained planted, although it failed to reach her frosty gaze. "Since you ask, Chase, let me be perfectly transparent. There are, in fact, a few…let's call them 'conditions'…that we'll want from you in exchange for this deal. Aside from your fabulous artwork, of course."

Resisting the urge to tell her where she could shove her "conditions," he folded his arms across his chest and leaned in toward her. "What do you want?"

She sat behind her desk and rested her elbows on top the dark mahogany, propping her chin on her folded fingers. "The conditions," she continued, "relate to Autumn Rivette."

His jaw tensed, and he wondered if his face revealed the toxic thoughts churning in his mind. Not that he gave a shit.

"Autumn's coding is part of what makes the art stand out," he said evenly, not bothering to hide his irritation. "Makes it special. Without that, it's just a whole lot of fancy glass."

"Hardly," Maryanne shot back. She dropped any pretense of pleasantries as the smile disappeared. "Let me be perfectly clear. Coding aside—and frankly, there are plenty of people with those skills around—the infatuation you seem to have developed for the IT help needs to go. It's not good for the White Ibis, and it's certainly not going to be tolerated as it pertains to this deal. We just can't afford it."

IT help? That bitch. His urge to careen around her desk and put his giant hands around her skinny bird neck to throttle her was almost irresistible.

He balled his hands into tight fists and used the meditative techniques he'd learned long ago from his parents to diffuse the anger. He wouldn't let her gain the upper hand by allowing his emotions to rule his thinking. "Explain how my personal business is any of yours."

"When it affects the hotel, it's a lot of people's business. Mine, hotel management, and the investors fronting millions of dollars to build these properties and the brand behind them."

She opened the folder and withdrew several sheets of paper neatly clipped together. "You'll get details of the proposal in this contract," she continued, her tapered nail tapping the papers. "But as to your question, let me put it this way. Chase Durand, the artist, creates fascinating, unique pieces of beauty that our wealthy patrons are going to want to own—plain and simple. But the mystique of any artist—the aura surrounding him—adds value to the artwork like nothing else."

She swung her chair around to sit parallel to her desk and re-crossed her legs. "Part of *your* mystique is that you're a muscled, tattooed, gorgeous, and talented bad-boy who also happens to be single. Unattached—and potentially available. Women flock to you like birds to a wire. We want that. It draws in the crowd, and a crowd brings money. For everyone."

She leveled a chilly stare. "But if you're shacking up with the hired help and it becomes widely known—*poof*! The power of your appeal decreases considerably." She shrugged as if to convey how sorry she was about the unfortunate circumstances.

The meditative effects started to evaporate as simmering anger took hold. A muscle twitched in the back of his jaw. "So in this so-called deal of yours, I'm supposed to be a monk?"

"Well, no, of course not," she said, waving a hand. "But let me put it this way. You're going to be a star, Chase. Newspapers, TV, live-stream interviews. People will be talking about you. Women will be lusting after you. If you're going to be linked to anyone, it needs to be a gorgeous, glamorous, enviable woman. A stunning runway model. A beautiful actress. Someone who'd turn you both into a true celebrity power couple. But an IT consultant?" She wrinkled her nose as if assaulted by a pile of steaming cow dung. "We just can't have that."

Chase's hands shook as boiling anger made him feel like a pressure cooker ready to explode. He ground his teeth, determined to bite back the string of nasty he wanted to scream in her face. What a disgusting, conniving, opportunistic *witch*. He'd met some revolting people in his life, but no one on planet Earth turned his stomach more than Maryanne Boudreaux. She was damn lucky he was a gentleman. 'Cause if not…

With forced calm, he picked up his jacket and slipped it on.

"Don't forget this," Maryanne said sweetly, holding out the contract between her slim fingers.

"If I had a dog, I could use that paper to pick up his shit when I walked him," he said quietly. "But since I don't, you go ahead and keep it."

Maryanne's face transformed from smug to outraged in two seconds flat, and he didn't bother hiding his juvenile smile.

"You don't get the money without the contract," she reminded him.

"And you don't get my artwork," he countered. "So I guess we're even." Without waiting for her response, he turned on his heel and left.

****

The door slammed behind him as Chase stormed outside to the parking lot. He strapped on his helmet and fired up the bike, gunning the throttle as he took off like his ass was on fire.

The sultry air was as refreshing as a spring day compared to the toxic atmosphere in Maryanne's office. His mind spun, churning through events of the past hour. Holy *shit*. No one ruled his life or told him what to do. And no fucking way was someone going to tell him who he could be with. Or love.

A goofy grin turned up the corners of his mouth. He'd just given up over five million dollars for a tiny IT techie who'd burrowed her way into his heart, and it hadn't even been a tough call. Money is nice. He could use it. Who couldn't? It was a shitload of dough, the likes of which he never thought he'd see in two lifetimes. But whoever said "Cash is King" was dead wrong. Even five-million dollars wrong. Without a second thought, he'd given it all up for Autumn. Because he loved her.

He opened the throttle, and the cycle roared. Rows of giant, bald cypress trees lined the open road along the bayou. The rush of air streaming past his helmet drowned out the sounds of nature, but above him, fittingly enough, a white ibis circled as it surveyed the landscape.

Yeah. He nodded to himself. It was true. He loved Autumn. Her brains, her beauty, her body. Her incredible personality. The strength she carried in every cell of her body to overcome her shitty childhood. Her smart mouth, her sense of humor. The dark sexy look in her eyes when he made love to her. Money or not, no one, least of all Maryanne, was going to tell him he had to give that up.

Suddenly, he knew exactly where he was going, and it sure as hell wasn't farther away from the hotel. He needed to get his ass back there, find Autumn, and do everything he needed to do in order to see that sexy look in her eyes as fast as possible.

****

"Down on your knees, wench. Service your Master!"

Hiding a tired sigh, Maryanne sank to the floor like an obedient servant and dutifully took Mason's flaccid dick between her lips. As she worked on getting him up so she could get this over with, she glanced at her watch. *Damn.* Nearly midnight. She'd wanted to be in bed early tonight.

It had been such an exasperating day, particularly the meeting with Chase. She couldn't believe the money hadn't been enough to make him kick that smarmy little shit, Autumn, to the curb. Not many years ago, he'd practically been a homeless bum. What the hell more did she need to do?

"Oh yeah, wench! Just like that." Mason's stubby fingers tugged at her hair.

"Mmm," she hummed excitedly. He loved it when he thought he drove her wild. He was like any stupid man, so easily manipulated. Any man except Chase Durand.

She grasped one hand around Mason's now-erect cock and pumped hard as she ran her tongue around the tip and tasted salty pre-cum. Good. He'd almost arrived at the promised land.

Seconds later, he reached nirvana. She looked up from her position on the floor, watching his head fall back and his mouth drop open as the orgasm ripped a long, low groan from his throat. He bucked his hips against her as he rode out the climax, his fingers pinching and twisting hard on his own nipples.

The second he'd finished, she stood, casting her gaze around the room for her discarded clothes.

"Where do you think you're going?" he panted, still catching his breath.

An unusual note of confidence in his tone gave her pause. "It's late, Mason. I need to get home."

"But we're not finished."

"Oh, I'm finished, all right." She pulled on her wrinkled skirt and fished through the pile of clothes for her bra and blouse. Once dressed, she took a seat to pull on her shoes when his butter soft fingers wrapped around her wrist, the grip unexpectedly strong.

"I have a surprise for you, Slave. But only if you

obey."

"Mason, really, I—"

"It's about Autumn."

She'd asked him several weeks ago if there was any dirt on that little tramp that she could use as leverage over Chase. So far, he hadn't produced a thing, despite her sharp-edged reminders that there was a price to pay if he wanted more of her ass. Had he finally come through with something?

"Tell me!"

Mason shook his finger at her like scolding an errant child, clucking his tongue to make a *tsk*-ing sound.

"Patience, greedy little Slave. First, you need to hear what I went through to get this information—and how I expect to be properly rewarded for it."

He didn't explain what reward he wanted, nor did he need to. Her continuation as his "slave" suited his perverted little mind just fine.

She wanted to scream at him to tell her what he knew, but it would only make him clam up and torment her. So she let her mind drift as he babbled on about nonsense and all of his supposed Herculean effort, until at last he got around to spilling the goods.

Minutes later, she grinned like a child at Christmas.

"Not bad, right?" Mason brimmed with smug satisfaction. "I told you I'd come through."

He'd taken his sweet time, she thought, but she wasn't going to start quibbling. Mason could have his little moment. The dirt he'd dug up was a gold mine. A prison record. A fucking prison record! This was like Christmas and New Year's and birthdays and every other holiday on the planet wrapped in a gigantic bow and placed at her feet—hers to do with whatever she wanted. And boy, did she ever know *exactly* what she wanted to do with it.

"You're the best." She slid off the bed and glanced in the mirror as she collected her purse. Her lipstick was gone, mascara smeared, and one side of her hair clumped together with what she could only assume was a jolt of his jizz. She couldn't care less. Nothing could ruin her stellar mood.

Blowing kisses at Mason, she sailed out of the room, down the stairway, and out the front door.

Her problems with Autumn were finally over.

Chapter Seventeen

Fists slammed against the front door like thunderclaps, causing her faithful lap cat, Zipdrive, to spring from her perch on Autumn's lap, back arched and tail puffed thick as a feather duster. Beau let loose excited barks and raced to the window to see who was there.

"I'm coming, I'm coming," Autumn grumbled, rising from the couch. She'd just settled down with a giant bowl of buttery popcorn and a DVR full of mindless TV shows to catch up on. The interruption wasn't exactly welcome. Another bang. *Who the—*

"Autumn," a rumble strip voice said. "I need to see you."

"Chase?" She hurried across the room. What the heck was he doing here? He said he'd be jailed in a meeting with Maryanne for a bit and then needed to spend time in his studio blowing pieces for a new project. They'd made plans to see each other tomorrow night, but…

The second she flung the door open, Chase devoured her. His warm mouth crashed down on her lips as he crushed her in his embrace. He slipped both palms beneath her shirt, coarse calluses dragging over her skin. With a flick of his fingers, he unhooked her bra. Cool air rushed in, immediately replaced by the rough caress of his palms on her breasts.

He kicked the door shut and then backed her into the living room until her ass hit the wall.

"Exactly where I want you," he murmured, sliding a teasing finger slowly down her arm. But before closing the gap between them, he leaned down beside him to scratch Beau's ears.

The Bernese no longer viewed Chase as a threat, and Autumn knew Chase wanted to ensure things stayed that way. *Guess he plans to keep coming over.* The thought warmed her imagination, and then Chase warmed her body.

A contended moan slipped through her lips when he began nibbling her throat. Her head settled back against the wall and her eyes slid shut. She easily gave herself up to his decadent assault. Questions would all be answered in time. Right now, her brain was mud. All she could do was feel—the tingling in her breasts, her aching nipples, her knees growing weak as water.

Without warning, he grabbed hold of the New Orleans Saints jersey she wore and scooped it up and over her head, flinging it to the corner. Her already unhooked bra slid down her arms. She tossed it aside to join the jersey.

His gaze scorched her bare breasts and stiff nipples.

"Nice," he murmured, rolling the sensitive buds between his forefinger and thumb.

Lust from his rough grip engulfed her, surging through her body and making her whole body shake. Her ragged moan echoed in her ears.

"Need you now," she growled, tugging at his leather belt.

Her impatience was outmatched only by Chase's.

With a light slap, he swatted away her eager fingers and shifted their positions so he could rest his weight against the wall. In seconds, he undid his belt and button and jerked down the zipper.

"Take me," he ground out, his hand pressing on the top of her head.

She sank to her knees, her hands gripping his jeans to slide them down his legs. She did the same with his boxers, freeing his stiff cock. Heat and his musky scent surrounded her. She took him between her lips, wetting his length with her tongue.

"Holy *shit*." His breaths came in ragged, shallow gasps, panting like a runner.

He gripped the back of her hair as she sucked, a sharp sensual tug racing like a line of fire from her scalp to her throbbing pussy. With practiced ease, she relaxed her throat and drew him in deep. His sharp hiss was followed by a long, low groan as she used one hand to tease his balls with her fingertips while the other hand pumped the base of his cock as she sucked. She looked up to see his pupils wide and black as tar while he watched.

"You're so fucking gorgeous," he murmured. "Your wet, beautiful mouth around my cock." His giant palm cupped her face, and with his thumb, he brushed aside a loose strand of hair impeding his view.

Praise flushed her skin hot and spurred her on. He thrust against her, and she swirled her tongue around his length, making him wet, sliding him deeper into her mouth. Unexpectedly, he pulled away.

"Get up here," he growled. "Need to be inside you. *Now.*" He shoved both hands beneath her arms and hauled her to her feet.

Excitement quickened her pace. With impatient fingers, she yanked the drawstring around her sweats and shoved them down her legs, then ditched her panties as well.

At the same time, he toed off his boots and kicked aside his jeans and boxers from where they were pooled at his feet. Then he pulled off his shirt.

Her breath caught in her throat, never tiring at the sight of his ripped physique. Abs like a column of bricks down his stomach, pecs hard as granite. She placed both palms on his chest, the scorching heat infusing her.

Suddenly, he bent and lifted her, a steely bicep beneath each thigh. "Wrap your legs around me," he ordered. He shifted their positions so her back was once more to the wall, his mammoth body trapping her with no chance for escape.

With a rush of heady excitement, she obeyed his command, coiling both thighs around his waist. The heat of his stiff cock teased as it slipped between the crack of her ass. She ground against it.

A low growl was forced from Chase. "Greedy little tease."

"Fuck, yes," she groaned. Her pussy throbbed, begging for relief. "Give me what I want."

"Tell me."

"Your. Giant. Cock." She leaned forward, her lips against his shoulder. Without hesitation, she bit his salty flesh. "Give it to me. *Now!*"

He shifted her weight to one arm, using his free hand to grab his cock. He aimed it toward her pussy and slammed into her.

"Ah!" She groaned as she was filled, moisture

streaming down her thighs as Chase thrust hard. She gyrated against him, seeking the delicious friction against her swollen clit that would shoot her to the moon. Sharp tingles streaked through her pebbled nipples as they brushed Chase's chest with every pump. She leaned forward, needing the taste of his sweaty skin on her lips. With the tip of her tongue, she traced a wet path up the side of his neck, then planted her lips against his throat and sucked, savoring his salty tang.

He thrust hard in response. Hot breath whooshed past her ear. Then, without warning, she slid down Chase's sculpted body and her feet touched solid ground. His magnificent cock was withdrawn from her slick pussy, its absence a cruel kind of torture. But before she could cry out in protest, Chase's strong fingers gripped the sides of her waist as he turned her to face the wall. She placed both hands flat against it, the wood cool against her hot palms.

Fiery heat burned her ass as Chase delivered a stinging slap. Her clit throbbed in response, and she wriggled like a cat ready to pounce as she begged for more. "Again!"

He held her in place with one steely hand against her back as he landed blow after incredible blow. Pulsing waves of ecstasy flowed through her with every sharp smack of his palm against her bare bottom.

A drop of wetness landed on her back, and she looked behind her at Chase, bringing his features into focus. Beads of sweat dotted his forehead and trailed down his chest.

"Need you back in me," she said, and when he didn't immediately respond she added, "*Now*."

A corner of his lip lifted in a teasing grin. "Tiny

Techie's giving the orders?"

"When I want something I do, Mountain Man. Now give it to me."

No need for her to ask twice. Chase took hold of his cock and circled the tip around her eager pussy, getting it wet. With a single thrust, he buried himself deep.

Her legs shook as he pistoned hard, stretching her, filling every inch. But still she wanted more, flooded by an overwhelming primal need for him. She arched her back and pressed against him when he thrust forward, the sharp slaps of skin on skin joining the sounds of their low, throaty groans.

Chase's breaths came faster and more shallow. She knew he was close, ready to explode, but he'd hold off until she found her own release.

Once more she looked behind to lock her gaze with his. One side of her mouth lifted in a teasing smile as she slipped her middle finger between her lips. She drew the digit in her mouth, her tongue swirling around her finger and coating it with moisture. Just as she wanted. Then she withdrew her finger and turned once more to face the wall. She slipped her hand over her breasts and then down the front of her body until she reached her needy clit. Her wet finger swept across the swollen bud as she masturbated while Chase continued thrusting against her.

"Oh *fuuuck*," she heard him groan. "You kill me, you hot little tease."

Strands of her hair had pulled loose from her messy bun and now fell like a curtain around her face as Chase rocked her hard against his cock. Blistering arousal roared through her and her muscles clenched tight, needing the delicious friction of his rock-hard length against her slippery walls.

In a low, throaty growl, Chase said, "Come for me, Autumn. Show me how much you love it."

Eager to please, she increased her pace, her fingers rubbing in fast little circles, back and forth over her swollen bud. Need for release grew, an all-consuming hunger barreling toward her. Chase ground his hips against her, burying himself deeper into her wet pussy with every thrust. Sweat poured down her body, salty trails running between her breasts and the backs of her knees.

He set a final, punishing pace, his cock ramming faster, his balls slapping hard. She spanked her clit with the flats of her fingers, chasing the orgasm that lingered just beyond reach. Then Chase slipped the tip of his finger into her ass in a new invasion, gently probing. Molten lust shot through her blood.

"*Yes!*" She pushed against him, shoving his finger deeper, the welcome penetration just what she needed to fly over the edge.

She ground hard against his cock and his finger. Pulses deep within her core throbbed. Chase wasn't even touching her breasts, but her sensitive nipples tingled.

Every inch of her skin, every pore, every last nerve was achingly alive, desire roaring through her body. Her eyes fluttered shut. She pushed back on Chase's finger and screamed as mind-blowing release at last came crashing over her. She rode the waves, her pussy clenching hard, the pulses seeming to last to eternity.

With one final effort, Chase slammed into her, grinding before he suddenly stilled, his deep guttural groans joining her lusty sighs.

Her thighs started shaking. She straightened and turned to face Chase.

"I'm guessing this is what a newborn colt feels like," she joked, her wobbly legs barely supporting her as she made it just in time to her couch.

Chase joined her, drawing her toward him so she could settle against his massive chest. His heartbeat hadn't yet fully slowed, and the heavy thumps raced against her ear. "Damn, woman. You nearly killed me."

She grinned but was slightly mortified at the way her cheeks burned from the compliment. At least he couldn't see her as she rested against his chest. "That's how it works, Mountain Man. David conquered Goliath, you know."

"Is that so?" He shifted to lift her slightly away from him, a serious expression on his face.

Alarm bells clanged as her nerves jittered. She didn't do serious. It meant bad things. Bad news, bad people. She scooted off the couch and fished around for her clothes.

"You hungry?" She didn't look at him, afraid that if she did she'd see something she'd rather not.

"Autumn, I wanted to tell you—"

"'Cause I'm *starving*." She hopped around on one foot as she pulled on her sweats. "I was just about to devour a giant bowl of buttery popcorn before you showed up and screwed up my plans…and me! Ha."

Her rushed tone and fake laughter were from nerves, but if she kept talking, she'd steamroll over whatever he was going to tell her. Then they could both pretend he'd never even said anything at all. "So you can either have some of my popcorn, or you need to be picking up that phone and ordering pizza. Good thing I happen to have a six pack chilling in the fridge. And if you're nice, I *might* be willing to share. It's not a sure bet or anything. I'm just sayin'."

Chase stayed quiet, and finally she did, too. If she kept on rambling, she'd begin sounding hysterical. What the *hell* was the matter with her? She didn't know why Chase's serious expression turned her blood to ice. They'd just had the most amazing sex on planet Earth, and from the way he'd banged down her front door, it seemed like that's what he'd come for in the first place. So why was she freaking like a pre-pubescent teen who discovers her first zit?

He looked at her for a long, quiet moment, those beautiful, sea-green eyes seeming to drink her down. He said nothing, although a faint, almost wistful smile gently parted his lips. She wondered if it was related to what he'd been about to say.

Chase pushed himself up from the couch. "I'm ripe as a yak's butt from all that sweating," he said. "You don't mind if I grab a quick shower before we get down to the serious business of devouring a giant, mushroom-onion pizza, do you?"

"Be my guest. Fresh towels in the closet to the right of the bathroom."

"I won't take long."

"Okay." She paused, then took a breath and added without thinking, "Good."

****

The scorching water pounded Chase's body like a waterfall against rocks, relaxing his tight muscles. He bent to let the water pummel his head and closed his eyes as he thought about Autumn's behavior just now.

Skittish as a feral cat.

He'd wanted to tell her about the conversation with Maryanne and get her opinion on it. But she must have assumed it was going to be something else, something she didn't want to hear. It was as if she'd seen a certain look on his face or in his eyes that had made her race for the hills. *Damnit.*

He flipped off the water and stepped out of the shower, toweling dry. Autumn's behavior was a fresh reminder that he had to take things slow with her. He knew she cared about him. But, as he'd recently realized, his own feelings back at her ran deeper. Unlike Autumn, though, it didn't scare him at all.

With the corner of the towel, he wiped steam from the mirror. The reflected image held a pensive expression as he thought about his childhood. Unconventional as his parents were, they'd never skimped on sharing their feelings. He and his siblings always knew how much they were loved and never shied from expressing those feelings themselves.

But Autumn hadn't grown up that way. The "L" word was as scarce in her household as it was commonplace in his. He needed to remember that. If he told her too early, he'd damage the trust between them.

Eventually, his little techie was going to have to get used to hearing him tell her how he felt. He might even have to train her a bit.

He grinned as he pulled on his boxers and jeans. Training Autumn could be a helluva lot of fun. Blood rushed to his groin. *Down, boy.* After the mind-blowing sex they'd just had, he was floored that his cock had started perking up so soon. Then again, Autumn did have that effect on him.

His cell buzzed in his pocket as he started down the stairs, but he ignored it. Whoever it was could call later. Pizza loomed in his future, and his growling stomach was damn happy about it.

He found Autumn in the kitchen, feeding Zip and Beau, and freshening their water dishes. He wrapped his arms around her as she stood at the sink, filling the bowl. She'd gotten dressed but had thankfully left off her shoes so he could catch a glimpse of her pretty pink toes.

"Don't get all cuddly with me, Mountain Man," she said in a fake, annoyed tone. "You promised to order pizza, remember?"

"How could I forget? You threatened to make my dinner a bowl of popcorn otherwise."

"*Buttery* popcorn," she emphasized, reaching for a towel to dry her hands. She turned in his arms and leaned into his chest. "Mmmm, what's that smell? Lavender and gardenia shower gel? I never would have pegged you as the type."

"Very funny. It's all you had in your shower."

"Actually…" A surprising faint blush tinged her cheeks. "I bought some, um, you know. Guy soap. Forgot to tell you." There was no missing the embarrassed way she cast her eyes to the floor.

A warm surge of pleasure shot through his veins, but he tamped it down. *Slow, remember*. Instead he made his voice purposely menacing. "Guy soap? You expecting someone?"

"Well, it's not for the dog."

"Is that so? Well, let me tell you something. You let this mystery person of yours know that he needs to keep his hands off my guy soap."

A half smirk tugged at her lips. "No problem, Mountain Man. Now order me pizza, or it's back to gardenias for you."

He pulled his phone from his pocket, grinning, but a frown rushed in to take its place as he eyed the phone screen. *What the...*

Two missed calls, both from his brother, Wolf. The first one had come while he'd been in the shower. The second was the one buzzing in his pocket just a minute ago.

"Something wrong?" Autumn frowned.

"Probably not," he said, tapping the voicemail icon. "But Wolf doesn't call often, so..."

He put the phone to his ear and listened. His brother's message was short and to the point, yet by the time it ended Chase's hands were shaking. He swallowed against a lump of fear in his throat.

"Chase?" Autumn stepped closer. "What is it?"

He slid the phone back in his pocket and released a breath. "I have to go, Autumn. My mom's been hurt."

She went still. "Bad?"

He grabbed his leather jacket from where he'd tossed it on a chair. "I don't know yet. She was hiking in Bighorn with friends. Wolf said she fell from a cliff and hurt her back. She's in the hospital."

"Oh, my God." She trailed after him as he jammed his feet in his boots.

"She's stable. But her back is messed up. Wolf said..." The fear welled again, bigger this time. "He said she might be paralyzed."

Chapter Eighteen

Two days passed before Autumn heard anything from Chase. Two days as maddening and endless as a line at the post office. Or dial-up Wi-Fi. She did everything she could think of to pass the time. She dove into work. Made her house antiseptic clean. Took Beau on marathon walks. Still, the nights haunted her like a thief, robbing her of sleep as her worried mind refused to power down.

She allowed herself to send a single text, a simple one-liner letting him know she was thinking about him. Chase needed to focus on his family and not get pelted with texts or calls. Yet in the wee hours of the night, the ones where every problem gets blown up and expanded to fifty times its actual worth, she tossed and turned. Had he thought about her? Missed her? Had she even once come to his mind?

Then she'd tell herself to stop with the nonsense and grow up. Her self-doubt was *so* not what anyone needed right now. Not Chase. Not her.

On day three of his absence, as she sat in her office, staring aimlessly at the computer, her pocket buzzed. She grabbed the phone and almost cried with relief when she saw it was Chase.

"Hey." She rose from the chair and shut the door. The late hour meant most people had already gone home, but she wasn't taking chances.

"Hey." Tiredness coated his voice. Sleep had probably been a no-show the last forty-eight hours.

"Tell me what's going on. How's your mom?"

"Stable. She'll be released in a few days. The good news is she can move her legs, so she'll be able to walk."

Relief flooded her. "Thank God."

"Yeah." The faint sound in the background of a doctor being paged told her Chase was still at the hospital.

"Have you gotten any sleep yourself? Anything to eat?"

Surprisingly, he chuckled. "Don't worry about me, babe. We're all here, the kids plus my dad. Between my sibs and extended family and friends, there's enough food back at my parent's place to feed the state of Montana." He released a tired sigh.

She closed her eyes against the phone, wishing she could feel that breath on her cheek.

"I miss you," he said. "Wish you were here."

"Miss you, too," she whispered. A lone tear leaked from the corner of her eye and slowly trickled down the side of her nose. Impatiently, she swiped it away.

His deep voice came back at her through the airwaves. "I'm going to be here for awhile yet."

She crushed the disappointment squeezing her heart. No way would she add to his burden with her melancholy shit. Chase had plenty else to deal with.

"When I get back," he continued, "I have some things I want to talk to you about. I meant to when I was at your place the other day but didn't get the chance."

More like she didn't give him the chance. Memory

assaulted her. The serious expression on his face. Those horror-movie scary words, *I wanted to tell you...*" She cringed, thinking back on the way she'd gone off the rails, shutting him down faster than Maryanne killing a good mood. It had worked, too. He'd held off telling her whatever was on his mind. Except her stupid behavior hadn't made it go away. Whatever it was still lingered, and Chase still wanted to talk. *Shit.*

"You can just tell me whatever you need to now," she said, forcing calm into her voice. "It's cool."

"No, I want us to talk in person. I need to—"

"Chase, the doc wants to talk to us about mom," a male voice said, the pitch similar to Chase's voice although not as deep. Probably one of his brothers.

"Chase?" she asked.

Nothing. A faint garbled conversation was all she could hear.

After a minute, he finally came back on the line. "Autumn, listen. I gotta bail. The doctor's here and wants to speak with the family."

"Okay, but—"

"Later. I'll call when I can."

Two beeps rang in her ear, and the line went dead.

She sank back in her chair and set her phone on the desk. Her gaze strayed to her computer screen where she'd been working right when Chase called, but the flashing lights and blinking cursor did nothing to catch her attention. All she could think about was that mysterious "thing" he'd now twice brought up.

Logically, she told herself it couldn't be anything bad. Three days ago, he'd come pounding on her door in dire need of her body. The heat between them burned lava-hot and showed no signs of cooling. On top of that, he'd told her he cared for her. And he'd called her babe. So why was she getting all worked up?

Because you're scared shitless it's all going to go away.

She let out a shaky breath. Her relationship with Chase was the best thing that had ever happened to her. Her White Ibis job, the cute little bungalow she'd managed to buy all on her own—those were nice things. They made her happy. But they were nothing compared to a relationship with someone who actually cared about her. Who one day might sorta love her, too. The thought of that ending, of Chase not being a part of her life…

She swallowed against the lump of solid fear closing up her throat and shut her eyes, wanting more than anything to block that damn thought or make it disappear entirely. Of course, it didn't work.

A sharp knock startled her, and her eyes popped open.

"Autumn? Are you in there?" Maryanne's voice pierced Autumn's brain like someone jamming a screwdriver in her head. *Crap.*

"Hold on." Autumn got up and twisted the lock.

The door flew open, and Maryanne stood before her, strapped in a fire-engine-red pencil skirt and billowy, white, silk blouse. A fierce scowl turned her scarlet lips into a thin gash across her face. "What are you doing in here so late?" she demanded, as if Autumn had committed some sort of crime.

"It's my office. I work here."

A vein pulsed on the left side of the designer's neck. Without being invited, she walked into the room and took a seat in one of the chairs opposite Autumn's desk.

"I have a lot of shit to do, Maryanne, and meeting with you wasn't on the agenda."

"It is now. I've been planning on scheduling time with you. But we're both still here, so let's just meet now."

"I told you, I've got things to do."

"Luckily, this won't take long."

With a loud sigh, Autumn turned from her screen to face her nemesis. "What do you want?"

Maryanne eyed a crumb on her chair and casually flicked it away, taking her time. Then she crossed her legs and cleared her throat before resting folded hands in her meticulously pressed skirt. "You're not a very...*refined*...kind of girl, are you?"

"What the hell does that mean?"

"Exactly." She sighed like a teacher resigned to her student's poor performance. "Just as I've come to expect from you."

"Frankly, I don't care what you expect from me. Or even whether or not you like me. I don't report to you. As long as I'm doing my job, you and I have nothing to talk about.

"Well, that's where you're wrong, Autumn." She cast a simpering smile. "We do have one thing to talk about."

"Which is?"

"Chase Durand."

Fuck. Could this be related to whatever Chase was going to bring up? Knots of fear twisted in her gut, but it'd be a cold day in hell before she'd ever let Maryanne see it. She sat back in her chair and mustered up what she hoped was a bored expression. *That's it. Calm and casual.* "What about him?"

"Let's cut to the *Chase*, Autumn." Maryanne giggled at her little joke before her expression turned fierce. "The White Ibis backers have invested an enormous amount of money to bring Chase's art to the hotel. Financial guys like to see a healthy return on their investment."

Autumn smiled through clenched teeth. "And this has to do with me, because…?"

The designer leaned forward and rested her elbows on Autumn's desk, piercing her with narrowed eyes. "Because you've got a little crush on him. You might even be thinking of him as your guy."

"He *is* my guy," Autumn shot back.

"And that's what we need to talk about." Maryanne smoothed both palms along her perfectly coiffed hair. Her tone turned casual. "Chase and I already discussed this right before he left. So he's aware that we're having this conversation."

That knot of fear turned venomous, coiling in Autumn's gut. This had to be related to what Chase wanted to tell her.

Maryanne leaned in toward the desk. "You've been keeping something from us, haven't you?"

"I keep pretty much everything about myself from you, Maryanne. In case you haven't noticed, we're not really BFFs."

The designer cast a tight smile. "Aren't you the funny one? Yes, I've certainly noticed we're not BFFs as you put it. Frankly, I'd rather be friends with a cockroach than with you. And I'm guessing that suits the both of us just fine."

"Probably the only thing we actually agree on."

"No doubt." Her lips curled in a tight smile. "However, getting back to you. Let's talk about that little juvie record of yours, shall we?"

Autumn's throat turned to dust as a bolt of icy fear arrowed down her spine. How the hell could Maryanne—

"My goodness, I'm thirsty. Got anything to drink around here?"

She knew Maryanne purposely stalled, letting her words sink in to draw out Autumn's anxiety. Because as much as Maryanne was a repulsive, repugnant piece of slime, she was, to her credit, as clever as a fox with no problem playing dirty.

"I'm not a damn hostess, Maryanne. Get yourself a drink somewhere else. Just say what's on your mind and quit wasting time."

The designer gave Autumn a curt nod. "Fine. Let me put it this way. You have a juvenile record you've been hiding from us. Time in the slammer for hacking into the Louisiana prison system. Changing inmate records. Sound familiar?"

A thick coating of sweat greased Autumn's palms. Goosebumps prickled her scalp and raised the hairs on the back of her neck. She was suddenly on a crazy carousel ride from hell, spinning wildly out of control. Everything that had once made sense disintegrated to ash. How did Maryanne know? How the *hell* could she have known?

Autumn swallowed and licked her parched lips. With deliberate purpose, she inhaled, filling her lungs like a balloon before slowly pushing out the air. "I don't know what you're talking about."

The designer raised an aggressively plucked

247

eyebrow. "Oh, really? You're going to play that game?" She shook her head. "You know everything I'm telling you is true. Let's not dally and force ourselves to be in the same room together any longer than necessary."

"I don't have a juvenile record."

"But you *did* have one."

Autumn's hands gripped the sides of her chair as she strove for calm. "That record was expunged," she ground out through clenched teeth.

"But of course, not destroyed," Maryanne replied sweetly. "Not in our proud state of Louisiana. And goodness, Autumn. You committed a *felony*. You didn't actually think that record just entirely went away, did you?"

Autumn clamped her mouth shut. Silence at this point seemed her best ally.

Maryanne rested one arm along the back of her chair. To an outside viewer, she probably looked like a woman having a routine chat about everyday matters. Upcoming weekend plans. A new restaurant she'd tried. But the casual pose belied a savage intensity in the designer's icy stare. "Hiding that type of information could be grounds for termination. As you know."

So that was it. It was what Maryanne was gunning for since the day they'd met. Autumn gnawed her inside cheek, thinking. If Chase already knew this, is it what he'd wanted to talk to her about ahead of time? To warn her that this was coming?

A sudden thought injected her with a sense of dread. Rather than wanting to warn her, had Chase been trying to tell her goodbye? He'd seemed so insistent those two separate times as he'd brought up his need to talk to her. And he wanted to do it in person, too.

As Autumn had done all her life when dealing with shit thrown at her, she steeled her spine and faced down her enemy, a stick-thin, officious interior designer on a megalomaniac power trip. Didn't really matter who or what the enemy was, though. She could deal with it. Always had, always would.

Autumn rose from the chair and cleared her throat. "Okay, Maryanne. You win. I'll be out before dark. Put Keith in charge. He's the strongest on my team and the best natural leader."

Instead of flashing a satisfied smirk, Maryanne frowned and shook her head. "You're leaving?" She managed to sound surprised.

"I thought—"

"I'm not having you fired. Not yet." Maryanne stood as well. In her severe pencil skirt and sky-high stilettos, with hair pulled back in a tight, stern bun, she towered over Autumn like a school-marm from hell. "Chase is your biggest fan, and that saves your ass. He claims to need you for his art. Fine, he can have that.

"But let me be very clear; you will *work* for him, and that's all you'll do. No dating. No pretending you are a couple. No emotional or romantic involvement *whatsoever*. If I find out you're still throwing yourself at him, our next conversation will be very different. Not only will this job of yours be gone, but I'll make sure you never work again in the entire state of Louisiana." Her face contorted with rage, white hot, seething fury, her lips pressed so tightly they nearly disappeared as sparks flew from her eyes.

"I will end your career as you know it, Autumn," she spat, stepping so close her cloying perfume choked the air like smog. "My connections are deep, and my influence is strong. And then there's social media. You being the tech type know all about that, right? Amazing what gets leaked to the public. Like expunged criminal records." She leaned down, her face only inches away. "Know what I mean?"

Rage boiled Autumn's blood like rocket fuel. The urge to slap the smug grin off Maryanne's heavily lipsticked mouth was almost impossible to resist. She had to get out of there. One more second in the same room and she'd add assault and battery to her record.

"I hear you," she mumbled, slapping down the lid on her laptop and shoving it into her carrying case.

"Excellent." Maryanne clapped her palms against one another like she was brushing off dirt. Or an unpleasant conversation.

Autumn pushed passed her, racing out of her office, down the hallway and out the side door to the parking lot. The summer heat wrapped its humid arms around her as she stalked toward her car. She gulped in huge mouthfuls of air, her chest heaving as a single, heart-shattering thought churned in her mind. *Chase knew. Chase knew. Chase knew.*

He'd been aware that Maryanne was going to talk to her and tell her that she and Chase were finished. He'd raced away to help his mother, conveniently out of town when Maryanne spoke with her. Was the accident even true? Or was it just an easy excuse for Chase to avoid her, letting the sting of their breakup ease before he faced her?

She shook her head. No way. The accident couldn't be faked. Could it? For crap's sake, he'd called her from the hospital. But was that just a ruse, him trying to pretend everything was normal until the coast was clear and he knew Maryanne had talked to her?

Sweat poured down her face. Thick, toxic bile roiled in her stomach as heavy saliva coated her mouth. Seconds later she heaved, the contents of her stomach splashing the parking lot, droplets hitting her shoes. A wail pierced the air, the scared, miserable pain of an injured animal. Except she was the one who'd made it.

Her thoughts were twisted, like they'd been written on a carnival funny mirror and reflected back at her all crazy and jumbled. She needed to get home and sleep, sink gratefully into oblivion for a few hours. Or days.

She stabbed the button on her key fob to unlock the car, swiping a hand over her face before pulling open the door. Working late had one advantage: the nighttime cloaked her in darkness so no one could see the hot tears pouring down her cheeks.

****

"Damnit, where the hell is she?" Fire from the kilns roared in the background, but the sweat pouring down Chase's back wasn't from the heat. It was anger and frustration, pure and simple. His entire body shook. He paced the floor, kicking away the punty he'd dropped seconds ago when he learned that Autumn wasn't anywhere to be found. Fortunately, he managed to stop himself from hurling his phone against the wall.

"She's, ah, taking care of some coding for the purchasing system," Keith Sanchez said.

The unease in Keith's voice pierced Chase's conscience with a stab of guilt, but not enough to calm him down. Autumn was avoiding him, and he couldn't figure why.

Damn it all to hell. He'd been back a week and still hadn't seen her. His texts to her were met with crickets or one-word bits if she even bothered answering. If he needed help with one of the installations, she sent someone else. He'd been tempted just to show up at her place uninvited, but a voice in his head warned that it was a bad idea. The feelings growing between them were new and raw, and like a freshly bloomed flower, easily prone to being crushed. Something had happened while he'd been gone. But what?

"She said I should help you with whatever you needed if you called," Keith continued.

"No, man. It's okay. When you see Autumn, just tell her I was looking for her, would you?"

"No problem. I'll tell her."

Chase clicked off and shoved the phone in his back pocket. The muted whoosh of fire in the kiln reminded him that he'd been planning to start blowing some pieces for a new idea he'd been mulling over, a creation inspired by the four seasons. He'd thought he'd start with autumn. But now with this...*something*...between them, he needed to clear the air before his muse came back to visit.

He whipped off the safety glasses perched on top of his head and set his jaw. *Fuck it.* This shit had to end. The hotel was big, yeah, but if he had to search every damn inch of it to find Autumn, he would. There was too much between them to just throw it away on something he was sure was some sort of misunderstanding.

And if he was a betting man, the odds were almost a hundred percent in his favor that he could peg the cause of what was going on with Autumn on one very irritating, self-serving, manipulative interior designer.

Chapter Nineteen

"Try this. It'll make you feel better," Pat said to Autumn.

An assortment of biscotti—almond, vanilla, chocolate, lemon, and coconut—were artfully arranged on a square, white plate offset with elaborate scrolls of caramel and chocolate.

"I'm fine, Pat."

"And I'm the pope." The chef scowled at Autumn as she joined her at the table.

They were the sole occupants in the dining room, the main restaurant having closed over an hour ago as the clock approached midnight. In the days following her conversation with Maryanne, Autumn had avoided going home after work. Her mind just whirled and conjured up reams of unpleasant thoughts if she sat around at home. Even Zip and Beau had failed to put a smile on her face. Much as she hated to admit it, she guessed this was probably what a broken heart felt like.

Sappy B.S. She told herself to stop thinking about Chase, which of course, only made her think of nothing but Chase. Since the conversation with Devil Lady a week ago, she'd tried focusing only on work. She'd directed her guys to deal with anything Chase wanted, going out of her way to avoid him until she felt she'd be able to hold it together long enough to face him. She wanted to appear tough and confident, unaffected by the sting of his rejection. But she was pretty damn far from feeling that way, so she went with option two: outright avoidance.

Twice she'd spotted him in the hotel since he'd been back, her heart snapping in two when she heard his gravelly voice or cast her gaze over his jaw-dropping body. But Maryanne would make good on her promise to get rid of her if she suspected Chase and she were still seeing each other. Autumn wanted to keep her job and keep her nose clean and out of jail.

She plucked a lemon biscotti from the plate and angrily bit off the end. Somehow, Devil Lady had discovered information that was supposed to have been suppressed forever. Autumn could argue Maryanne shouldn't have had access and was using the information illegally, but it wouldn't matter. If the designer let word get out about Autumn's record, it was game over.

Future employers would suddenly find candidates more "qualified," their convenient excuse for not wanting to hire a felon. Even beyond that, Autumn had no doubt that someone as conniving as Maryanne could absolutely put her ass back in the slammer if she was so inclined. So she did as she was told and kept her distance from Chase.

She didn't give Pat specifics, but her friend knew she was hurting. So Pat did what any good chef would do—she fed Autumn. They'd developed a late-night routine. Autumn visited Pat in the empty restaurant after closing and grabbed a midnight snack while she talked about anything and everything except what was really on her mind. And Pat, being the supportive friend she was, just let Autumn talk.

"So what else is going on besides you being miserable?" Pat asked.

The chef's no-nonsense attitude made Autumn smile. "Well, besides me being miserable, I've made an appointment with a new hair stylist."

"*What?*"

"I need something different. My hair's so long, it's always in the way. Thought I'd shake things up a bit and get it cut."

"You cut that hair, and I'll smash a lemon meringue pie in your face."

"Whoa! Call the cops. Violent chef making dangerous pastry threats."

"I'm serious, Autumn." Pat's voice remained firm. "That's a horrible decision. Your hair is the envy of every woman who's ever existed. You can't just make some random impulse decision to cut off a treasure like that. It'd be like hacking off the Mona Lisa's smile."

"That's a little extreme, don't you think?"

"Not at all. She's absolutely right," said a deep, gravelly, heartbreaking voice.

Autumn's breath whooshed from her lungs as her heart flipped. She knew she'd see Chase eventually, but she'd wanted it to be on her terms, when she was ready. No such luck. He'd found her, and they'd be talking.

Quicker than a jack-in-the-box busting through its top, Pat shot out of her chair and extended her arm to Chase, indicating the seat was free. "Make yourself comfortable," she said. "I need to get in the back and clean up."

"I can leave, Pat," Autumn mumbled, managing to find her voice. "I'll just be in your way."

"Eat your biscotti, Autumn," Pat said. "See you

later, Chase."

Autumn looked up, not missing the glances exchanged between Pat and Chase just before he took the recently vacated seat. He settled in like he'd planned on being there for awhile.

Her stomach twisted, a jumpy jumbled combination of excitement, nerves, and longing all vying for attention. She couldn't pull her gaze away from him. Chase made her feel so warm and protected. How she wanted to just sink into his powerful arms and forget every nasty word Maryanne had ever uttered. Pretend like it never happened.

Except it had. And Chase apparently knew.

His gaze roamed along her body, but he maintained distance, making no effort to touch her or kiss her. "So."

That was it—just a single word. But it said so much. He knew something was going on with her, and he patiently awaited her explanation. He didn't push, but he also didn't budge. Neither one of them would be going anywhere until they'd had it out.

"Biscotti?" She cringed at her own stupid comment. What the hell. They weren't exactly at a tea party. But inadvertently, she'd added a dash of comic relief to the strained atmosphere.

Chase visibly relaxed in his seat and a faint grin curled his lip. "Thanks, but I'm stuffed."

His smile was contagious, and she couldn't help it as she flashed one right back at him. Maybe they both just needed to lighten up.

"Tell me what's going on, Autumn."

"I—"

"And don't bullshit. I want the truth."

She sighed; he was right. Time to face the music.

In a soft, halting voice, Autumn told him about the conversation with Maryanne. How the designer had said in no uncertain terms that Autumn needed to stop seeing Chase. That their relationship, according to Maryanne, was limited to strictly business. And that if they kept seeing each other intimately, Autumn was history.

Chase stayed quiet but listened intently, his arms on the table as he leaned forward. His face clouded with anger as his eyes narrowed. He bounced his leg up and down like his veins were made of rubber bands. A muscle twitched in the back of his clenched jaw. "How did she know about your record? I thought juvie stuff was private."

He didn't ask specifics about why she had a record or what bad thing she'd done to get it. His focus was all about the violation of her privacy. Autumn nearly wept with relief. But of course, that's how he would be. Chase had never judged her before and wasn't about to start now.

"I don't know," she admitted. "You're right; it's supposed to be private. The record was expunged."

"Which only means it's not available for the general public to see. In Louisiana, it's not physically destroyed, so the record's still accessible to law enforcement and criminal justice agencies. Some state agencies, too."

"I know. But Maryanne's none of those."

"So someone on the inside leaked the information."

Autumn had gone over and over the conversation with Maryanne, wondering the same thing. How in the hell had Maryanne learned what she had? Who'd given her the intel?

She looked up at Chase, drawing strength from his calm gaze. All at once, her breath stuck fast in her throat and her mouth dropped open. A rush of understanding flooded her body like water breaching a dam, and in that moment, she knew. She *knew* that everything Maryanne told her was a lie. Chase wasn't going to ditch her. She didn't know what he'd wanted to tell her before he left, but it wasn't goodbye. They weren't ending. If nothing, their bond had just kept growing stronger.

She pushed out words from her dry throat. "I—"

"You don't have to tell me why you have a record."

"You a mind reader now or something?"

"I know my woman."

His woman. Holy crap. That might even top "babe."

Absently she crumbled a piece of biscotti between her thumb and forefinger as she took a deep breath. "But what if I want to tell you?"

"Then you should."

Calm, uncomplicated. His whole-hearted acceptance of her came without question. Or terms. Chase took her with everything she brought along. Dodgy past. Prickly attitude. None of it seemed to matter. No wonder he could turn her into a puddle faster than Dorothy dousing the Wicked Witch with a bucket of water.

But Autumn realized that the unreserved, no-questions-asked way he cared about her was something she'd longed for her entire life. It was what had led her to having the damn juvie record in the first place.

She drew a breath, readying to spill the truth.

Pat shoved through the swinging doors. "I gotta go, Autumn."

"Oh." She started to rise from her chair. "Okay, we'll follow you and—"

"So go out through the kitchen when you leave. That door'll lock behind you." Pat flashed Autumn a grin. "All the other doors are secured. Have fun, you two. Night-night."

Without another word, the head chef went back into the kitchen. Seconds later, lights from the kitchen went dark, and the muffled slam of a door indicated Pat had left the building.

Autumn sat back down in her chair and looked at Chase. "You want to stay?"

"Why not? I've got coffee, and cookies, and a beautiful woman about to tell me a story."

Hell's balls. For a cycle-riding bad-ass, he sure had a way with words.

"Don't know how good of a story it'll be, Mountain Man." She released a quiet breath. "But here goes."

She eyed him as he sat, calm as a hidden pond, quietly waiting for her to start spilling the beans and tell him whatever she wanted. Time to take the plunge. "So, um, Rick. My foster father."

"The douchebag who took you to Vegas." Anger clipped his words.

"Well, yeah. But like I told you, once in awhile he could actually be okay. Relatively speaking."

"I remember."

"The threat from those guys in Vegas freaked him enough to want to try going straight. He was even what you might call 'nice' to me for awhile. Got his old lady, Nancy, off my back and told her to stop ragging on me all the time. Sorta acted like a dad."

"Which you'd always wanted."

"Yeah. So for awhile after we moved here, things were all right. He got a job working third shift in an auto parts factory. But even though he worked a lot of hours, it didn't pay much. We were always struggling to pay bills, stuff like that."

"I'm guessing the good times didn't last."

"They did for a little bit. He was trying. I like to think so, anyway. But the job didn't pay as much as we needed. Rent fell behind, and the landlord threatened to kick us out. So Rick started dealing."

Her finger idly traced the rim of her biscotti plate as she thought back on those days. It wasn't Vegas, but it wasn't good. "Primarily weed, but pills, too."

Chase's face clouded. "Don't tell me he made you sell, too?"

"No. He actually had some sort of principles in what he sold and to who. Misguided as that probably sounds."

"Maybe. Tell me more."

"Well, it was in the days before medical marijuana laws. The only way to get weed for any reason was through an illegal dealer. But Rick had this idea that he'd restrict his buyers to people who wanted the drugs for legit medical reasons. Like relief from nerve pain. Or migraines. I guess, in his mind, it helped him justify what he was doing."

"If that's true, then I don't see it as misguided," Chase said quietly. "At least he was trying."

"That's how I saw it, too," Autumn said. "But it

was still illegal. And he got busted."

"Figured that was coming."

She nibbled at her bottom lip, anger simmering as she remembered what had happened to her foster dad— and everything else that followed. "One day, Rick was contacted by a guy who'd said he needed marijuana for his wife. She had cancer and couldn't stand the nausea from chemo. They met close to where the guy lived. The area was sketchy, but Rick never let people come to our place. He always went to the buyer. But this particular neighborhood had problems with crime, and the cops kept an eye on it."

"Which I assume is how they found him."

She nodded. "He and the buyer were in a park, it was dark out, and cops were patrolling the area. They saw the exchange and arrested him on the spot. Hauled his ass to jail and kept him there for over a month. We were only lucky it wasn't longer."

"Did you lose your apartment?"

"Sure did. The landlord kicked out Nancy and me. We had to go to a shelter until Rick got out and found us a place to live."

Chase leaned forward, taking Autumn's hands in his. He said nothing, but words weren't required. The warmth of his touch provided her with comfort to face the agonizing memories.

"When he got out of jail, he swore he'd go straight and put all the illegal con shit and drug dealing in the past. He was true to his word. Within the first few weeks of being out of jail, he sent over a hundred job applications."

"And let me guess," Chase said quietly. "Not a single call."

"It's so messed up," she said, hearing the bite of anger in her tone. "Every prisoner in this country actually serves *two* sentences—one in jail, and one on the outside where people treat you like a criminal even after you've paid for your mistake. Rick didn't even get a chance. Not one interview. Not one call. Nothing. He was like a biblical leper. No one would touch him. He had to be open about his felony record on the job application, but as soon as that info was known, he was damn *persona non grata.*"

"Ex-drug dealers aren't such desirable job candidates."

She sat back in her chair, slipping her hands out of Chase's warm grasp. Even his touch couldn't reach the chill of the dark memories swirling in her mind. She let out a long breath, anxious to finish the story and put it behind her. It would be the last time she told it. To anyone.

"Even with the job struggles, he was still being fairly nice to me. You know, like a dad. He would ask about what I did at school and even made dinner a couple of times. I could tell he was trying, but the frustration was beating him down. Nothing worked. So, I—ah. I decided to do something about it."

"Meaning?"

She shrugged. "He wasn't getting hired because of his record. So I made the record disappear."

Chase's eyebrows shot up. "What?"

"I hacked into the Louisiana prison system and deleted everything in there about him. Made it like the arrest and jail time never happened."

"Holy shit." Chase shook his head like he couldn't believe what he'd heard. "Damn, have you ever got some talent, Autumn. You really are amazing."

She gave him a smile but felt the strain behind it. "Not that amazing," she said quietly. "I didn't know enough at the time how to completely erase my virtual footprints. So I got caught."

"And thrown into juvie."

"Yep. That's what gave me a record. But for once in my life, I kind of caught a break. Even though what I did wasn't legal, the judge was impressed with my abilities. That's what she told me, anyway."

"Smart judge."

"She said what I did exposed flaws in their IT security and had ultimately made it better. The fact that I was able to break in means I had a…um." Her face heated, and she cast her gaze to the floor. "She said I had a natural gift."

"You do. And by the way…"

When he didn't continue, she looked up and met his eyes.

"It's nothing to be embarrassed about."

"Who says I'm embarrassed?" She crossed her arms over her chest.

"Your tomato-colored cheeks are a decent clue."

From the heat scorching her face, Chase was right.

For the first fifteen years of her life, she'd never had a single word of encouragement or praise from a parent or adult mentor. Never had anyone tell her she was awesome. Or amazing. So she'd never gotten comfortable hearing compliments and was even more uneasy having to talk up her skills.

"Anyway," she said, brushing aside his praise, "the judge gave me the minimum sentence she could under the law. I served my time, but when I came out, I learned that the judge had recommended I get placed in advanced IT classes in high school. For the first time in my life, I actually liked going to school."

"It's always fun to do something you're good at."

"For sure. I went on to college and majored in computer engineering. Now, I have this job. But before all that, I petitioned the courts to have my juvie record expunged, and I received confirmation that it had happened. So how Maryanne learned about it…" She sat back, nibbling her bottom lip. "Only thing I can figure is that someone gave it to her."

"Had to," Chase agreed. "But who?"

"And why?" Her body trembled with frustration. "What the hell is the point? Why does Maryanne have it out for me so bad? I didn't do shit to her."

Chase drained the last of his coffee and polished off three of Pat's almond cookies before giving her a nod, like he'd come to some sort of decision. "I know why," he said quietly. "And I've been wanting to talk to you about it."

****

Chase hadn't meant to sound the alarm bell, but from Autumn's saucer-wide eyes and tightly clenched fists he might as well have set off an air raid siren. The second the words left his mouth, she froze. Sitting statue-stiff in her chair, her hardened expression looked as if she were bracing for bad news while erecting walls to ward off the enemy.

"You had said before you had something you wanted to talk to me about," she said quietly. "But you wanted to do it in person."

"Yeah." He frowned.

"Okay. So, what?" A nervous edginess had crept

into her tone. Her words were short, like she wanted to get the conversation over with as fast as possible. But she couldn't know what he was going to say. Unless—

"Did Maryanne talk to you?" he asked.

Autumn flinched. He'd hit a nerve.

"Figured that's what made you scarce as a ghost." A vein pulsed on the side of his face as a crushing urge to smash something came over him. "What'd she talk about?"

Autumn looked at him with haunted eyes but kept quiet. Clearly, Maryanne had said something. But only Autumn knew, and she wasn't talking. At least not yet. He sat back. Better to just say what he wanted and take it from there.

"Look," he began gently, "I've been wanting to tell you something Maryanne discussed with me a few weeks ago. It's been weighing on my mind, and I need your opinion."

She nodded. "Okay."

As quickly as he could, he went through the conversation he'd had with Maryanne right before getting the phone call about his mother. He told Autumn everything, including details of the deal he'd been offered and the terms surrounding it.

He finally relayed Maryanne's ultimatum that he make a choice between the lucrative hotel deal and his relationship with Autumn, and a storm swirled in Autumn's beautiful baby-blues. She pressed her lips tightly together and curled her fingers into fists. But she stayed silent, never once interrupting as he made it to the end of the story.

When he paused for a break, she said, "Five million dollars is a shitload of money."

"No doubt about it."

"But you didn't take it."

He shook his head. "Wasn't even a thought in my mind. No one dictates my life. *Ever*. I do what I want." He sat forward, taking her hands in his. "And see who I want."

If Autumn's mind were transparent, he swore he would have seen a million cogs and wheels spinning like tops as she processed what he told her. "But—"

"No 'buts,' Autumn." He caught her worried gaze and held it. His voice was raw, matching the honesty of the next words out of his mouth. "No deal is worth it if it means I can't be with you."

She slipped her hands from his, absently picking at a loose thread on her jeans as she stared off in the distance. The only sound was the quiet ticking of an old-style clock on the far wall. He let her take all the time she needed, by now knowing Autumn's sometimes skittish nature when he laid an emotional heavy on her. She needed to process.

"So." At last, she returned her gaze to him. "In her mind, you're a living, breathing cash cow. Her ticket to fame and a crap load of fortune. She dangles money over your head to make sure you stay just as you are— hot, brilliant, bad-boy artist."

"Don't forget single."

"Making you an even more lucrative asset."

"Which is why she's trying to get you out of my life." He shook his head. "There's no end to that woman's greed and ambition."

"Sure as hell isn't. She—" Autumn frowned, deep furrows in her brow as if an unpleasant thought had just occurred to her.

"Babe? What is it?"

Her lips parted and she looked at him, words forming but not yet spoken. Unease notched up his heartbeat.

Finally she took in a sharp breath. "You need to take that money."

He shook his head. "No, I already told Maryanne—"

"You need it, Chase. For your mother."

What the hell? Had Autumn turned into a damn mind reader? He clenched his fists, nerves firing. Truth is, she'd hit the nail on the head. His mom faced expensive back surgery. Ever the bohemian, she'd never bothered with insurance. Chase wanted to help, but he couldn't pull money from a monkey's ass. Maryanne's lucrative contract had tempted him like Eve with an apple.

But as much as he needed the cash, he couldn't take the contract, not with the marionette strings Maryanne had attached. She'd be jerking him around like her own personal puppet. Most importantly, jerking him *away* from Autumn. No way was that ever going to happen. So he hadn't signed the contract and had kissed the money goodbye. Best five million bucks he'd ever had the pleasure to lose.

He waved a hand. "Forget about that. I'll figure it out."

"But it's *been* figured out. Maryanne's handing it to you with the flick of her pen. Sign the contract, problem solved."

His eyes narrowed as anger stirred in his gut like sludge. Autumn's craziness was starting to piss him off. Did she think he could end things with them just like that, without a second thought? Was what they had between them so meaningless to her?

He was about to say something when he noticed how she'd drawn her arms across her chest like a protective shield and the quick, shallow puffs of air from between her parted lips. The words died on his tongue.

Autumn was scared. Right now, he was seeing the girl who'd been denied love all her life and would do anything to get it. Breaking the law and serving time was worth it if it meant a hug. She hated being that fucking vulnerable. Who wouldn't? Autumn's default solution to preventing emotional pain was to remove the object causing it. In this case, their relationship. In that way, she erased the possibility of falling in love and then losing everything.

He stood, held out his arms. "C'mere."

Like an obstinate mule, she shook her head, and his suspicions were confirmed. She was scared.

"I said, 'come here,'" he repeated, keeping his words calm but firm. "I need you, Autumn."

She blinked back the tears as she stood and buried her face in his chest. Her tiny frame trembled in his arms, his normally steely girl a scared bundle of nerves. He held her close, his hands smoothing along her back to calm her. After only a minute, she seemed to have collected herself and gently eased out of his embrace. They took their seats again.

Chase said, "Far as I'm concerned, the damn woman's blackmailing the both of us."

Autumn frowned. "Blackmailing?"

"Sure. Your job, my future earnings. She's putting conditions on things she has no right to do just to make sure we're not together. Which, by the way, isn't going to happen."

The soft smile Autumn gave him sent more heat rushing through him than a blast from his glory hole. Damn. His Techie was turning him into one mushy SOB.

"Here's the thing," he continued. "We can assume she's getting the information she has on you from someone on the inside."

"Has to be," Autumn agreed. "A cop, a judge— someone like that. They're the only ones who have access to expunged records. But they're breaking the law big time by sharing it."

"And she's breaking the law by using it against you."

She chomped on a piece of vanilla biscotti and tossed the rest onto a plate. "Tough to prove. It's my word against hers, and who'd believe a high-level, interior designer would spend her time threatening the IT help?"

"Everyone, that's who. Once we show them proof."

Autumn let out a disparaging snort. "You gonna wave your magic wand and make it appear out of thin air?"

"Nope. I'm gonna make Maryanne give it to me."

"By…?"

"By letting her think we're doing what she wants."

Wariness crept across Autumn's face. Her eyes widened, and she started that nervous lip biting thing she did. "You mean we break up?"

"We *pretend* to break up. Give her what she wants so we can do some digging and find out what the hell's going on." He took some biscotti for himself, biting down. Weirdly enough, he was suddenly hungry. Maybe the ideas spinning in his mind were causing it.

"She's treading some seriously dangerous waters," he continued. "Using illegally obtained information against you can land her skinny butt in the slammer."

"I know. But she's careful not to put anything on paper. If she's confronted, she'll deny she ever said anything."

"Which means we need to get proof of what we already know."

Autumn nodded. "If she's using this against me, who knows what else she'll do, or how far she'll go? She's a soul-sucking narcissist on a power trip, and nothing's going to stop her."

"Except us."

His quiet reassurance eased worry lines from her forehead, and her tense posture relaxed as she sat back in her chair.

"I'm Maryanne's ticket to happy land. She looks at me and she sees dollar signs. So let me use that against her."

"By…?"

"By pretending that I'm in on her deal. Make nicey-nice with her and get her to open up."

"Just as long as it's not her damn legs doing the opening."

His deep rumbly chuckle filled the empty restaurant. "Hmmm," he said, reaching out to grasp her wrist and draw her forward. He dotted soft kisses along the inside of her arm. "I think someone's getting jealous."

"I think someone's getting smug," she countered.

He sprinkled kisses up to her throat, lightly sucking her skin before using his teeth to nibble her silky flesh. Her soft moans stirred his cock. "Why not? I know you like me, Techie."

He stood, slipping his hands beneath her arms to pull her out of her chair. He hauled her up onto the table, wrapping her thighs around his waist. He shoved aside the biscotti plates and pressed her down so she was lying on the table. Her beautiful breasts heaved with every shuddering breath she took. He slid his palms over them, pinching her stiff nipples through her top and bra.

"*Maybe* I like you," she whispered, her eyelids drifting closed as she gave herself up to his assault.

"More than 'maybe,'" he insisted.

Shoving both hands beneath her top, he eased his fingers around her back and flicked open her bra, then pushed both the T-shirt and bra up and over her head. After tossing them aside, he pulled sharply at the shoestrings on each of her sneakered feet and yanked off the shoes.

Time for the jeans. Not bothering with being gentle, he jerked open the top button and pulled down fast and hard to haul them off. He tossed them aside and pulled down the flimsy material of her panties with a forceful jerk.

"Mmm." He eyed her exposed pussy. "I like what I see."

She propped herself on her elbows so she could peer down her body at him. "Yeah?" she drawled. "So what do you want to do with it?"

"Have you show me how much you like me."

"What?"

"Put your feet on the table."

She hesitated.

He growled. "Do it."

A sharp intake of her breath revealed her excitement. He knew she liked it when he grew forceful. She lifted both feet and propped them on the edge of the table, offering a sneak peek of her naked pussy between the slight opening of her legs.

"Spread your thighs."

Her lips curled in a smile as she obeyed, showing him her wet pussy lips unfurling like a flower before the sun.

His heartbeat jolted like he'd just been struck by lightning. He licked suddenly dry lips. "Excellent. Now," he said, stepping forward to position himself between her thighs, "I'm going to stick my fingers in that beautiful cunt of yours. I'm going to feel your tight walls around me, and I'm going to get my proof of how much you like me when my fingers get drenched. And then you're going to admit it."

Her eyes were the color of pitch as a soft moan slid from her parted lips. Her tongued darted out to lick them, and she swallowed. "You sure about that?"

"Damn sure." He ran a finger along the inside of her thigh, feather light. Goose bumps pebbled her skin. "Keep those thighs parted," he snarled.

Her long, low moan filled the restaurant. She struggled to keep her legs wide as he ruthlessly teased the sensitive skin. His fingers trailed down her leg to her core. He drew circles around her mound, tracing over her plump outer lips. She gyrated on the table, thrusting her hips toward him.

"Keep still, you dirty girl. I know you want me

pumping you hard." He slid his middle finger through her crease, her slick juices coating him.

"You don't know shit," she ground out while she spread her thighs wider.

"Don't I?" He lifted his hand to show her his slick finger. "Then what's this all about?"

When she stayed mulishly silent, he leaned forward and painted her lips with her own juices. "Suck it."

Without hesitation, she opened her lips, and he slipped his finger in her mouth. Her warm, wet tongue circled his finger, licking away the proof of her excitement.

Suddenly, those wet lips were too much for him to resist. He withdrew his finger and dipped down for a deep, soul-stirring kiss. Lust scorched his blood as his stiff cock pressed painfully against his jeans. He wanted her lips wrapped around his cock, teasing it just like she had done with his finger. But that was for later. Now was for Autumn.

He shifted his position to one side to slip his hand between their bodies. Heat from between her legs drifted over his hand, so he knew exactly where to aim. He drove two fingers into Autumn's core.

"Ah!" A groan slipped from her lips as she writhed on the table. "Harder," she begged. "Fuck me harder, Mountain Man. Need you deep."

He did the opposite, stopping cold as he slid his fingers out.

Her eyes popped open. "What the—"

"Tell me what I want to hear, Autumn." Without dropping her gaze, his hand cupped the bulge in his jeans. "You want this?"

She licked her lips. "Maybe."

He chuckled. Stubborn as a cranky mule. With both hands, he lifted his shirt up and over his head, tossing it aside. Her breath hitched, but he ignored it as he popped the button on his jeans and slid them down his legs, then did the same with his boxers. Standing naked in front of her, he fisted his cock.

"You said you wanted it hard." He slid his hand over the head where a drop of pre-cum glistened at the tip. "And deep."

He increased his pace and kept his grip firm. He ached like hell to bury himself in Autumn's tight, wet walls, but not until she said what he wanted to hear.

"So give it to me," she croaked in a dry voice.

"You know the price of admission." He didn't bother hiding a groan; instead, he continued pleasuring himself, showing her what she was missing. "The truth."

She pushed herself up from the table, sitting on the end as she watched him stroke his dick, her eyes dark and glittering with desire.

"Let me give this to you, Autumn. Let me drive myself deep inside you until you're begging for more, until you scream with release."

Her hand slid down her body until she reached her core. She spread her legs and slid two fingers into her wet pussy, matching her own thrusts with his. "You'll make me come?"

"You know I will." He growled, pumping harder.

She matched his pace. "You'll make me scream?"

"Like a howler monkey."

She groaned, her fingers slapping hard against her clit. "Then do it," she ordered, although the hitch in her voice revealed she was far from feeling bossy. More like desperate.

He felt the same way but needed to stay strong and stick with what he wanted. "Then say it," he ground out, continuing to fist his cock.

She moaned long and low, her eyes fluttering shut as she rolled her hips forward on the table. "I want you, Chase," she whispered. "I want you to pound me with your awesome dick. Because…" She whimpered as her fingers worked over her slick swollen clit. "Because I like you, damnit. A lot."

"Then your wish is my command." He stepped between her spread thighs, grabbed her hips, and buried himself balls-deep in her slick heat.

She let out a stream of groans as she held herself steady on the table to match his pounding pace. Her slick, vaginal walls gripped his cock like a vise. With her thumb and forefinger, she pinched her nipples hard as she rocked against him. Pure unconcealed lust cascaded over her face—wet lips parted, eyes shut, loud moans bouncing off the walls of the empty restaurant. He'd never seen anyone more beautiful.

"Look at me, Autumn." His hoarse voice was thick with lust. "I want you to watch me when you come."

Slowly, she opened her eyes, her normal baby-blues now ebony dark as she fixed her gaze on him.

"That's it," he praised. "Now, stay with me. Stay with me and let yourself go."

He pushed the pace, pounding hard. She met him thrust for thrust, her hips rocking against him, legs wrapped tight about his waist. Her hair had come loose from its pinup and spilled behind her back like waves of blonde silk.

He slid a hand to her breast, cupping hard before

pinching her nipple. She cried out from the pain, then groaned from the pleasure. By how hard and fast she ground against him, he knew she was close. He slipped a hand between their bodies and fingered her swollen clit.

Two seconds later, she exploded, her head falling back as release consumed her. She screamed as it took hold, her fingernails digging painfully in his shoulder as she grabbed him like a lifeline. Two more hard pumps of his cock and he joined her, hot jets of cum shooting deep as her clenching pussy milked him.

When Autumn was finally spent, she rested her head against his chest. He was sure she could feel his pounding heartbeat against her ear. He wondered if she liked it.

"So." Her breathy voice sounded like she'd just run a marathon.

Pride puffed up his chest like a damn rooster. "Yeah?"

She pulled back from him. "If this is what break-up sex feels like, I want more."

He grinned and ruffled her gorgeously messed up, bed-head hair. "I like the way you think."

Chapter Twenty

"HR wants to see you." Keith Sanchez stood in the employee kitchen, eyeing a huge assortment of candy.

Baskets spilling over with free snacks for all the employees lined the counter, and Autumn knew he wasn't shy about taking advantage of the perk. How he managed to stay runner slim while eating pounds of junk was one of the world's great mysteries.

"They phoned down to the office a few minutes ago," he continued, reaching for the king-sized M&M's.

"Yeah, they texted me, too," she said, grabbing an orange seltzer from the fridge and twisting off the top. "Did they say what they want?"

"Negative. Just asked me to let you know they're looking for you." He ripped open his candy and shoveled handfuls into his mouth as he strolled out of the kitchen. "By the way, I finally got that overhead audio recording system working."

"The one in the conference rooms to record meetings?"

"Yep. Took a lot of damn testing, but I figured out the bug. Going to finish up the installation for the HR system now."

"Thanks, Keith. You're awesome."

"Remember that at review time."

She grinned as he left but remained in the kitchen,

resting a hip against the counter while drinking her water. Looking around to make sure she was alone, she pulled her phone from her back pocket and glanced at her texts. She'd read the most recent one from Chase about ten times and still felt a rush of warmth every time she did.

I can't stop thinking about all the dirty things I'm planning for that amazing body of yours. Signed, your ex.

Since their conversation two weeks ago, they'd made good on Chase's idea about "breaking up." They avoided each other in the hotel. If they happened to cross paths, they didn't stop to speak. They never texted each other on work phones.

It was tough as hell in the beginning. Memories of being abandoned by so many foster families when she was just a kid were brought to painful light again as she was "abandoned" by Chase.

Except she wasn't. If anything, his attention toward her was more amped up than ever before. They'd bought burner phones to use exclusively for texting and calling each other. Chase had promised that until they got to the bottom of the Maryanne mystery, he'd burn up her burner phone with scorching hot texts, and he'd made good on the promise. She blushed as she thought of some of the shit he'd texted her. What a gutter mind.

She slipped the burner back in her pocket and glanced at her work phone. The text from Human Resources glared at her. *Please stop by our office, Autumn.*

It was never anything good when the corporate cops needed to see you. Had Maryanne said something about Autumn's record? She *claimed* she wouldn't, but

Autumn trusted that snake of a designer as much as she trusted…well…a snake.

Slogging down the last of her seltzer, she tossed the bottle in the recycling bin and trudged toward the administration offices with the enthusiasm of a prisoner walking the plank.

The offices were as hushed as a library. Or a graveyard. Autumn cringed as she eyed the beige walls, beige carpet, and sterile, framed prints. One thing she knew for sure—these offices were absolutely *not* decorated by the Dragon Lady. Much as Autumn disliked Maryanne, she had to admit that the designer could help spruce up this dreary fiasco.

The HR area had a handful of desks in an open floor plan with offices surrounding the room's perimeter. Autumn approached the closest desk.

A surprisingly perky blonde greeted her. "Hi! Autumn, right?"

She frowned. "Yeah. How'd you know?"

"From the opening night reception. You were on stage with Chase Durand."

Ah, right. As his "girl."

"Oh, that. Well…we're not, you know, together anymore."

The blonde's perkiness tanked a peg. "Sorry to hear. You looked like such a cute couple."

Autumn shrugged. "It happens." Suddenly, she wanted nothing more than to change the conversation. Talk of a breakup with Chase, even a fake one, still managed to feel like someone was jamming push pins in her heart. "I got a text that you needed to see me?"

"Oh, right." She stood and walked over to where neat stacks of paper forms were arranged on a counter against the wall. "I can't wait until the HR system is activated," she said, walking back. "It's crazy that we're not able to do everything online."

"It's coming, actually," Autumn assured her. "One of my senior techs is on it right now."

"Excellent!" She sat back down behind her desk and pushed a single sheet of paper and a pen toward Autumn.

"Apparently, you never signed your acknowledgement receipt of the employee handbook." She frowned. "You *did* receive a copy of the handbook, didn't you?"

Seriously? *That's* what this was about? "Yeah," she said. "When I first got here."

"Okay, great. If you can just sign the form, we'll be all set." She flashed Autumn a smile. "I'm Jen, by the way."

"Good to meet you, Jen." Autumn scrawled her name across the bottom of the paper and slid it back across the desk.

"That's all you needed?"

"That's it. Pretty painless, right? Now I just have to stick it in the old-school employee paper file I'm embarrassed to say we actually keep."

Autumn was about to take a hike when a single world stopped her cold. *File?* She turned back toward Jen. "Just out of curiosity, are employees allowed to see their files, or are they super-secret, For HR Eyes Only?"

Jen laughed. "The rumors that get spread about HR could choke an elephant. No, they're not top-secret files. Any employee can see what's there. It's *your* file, after all." She rose from her chair. "Wanna see yours?"

"I wouldn't mind taking a peek."

"No prob." Jen had already crossed the room to the file drawer and was thumbing through the contents. "Rivette, right?"

"Yep."

Her forehead creased as she flipped through the files, growing more prominent with every passing second. "Hmmm…I can't figure out why—"

"You looking for Autumn Rivette's file?" another girl at the desk nearest Jen's asked.

"Yeah, Tiff. You know where it is?"

"I saw it on Mason's desk the other day. Might still be there."

"Mason's desk?" Jen frowned as she turned toward Tiff. "Why would Autumn's file be there?"

Dark-haired Tiff shrugged. "No idea. Maybe he was doing a general review of files in case EEOC auditors come knocking."

"Yeah, maybe. I guess." The doubt Autumn heard in Jen's voice matched her own.

"I'll go see if it's still there," Tiff continued. "Mason's out today, but I have the key to his office." She rooted through a drawer in her desk, grabbed a ring of keys and walked over to a closed door.

While Tiff was inside, Autumn refocused her attention on Jen. "Who's Mason?"

"He's a lawyer who works for the hotel's investment firm," Jen said.

Lawyer? "But he has an office here?"

"Sounds a little weird, I know. But he actually helps us out part-time with matters related to employment law. Making sure we do everything by the book. So the hotel gives him an office to use for the times when he's here."

"Found it!" Tiff emerged from the office with a pale-green file. "Still in the same place," she announced triumphantly, holding up the file like a prize winner showing off her trophy.

Tiff handed it to Autumn and nodded toward a row of chairs lining a far wall. "You can review it over there," she said. "Like Jen said, employees can see their files any time they want, but we require that they stay within HR. Otherwise, we'd probably never get any of them back."

"Okay, sure," Autumn mumbled, her attention already focused on the file. She took the closest chair and skimmed over the clipped papers. Employment application, resume, job description, offer letter, W-4. In a separate section were her I-9, results from her drug screen, and a background check that included a police report. *Bingo*.

She glanced up. Her new HR pals, Jen and Tiff, had their eyes glued to their computer screens as their painted nails tapped away on the keyboards. Autumn might as well have been invisible. Perfect.

Easily prying a finger beneath the metal fastener keeping the papers in place, she pulled the background check away from the other papers. The contents of the printout were pretty standard—credit report, driving record, education record, sex offender registry scan, criminal record. But then the hairs on the back of her neck stood up. She didn't believe what she was seeing.

Impatiently, she flipped the report over, scanning the other side. Empty. Again she turned the paper, re-reading the criminal record report. She did it a third time, but the result never changed.

Criminal Record: None.

She stayed pole stiff in her chair and focused exclusively on her breathing. In. Out. Slowly, evenly. *Ignore your slamming heartbeat, Autumn. Think of breathing.* Questions swirled about her mind, but she needed calm before she could process.

"You need anything over there?" Jen's face popped in view from around her computer screen.

"Nope, I'm good," Autumn said, pleased with how relaxed she sounded.

Jen flashed a smile and returned her focus to the screen.

Autumn glanced around the room, making certain she was totally ignored. With stealth-like quiet she slipped her phone from her pocket and snapped a picture of the criminal report. Then she stood and walked back over to the HR desks.

"Thanks," she said, handing the folder back to Jen. "So…it's just this one, right? There aren't other files you keep that employees aren't allowed to see?"

Jen shook her head. "Any medical information we might have is separate for privacy reasons, but otherwise, everything we have on file on any employee is all right there."

"Cool. Then I'm done."

"Just like I said, right?" Jen said with a wink. "No secrets."

Autumn gave her a big smile. "None at all."

Fast as her legs would carry her, she hustled over to an IT closet and shut herself inside before jerking the burner phone from her back pocket. Stabbing at the keys, she jammed out a text to Chase.

Something's up. Need to see you. IT closet on 4.

He responded in under thirty seconds.

I'm in my workshop. Be there fast as I can.

She heaved a sigh as she put her phone away. Knowing Chase was coming brought her anxiety down to a quiet roar. A smile tugged at her lips. She'd been calmed by her knight in shining chrome.

Minutes later, Chase swung the door open and her giant Mountain Man was standing before her, concern etched in the furrows on his brow.

"What's up, Babe? Got here fast as I could."

She wanted to joke about him breaking every speeding law on record to get there so fast but realized she didn't have it in her. Now that she was actually going to talk about her discovery, it seemed more real—and troubling—than before.

"I saw my employee file," she began, pulling out her phone and bringing up the picture she'd taken. "This was the printout of the criminal record."

He took the phone from her and looked over the photo. From his tight expression, he understood her alarm. "There's nothing else there? No other paper that could be filed somewhere else?"

"I asked. HR said everything's kept right there."

His eyes narrowed as anger seemed to vibrate out from every limb. "This is fucked."

"I know."

He handed her the phone and leaned back against one of the equipment racks. "If there's nothing in your file, where the hell did that bitch get the information on you?"

"Exactly what I want to know."

Chase absently stroked his chin as he thought, like a man contemplating whether or not he needed a shave.

He looked down at her, those gorgeous green eyes filled with concern and affection, immediately making her feel safe, her own mammoth bodyguard protecting her from harm.

"Someone obviously gave it to her," he said.

"Yeah," Autumn replied, the hum of anger zinging through her veins. "And I think I know who."

****

Autumn stood before Chase like a steel rod had replaced her spine. Resolve spewed from every pore. Despite the seriousness of the situation, Chase couldn't help the slight tug at his lips as he grinned. It seemed his Tiny Techie had reached her limit of putting up with shit from Maryanne.

"You found something out?" he asked.

"When I was in HR," she said, "and asked to see my file, they couldn't find it at first. Then it turned out my file was in Mason's office."

"Who's Mason?"

Surprisingly, she chuckled. "I was wondering if you'd know. I didn't. Turns out he works in HR part-time for the hotel. That's where his office is. And my personnel file was sitting right on his desk."

"Because…?"

"'Cause there's some shady shit going down is what I think. The chicks in HR seemed surprised. One of them said something about him reviewing files for an audit, but neither of them seemed to believe it."

She retrieved her phone from a nearby shelf. Quick as lightning, her fingers flew over the touch screen until she pulled up something before handing him her phone. "Take a look at that."

It showed the White Ibis' website, listing the

company's corporate executives. Chase scanned the faces listed but it told him nothing. "I don't get it."

"You don't see anyone named Mason, right?"

He glanced at it again. "You're right. I don't."

Autumn took her phone back and tapped some more. "While I was waiting for you to show up, I did some digging on Mason," she said. "If he was listed among the White Ibis big shots, he would have a bio on the website. He doesn't. So I found the website of the private equity dudes who financed this hotel."

She handed him her phone again, this time showing the profile page of Stonebridge & Silver private equity investors revealing photo after photo of wealthy, white, older men.

Chase drew his finger along the screen, scrolling down. Sure enough, smiling into the camera was a somewhat pudgy, somewhat balding guy named Mason Reed.

He looked away from the phone and down at Autumn. "I've seen this dude around the hotel."

"Plenty of times. And always with Maryanne." She gave a single nod toward the phone. "Check out his profile."

He scanned Mason Reed's bio, growing more pissed by the second. "Lawyer," he growled. "Representing the hotel's financers."

"*And* he represents the hotel itself in employment law matters," Autumn clarified. "Total conflict of interest, which sure as shit is why he's not listed on the hotel's website."

"That's royally fucked."

Autumn nodded. "What's also fucked is that lawyers know judges. Judges can access private documents sealed from the general public."

Realization washed over him with the force of a tidal wave. "Like expunged juvenile records."

"Yeah," she echoed quietly. "Like expunged juvenile records."

His fingers curled into fists. Fiery rage made him want to roar. Every molecule in his body demanded that he hunt down Maryanne and force her to confess what they both suspected. But he had to take things slow. They were doing a whole lot of speculation without any actual facts.

"Definitely possible," he said slowly, forcing himself to calm. "But we don't know for sure."

"You mean we don't have any proof to back up what we know for sure."

He couldn't hold back his grin. Nothing hotter on the planet than Autumn hell-bent on proving her point. "Even so, the fact is we'll need it."

"And I've got a plan to get it."

He raised an eyebrow. "Is that so?"

"It is, Mountain Man. And it involves you, so listen up."

"That slick mind of yours is scaring me, Techie."

For a moment, she looked down at the floor and fiddled with a strand of hair that had come loose from the messy sexy pile she had pinned behind her head. She still wasn't a champ at taking compliments. But he'd get her there eventually.

She looked up at him. "Here's the thing. Maryanne wants you to sign that contract, right? And you haven't done it yet. So here's our opportunity."

"Go on."

"It's like this. Offer to…um…you know, take her

to dinner. Use the contract as an excuse. Say you want to talk things over. Get her drunk, then pump her for intel. Play your cards right, and she'll tell you everything you want to know, including what's the deal behind her relationship with Mason and why he'd be helping her."

"*Maybe* she'll tell me."

"She will if you act like you deserve an Oscar. Tell her you thought over what she said, and you've realized she's right about me. That you think it's better for your career to have a model slung over your arm instead of just an IT chick. You could even say you've always felt there's something about me that I was hiding, but you could never put your finger on it. Give her an opening to drive a truck through and heap on the praise like a worshipper at the altar of Maryanne. I guarantee she'll flap her gums."

He whistled under his breath. "Damn, Techie. This just might work."

"Sure it will. She'll confirm your suspicions about me by telling you everything she knows about my record. Your job is to ask her where she got the dirt, and I bet the farm she'll tell you it came from Mason. Then just make sure your phone's recording every juicy detail." Autumn's eyes were bright, her cheeks flushed. She stood before him like a feisty soldier determined to do what's right even at her own personal expense.

Despite trying to stick with just the facts of the plan, he saw the hurt in her eyes when she talked about him having a model on his arm and referring to herself as "just an IT chick."

He curled his fingers into fists, his body humming with resolve. Autumn's plan made sense, but there was no way he was going through with it before making it crystal clear exactly how he felt about her. Who cared that they were standing in a tech closet? Maybe it was actually the most appropriate place of all.

"Okay," he said quietly. "It's a good plan, and I'll do it. I'll suffer through a night of hell."

She cracked a smile. "You'll survive."

"I will," he agreed, looking straight into her eyes. "'Cause I know I'm doing it for someone I love."

She remained still, her feet planted in place like they were fused to the floor. Her mouth parted, eyes turning sky wide, the surprise evident on every plane and curve of her gorgeous face. She nibbled at her cheek and then let out long breath, eyeing him accusingly. "Did you just drop the L bomb?"

"Yep."

"Well….um—"

"Doesn't require a response, Autumn. But you need to know how I feel. I don't want a damn model on my arm. I want you." He reached out a finger and slid a soft caress down her cheek. "Only you."

She closed her eyes against his touch and leaned into it. When she opened her eyes, there was a glistening sheen of tears she didn't try to hide. "I never had someone tell me that before," she whispered. "Not even once."

A lump like a damn egg stuck fast in his throat. No one should have to go through life without ever being told they were loved. The shit childhood Autumn had endured was a horse kick in the gut.

"Then I better make sure I tell you often," he said, raw emotion making his words more of a rumble strip than usual. "To make up for lost time."

"You don't have to."

"I want to." His arms slipped around her waist, and he pulled her close.

She clung to him, burying her face against his chest.

"I love you, Techie. Deal with it, cause you're going to be hearing that a lot."

Her quiet, muffled reply warmed him like a shot of whiskey.

"Okay."

Chapter Twenty-One

The red disc sailed through the air, dipping low before soaring straight, spinning perfectly parallel to the ground. Beau the Bernese stayed hot on its tail, awaiting the exact right moment to leap up and catch his prey. Autumn grinned. Bernese Mountain Dogs weren't typically the breed to dart after Frisbees, but Beau didn't care about playing by the rules.

He leapt up, snatching the round plastic disc from the air with long-practiced precision. As he trotted happily back with the Frisbee between his jaws, she had a fleeting longing for the amazing feeling of being a well-loved dog. Fed, sheltered, cared for, and one hundred percent perfectly happy to be chasing a Frisbee or even a plain ol' stick. No worries, no concerns about horrid pencil-thin, conniving women threatening to ruin a reputation that had taken years to build. She gave Beau a half-smile as she whipped the Frisbee for him to chase. No, Beau didn't have to think about any of that shit.

But since her conversation with Chase a week ago when he had agreed to have dinner with Maryanne, that was *all* she freakin' thought about. Well, no. That wasn't true. She shifted back and forth between thinking about the damn dinner and obsessing over him saying he loved her.

Her body heated, warmth filling every crack and

crevice of her heart. She'd told the truth about never having had those words directed at her before. Who would have said them? Her biological parents had given her up; social services had bounced her from one shitty foster family to the next. Even after she'd more or less settled with Rick and Nancy, neither of them had shown her feelings that could've remotely been mistaken for love. No, it had been clear from the get-go that they'd brought Autumn in their home to serve as a maid. Lucky her.

So when Chase had given her the "L" word, it'd nearly knocked her on her ass. But in a good way.

She whistled to Beau as he pawed at the ground, flinging dirt from his paws. God only knew what he was after, and she sure as hell didn't want any of his "presents" in her home.

"C'mon, big guy," she called.

He abandoned his mission and raced over to Autumn. She led him back to her car, they got in, and she gunned the engine. They had a half hour's drive home. Parks with open space were at a premium with all the surrounding bayous.

She kept the top up whenever Beau was with her, not taking the chance of her dog flying out of the car when she was cruising along the open highway. As he sprawled out and slept on the back seat, her thoughts drifted to where they always were these days—on Maryanne and Chase.

Chase had said the "L" word. A smile curved her lips. Helpless to stop it, she let it grow, feeling her cheeks bunch as she grinned from ear to ear.

He loves me. She said the words aloud, tasting them on her tongue.

A quick glance in the rearview mirror revealed Beau waking from his nap. He looked up, his big, brown doggy eyes filled with tenderness and yes, love. Her dog loved her. Now a human did, too.

"He loves me, Beau!"

The Bernese barked in reply.

She laughed at the absurdity of sitting in her car, confessing deep thoughts to her dog. But damn, it felt good. Chase loved her. He *loved* her. And without a doubt, she knew she loved him right back.

She'd tell him. Eventually. After he'd talked to Maryanne. When the timing was right. When…she swallowed, eyes on the road but thoughts miles away. *Admit it, Autumn.*

When you find the damn courage.

It was one thing to hear the words. Something else again to say them. But she would, because it was true. She loved Chase wholly, completely. She'd tell her Mountain Man how she felt, secure in the knowledge that those feelings were returned.

Sudden realization hit her with the force of a soaring comet.

She was no longer alone.

She braked hard and pulled onto the shoulder, heart beating fast. Once off the road, she killed the engine, needing a moment. Her hands shook despite a firm grip on the steering wheel. Short, quick breaths gusted in her ears.

She had lived her entire life with no parents and only a handful of friends. Like a ferocious junkyard dog, she'd survived childhood, juvie, and gang bangers in Vegas through wits and courage, but she'd always been alone.

Now when she wasn't even looking, her situation had changed forever. She had someone in her life to love her and protect her and to take away her loneliness. She had Chase.

Her breaths slowly calmed, thoughts of her man easing frayed nerves when he wasn't even by her side. *Guess that's what it meant to have a partner. Someone who completes you, who's there for you, who fights for you. Someone with whom you punch through life's troubles together.*

Her grip tightened on the steering wheel as she remembered that tonight was the night Chase and Devil Lady were having dinner. Curiously, the thought didn't cause the overwhelming dread that it always had before, because she and Chase had a plan. They were dealing with "The Maryanne situation" in a thoughtful, smart way that both felt confident would work. And if it did…

She turned the key over and started the engine. A single car sped past her on the highway. Once it cleared, she nosed off the shoulder and onto the highway, punching the gas to gain speed. Bald cypress trees stood sentinel tall in the bayou on her right-hand side. Water birds crept through reeds and circled overhead, seeking their next meal. She glanced at the clock on her dash. Nearly seven. The dinner hour. Nerves sizzled down her spine, yet she maintained a sense of calm. Chase was carrying out their plan. If everything went as they hoped, Maryanne was going down.

****

"Right this way, sir. Your party is already seated." With footsteps light as a whisper, the black-suited maitre d' led Chase through the elegant dining room.

They passed intimate tables of couples holding hands as they delicately nibbled at shockingly expensive, tiny portions of food served on square, white plates. Inwardly, he grumbled. It figured that Maryanne would choose this place. Over-the-top pretentiousness fit her like a glove.

As they approached the table where Devil Woman was already seated, his annoyance soared to new heights. Near their table stood a grand piano where a tuxedoed player plucked out grandiose classical music. There's no way his phone would pick up any of their conversation with a symphony concert raging in the background.

"Chase!" Maryanne's colossal smile radiated. "I've been looking forward to this like a girl on her first date." Her blatant flirtation sent the night careening from bad to worse.

When Chase didn't immediately take his seat, the maitre d' looked at him with concern. "Something the matter, sir?"

"Of course there isn't!" Maryanne sang out. Ignoring her, Chase turned to his ally and dug deep within to begin his award-worthy performance.

"The table is fine," he said smoothly, "except…well…" He gave Maryanne a wink. "The lady and I are actually celebrating, and ideally, I was hoping for something a bit…quieter, perhaps? If it's not too much trouble?"

"Ah." the maitre d' gave a knowing nod, as if he'd been presented with a particularly thorny problem that he alone could solve. With an almost imperceptible nod, he signaled to a waiter across the room, who came gliding toward them. "Martin, please prepare table twenty-two for this fine couple."

"Certainly." The waiter hurried away.

"It shall be ready momentarily, sir," the maitre d' said. "Won't you follow me?"

Before ushering them toward the new table, the man helped Maryanne out of her chair, making sure to capture the napkin resting on her knees before it tumbled to the floor. Chase glanced to where she'd been sitting. With satisfaction, he noted her nearly empty wineglass. Already one under her belt. With many more to come.

Like the most polished of gentlemen, he held out his arm for Maryanne as he led her toward their new table. She slung her wrist around his bicep, leaning into him much closer than she should have. *Just a couple of hours,* he reminded himself. But shit, they were going to feel like an eternity.

The selected table was in the back of the restaurant and mostly out of earshot of the piano music. Perfect.

Chase discreetly slipped the maitre d' a twenty. "Another glass of wine for the lady," he said, "And a bottle of your best champagne."

"Champagne!" Maryanne gushed. "How absolutely perfect."

As he took his seat, he slipped his phone from his pocket and flicked on the record feature. Then, pressing the center button to return the screen to black, he set his phone on the table near the corner of his side.

"Hope you don't mind," he said, nodding toward the device. "I only have it out so I don't miss a call from my brother. My mom had an appointment with the doctor to see if she'll need surgery on her back. He's supposed to let me know the results." He already knew that the docs were going to hold off on surgery. He and Wolf had spoken earlier that week. But the lie to Maryanne was a convenient excuse to keep his phone out on the table and in perfect position to record their dinner conversation.

"Oh, of course," Maryanne agreed, managing to drum up a concerned expression. "I certainly understand."

Their waiter arrived with champagne chilling in an ice bucket and Maryanne's second glass of white wine. Once the cork was popped and the glasses poured, he left them alone to look over the menus.

Maryanne lifted her champagne glass and tipped it toward Chase. "To us," she chirped. "And all the amazing work we're going to do together."

Chase clinked glasses with her and took the smallest of sips. He'd always been more of a beer-and-whiskey guy than champagne. But for Autumn, he'd single-handedly drink the restaurant's entire supply if that's what it took to get them the information they needed.

"Why don't we order?" he suggested, "so we can focus on enjoying ourselves."

"Oooh, I like the way you think, mister," Maryanne giggled, the sound like a pencil piercing his eardrum.

Chase curled his fingers into fists and released a long, slow breath, gathering sufficient mental strength to endure the evening. They placed orders with their waiter, and Chase nodded toward Maryanne's untouched glass of wine. "Drink up," he encouraged with a smile. "We're celebrating."

"Your wish is my command." With an oddly

unlady-like speed, she downed her wine in only a few sips before returning her attention to the champagne. "This is *so* delicious. I've always loved a good bottle of Dom Perignon."

"As have I," he assured her, although he'd never before had any bottle of Dom Perignon, good, bad, or otherwise. But it was the most expensive champagne on the menu, so he knew Maryanne would drink it down.

"Nice that we have something to celebrate," he said, taking charge of the conversation. He paused and added quietly, "I'm really grateful to you, Maryanne."

The waiter arrived to serve their first course. Right before he left, Chase asked for another bottle of champagne.

"Another bottle?" Maryanne's eyes were already beginning to glaze over but from her big smile Chase knew she'd have no qualms about continuing to drink. It was Dom Perignon, after all.

Chase, determined to steer the conversation where he needed it to go, repeated his earlier statement.

"I feel like you've been instrumental in helping my career."

Maryanne lifted her napkin and dotted the corners of her lips. "Oh yes, you were saying you were grateful, Chase. But why? All I've done is make sure your talent gets the respect and attention it deserves."

"It's more than that. You've also helped clarify my thinking and make sure I don't get caught up in something that's no good for me."

"Well, I just—"

"And there's no room for false modesty. You know exactly what I'm talking about. Or rather, who." He stoked the fire of her ego with heaps of praise, shamelessly piling it on. He released a breath. "Autumn."

"I know who you meant." Despite the volume of alcohol flowing through her veins, Maryanne's annoyance toward his Tiny Techie didn't appear to be at all dulled.

"I've upset you," he noted as her cheeks flushed. "Why?"

"Oh, I don't know, Chase. There's just something about Autumn that's always rubbed me the wrong way. She's such a little know-it-all. And I do mean 'little.'" She laughed before downing another healthy gulp. "I mean, what is she? Like four-foot-two? And nothing but a skank. Certainly not good enough for you."

Beneath the table, Chase's fingers curled into fists. He clenched his jaw, not trusting himself to say a single word. Never in his life had he hurt a woman, and he wasn't about to start now. But Maryanne's smug conceit tested his willpower to the extreme.

Fighting hard to maintain control, he took a sip of water and swallowed his fury. "I guess you were right all along," he said.

"Meaning?"

"I always kind of felt there was something a little off about Autumn. But I didn't want to admit it. She and I had hooked up, you know? And she seemed cool."

"Well, she's not, I can assure you."

His pulse jumped. "Yeah?"

"*Oooh,* yeah," Maryanne said with a knowing nod. "That girl's got skeletons in her closet that would put a graveyard to shame."

"Really? What do you—"

"Finished with the soup courses?"

Fuuuck. Chase cursed silently. Worst possible moment for the damn waiter to show up. "Yeah," he mumbled, wishing he could literally shove the man aside.

"Excellent." In seconds their bowls were cleared, and the waiter was gone, but the moment had been broken.

"But let's not talk about Autumn tonight," Maryanne pouted. "She's ruining our celebration."

"Well, yeah, but—"

"Your salads, madam and monsieur."

Damnit. Damnit. Damnit! Chase was positive smoke poured from his ears. Their waiter had exactly point five seconds to get the hell out of his face before he became the victim of a violent homicide.

What appeared to be artfully arranged swamp grass topped the plates. As with the soup, Maryanne dug in, but by this point, Chase's patience had reached its limit. Drastic measures were called for.

Grabbing his glass of champagne, he downed the contents in a single swallow, anything to dull his senses for what he was about to do. Releasing a breath, he reached across the table and grasped Maryanne's hand.

She looked up, surprise evident in her wide eyes. "Chase…?"

"Please," he said, "just so we can enjoy our celebration in style, finish saying what you were telling me about Autumn. I need to know."

Her fake-eyelashed gaze looked deeply into his as she clung to his hand. "You poor man," she cooed. "This is really tearing you up inside, isn't it?"

"You don't even know," he choked out. "Which is

why I—I'd feel so much better if I could just know the truth."

Maryanne gave his fingers a squeeze. "Since you put it that way, Chase, of course I'll tell you."

He gave her what he hoped what a relieved smile and held his breath. *C'mon, c'mon c'mon. Spill the beans.*

Maryanne glanced around before leaning in. "That girl's background is *loaded* with trouble," she began conspiratorially in a low voice.

"Such as?"

Her eyes gleamed. "Try 'time in juvie' on for size."

"Juvie?" Chase wrinkled his brow, feigning confusion. "Autumn's been to jail?"

"Sure has." Maryanne picked up her fork and stabbed at the salad, loading up a mouthful of swamp greens. "Should have stayed there far as I'm concerned."

"What…ah. I mean, what'd she do?"

"You don't need all those details, Chase. Spare yourself."

Oh, *hell* no. He sure as shit wouldn't be sparing himself. He tried a new tactic. "Like I said, I need to know."

"But—"

"I'm an artist, Maryanne. As you well know. And I can't create if I'm distracted. My brain starts focusing on shit I don't need, and I might as well close shop. Artistic creativity is deader than all those skeletons in Autumn's closet."

"I didn't realize that."

"That's why I'm sharing this with you." He leaned forward as if to tell her a great secret. "Almost no one knows this about me. But I'm choosing to tell you, because I know you'd understand. And if we're going to be partners, you gotta see where I'm coming from."

She smiled and batted her spider eyes. "I'm flattered."

"We've got a multi-hotel deal on the table that we both want to be successful. That's why my head needs to be clear before I can even think about signing on for a project of this size."

He pulled his hand away from hers and sat back in his chair, arms folded. "Now, please. Tell me everything you know about Autumn."

Maryanne downed her champagne glass—which he immediately refilled—and told him everything about Autumn's record, what it was for, how long she was in juvie, that she was released to foster parents.

She also admitted that she'd confronted Autumn about her record and the conversation between them that Chase already knew about. But to no surprise, Maryanne was quick to bathe herself in a halo of goodness. In her retelling of the conversation between her and Autumn, Maryanne made it seem as if her lavish benevolence was all that stood between Autumn either retaining her job or ending up back in the slammer.

When she finally paused to come up for air, Chase said, "It was nice of you to not fire her," he managed to choke out. "I need her for my art."

"Which is the only reason I held off," she assured him. "Otherwise, that girl woulda been gone."

Her words were getting dangerously slurred, so Chase knew he had to wrap this up quick.

At that moment, the waiter appeared with their

entrees. He set them down with a flourish and whisked away.

Chase ignored his food, instead directing them back to the conversation. "That explains a lot about her," he said, nodding. "I should say I'm surprised, but I guess I'm not. Like I said, I felt like there was something off about her. She's quiet, just like a person would be with a big secret."

"Sure," Maryanne agreed. "But you can't run away from your past."

"Actually, I do have a question about that."

"Oh?" She looked up, fork in midair. "What question?"

Careful he reminded himself. *This is the death blow.* "Well, I'd always thought that juvie records were, you know, private."

"They are. To most people."

"So how…?"

"I have my sources."

"Cops?"

"Nope!" She let out that annoying giggle again, and it took the will of a gladiator for him not to reach across the table and choke her like a chicken. Instead, he forced out a chuckle, as if happily playing along with her childish game.

"Umm…a newspaper reporter?"

"Good guess, but wrong again." She sliced off a bite of steak, and with her fork, slid it through the thick butter sauce swirled around her plate before lifting it to her lips. "Only one more guess!"

"Hmmm…" He pretended to consider his options, and then released a wide smile. "Oh, I know who it must be," he said happily, as if the thought had just occurred to him. "Mason Reed."

"Ding, ding, ding, ding!" She winked at him and gave him a delicate golf clap, making sure not to damage her nails. "Very good. But how did you guess?"

"I've seen him around the hotel a few times and knew that he's part of the VC group financing us. So I took a shot."

"And scored a hole-in-one!"

Chase gave her a smile and turned his attention to his food just to gather his thoughts. He had what he needed and could end the conversation right here. But if he could just get her to admit what her relationship was with Mason, he felt like it would be the final nail in the Maryanne coffin.

"There's one last thing I don't get," he said. "Why would Mason tell you this?"

"Because I hold a key senior management role in this organization, Chase," she responded primly, as if his question had been an insult.

"Oh, I know," he assured her. "But still. Why would Mason think you need to be spending your time on a trivial matter like Autumn's juvenile record? I mean, what would have prompted him to find out the information in the first place?" He frowned as if suddenly struck with an unpleasant thought. "Has he got a thing for her?"

"Oh, please," she said dismissively, "Don't get your manly self all worked up. Mason doesn't have a thing for Autumn. He's got a thing for *me*."

"You?"

"Don't act so shocked. I'm not a bad catch, Chase." She stabbed at her asparagus. "If you'd bothered to take notice."

Fuck. He let out a breath as "Proceed with Caution" flashed in his mind like a neon sign.

"No doubt," he said carefully. "But I still don't understand how that ties in with Mason thinking you'd even want that information in the first place. I mean, what do you care about Autumn's background?"

She downed the last of her champagne in a single swallow and sat back in her chair. "Isn't it obvious?"

"I'm not sophisticated like you, Maryanne. I blow glass for a living. Enlighten me."

"But that's just it. You don't just blow glass; you create astonishing art. Art that's going to make both of us filthy rich through this multi-property deal."

Her glassy eyes and flushed cheeks exposed the heavy volume of alcohol flowing through her blood, as did her rising tone. He glanced around the room, but so far no one seemed to be paying them any attention.

"I'm telling you," she continued angrily, "I've worked for *years* making this deal happen, and nothing—I repeat, *nothing*—is going to ruin it for me. Especially not an irritating little know-it-all IT skank like Autumn Rivette!" She chomped down on a mouthful of steak. "That little twit better watch her back, too."

"What do you mean?" His rage toward the designer began filtering into his words, like blood soaking through a bandage.

Luckily, Maryanne's drunkenness likely prevented her from noticing. "That's why I had Mason check into Autumn's background. I figured if there was anything worthwhile that I could use, he'd find it. And sure enough, he did!" She propped her elbows on the table and leaned in.

The alcohol was so strong on her breath that Chase felt as if he might ferment. But he guessed she was about to lay down some juicy gossip, so he gritted his teeth in a smile and nodded, encouraging her to continue.

"When he came across an old court document containing listings of juvenile convictions, he found Autumn's name. The record was sealed, but Mason knows an army of judges from his years practicing law. Even better, one of his old judge buddies owed him a favor from a time back in their years at Duke. That judge got ahold of Autumn's juvie record and passed it on to Mason." Her slim fingers wrapped around her champagne glass and for a moment she lifted it and held it aloft, as if in a silent salute to Mason's illegal deed.

"So let me get this straight—you'd use your knowledge of Autumn's juvenile record against her?"

"Damn right I would. And why not?"

"I guess cause last I checked, blackmail's illegal."

Maryanne shrugged as if that was a matter of no consequence. She looked up at him through glassy eyes while stabbing her fork in the air. "All's fair in love and war. We've both worked so hard, Chase. You with your art and me with this deal."

She lifted her napkin to dab at the corners of her mouth. "You said it yourself—something was off with Autumn. So of course, I'll do whatever's in my power to protect us both from her. And I was crystal clear when I talked to her. My ultra-talented, hot celebrity artist needs a gorgeous model on his arm, not some two-bit skank who tarnishes your appeal. I told her that if she continues throwing herself at you, I'd make damn sure she never works again in the state of Louisiana. All I'd have to do is release her little juvie record that Mason uncovered. And I would, too. Easy peasy!"

Nausea rose in his throat. He sat, speechless, silent as a mummy. He didn't blink, didn't breathe, didn't react in any way. His only salvation was the sole thought that Maryanne was digging her grave, every word out of her mouth like flinging dirt from the shovel, burying her deeper.

"Anyway," she continued, returning focus to her food, "this conversation has gone on long enough. I said I didn't want to talk about Autumn, and now I really have to put my foot down. This is turning my stomach and ruining our celebration."

He knew that was it. If he pressed harder, he'd only raise questions, and besides, there was no reason. Just as Autumn predicted, he'd gotten her drunk enough and she'd spilled the beans. He had everything he needed.

Drumming up a placating tone, he grasped her fingers where they rested atop the table.

"Then let's stop talking about her," he said soothingly. "It's our night, after all."

Her pinched face relaxed. "Now that's more like it."

With grim determination, he kept the conversation focused on everything besides the hotel and Autumn.

At last, three long hours after they'd first been seated, the excruciating dinner came to an end. Maryanne wobbled as he helped her to her feet. Clearly, she was in no condition to drive, so he had the restaurant call for a cab.

Only once she was safely tucked into the car with

instructions to the driver about where to take her could he relax. He watched the car get swallowed up by the black night, and at last, allowed himself a victorious breath.

He grabbed his phone—where the entire conversation with Maryanne was already uploaded into his cloud storage—and pulled up text messaging. He tapped out a single word text to Autumn, wishing he could see the smile on her face when she saw it.

Nailed.

Chapter Twenty-Two

Giles Noble wasn't a man to be fucked with. Six-foot-two, his body as lean and muscled in his fifties as it was back in college when he was the British national decathlete champion. The unstoppable drive that brought him armloads of trophies back then gave him bank vaults of cash now.

Chase eyed him from across the gleaming desk where they sat in Giles' office. Everything around them smelled of money. Not surprising, considering the source. After all, Giles was loaded. Filthy, stinking rich. His Midas touch with hedge funds had made him a millionaire several times over before he turned thirty, and he took that money to form one of the nation's premier venture capital investment groups specializing in luxury hotel development. His reputation was ferocious yet fair, well respected by those who worked for him. But now, he was pissed.

He shrugged off his expertly tailored suit jacket and tossed it to a nearby chair. For a moment, he sat at his desk without saying a word as he gazed out the window, the only sound in his palatial office his drumming fingers against the sleek glass top. He glanced over at Chase, nodding toward the phone sitting on the desk between them. "Play it once more," he said, his clipped British accent knifing through the silence.

For the third time, Chase picked up his phone and hit play. Maryanne's slurred words invaded the office.

"That's why I had Mason check into Autumn's background. I figured if there was anything worthwhile that I could use, he'd find it. And sure enough, he did!"

"So let me get this straight. You'd use your knowledge of her juvenile record against her?"

"Damn right I would. And why not?"

"I guess 'cause last I checked, blackmail's illegal."

"Shut it off. I've heard enough." Giles leaned back in his chair and folded his arms across his chest. "Bloody fucking hell."

Chase slid his phone into his jacket pocket. "She's a piece of work."

"With a pissy attitude." Giles reached into a drawer and pulled out a bottle of high-priced whiskey and two glasses. Without asking whether Chase wanted any, he poured them both a stiff belt.

"I put up with her shit for what she brings to our development projects," Giles continued after taking a swallow. "She knows what she's doing, and her drive is relentless. But if this were to get out…" He shook his head and let out a long breath. "Damnit to hell. Our entire deal is in jeopardy."

"Yep."

"This goes up in smoke, and the investors will have my head. Which is why there's no way in hell that's going to happen." He downed the rest of his drink and poured another before leaning forward to rest his chin on steepled fingers. His blue eyes, sharp and cold as ice chips, lasered on Chase. "Will Autumn sue?"

Chase paused before answering, playing his cards carefully. "Up to you."

"As if I have a bloody choice."

"There's always a choice. Which one you take is what matters."

Giles allowed a small grin to tug at his lips. "You sure there's no secret philosophy degree in that artistic background of yours?"

Chase shrugged. "I'm just a guy who blows glass."

"Sure you are. And I'm just a bloke from England who likes spending money." He pushed back from his chair and rose, walking over to where he'd tossed his suit jacket. Fishing inside, he withdrew his phone and punched in a number. "Get me Ramos." His words were quiet but filled with command.

"Jose? It's Giles." A pause. "Fine, fine. She's in her first year at Oxford, making her old man proud. Listen, I've got a situation. It's urgent and needs utmost discretion. Meet me at the White Ibis immediately. Right. Okay, thanks, mate. I owe you."

He jabbed at the phone and ended the call. Grabbing his jacket from the chair he slid it on and nodded at Chase. "Let's go. Detective Ramos is on his way."

****

Excitement. Anticipation. Disbelief. Autumn's emotions swirled around her like kicked-up debris from a category five tornado. Which, all things considered, was appropriate when a shitstorm is about to hit the fan.

She paced the room, listening for sounds at the door. Maryanne and Mason were due any minute.

The plan Chase and the detectives had outlined was simple. Under the guise of telling Maryanne that she had a sensitive employee matter to discuss, Autumn had insisted that both the head designer and the employment attorney meet her in one of the staff conference rooms. She had left out the part about them having company.

Giles Noble, the detective, and half a dozen cops kept silent vigil off to the side of the room. Chase stood at Autumn's side. They had agreed that she'd do most of the talking, but he was her quiet, giant mountain of confidence. Her pillar of emotional strength, never for a minute letting her face trouble alone.

Sharp clicks approaching the doorway told her that the ice woman cometh. She and Chase took seats at the large center table, and as they did so, he grasped her hand and gave it a reassuring squeeze. Show time.

Without bothering to knock, Maryanne barreled into the conference room with Mason Reed trailing her heels like an obedient dog. When she spotted the assembled crowd, she halted mid-step. Composure slid from her face, morphing to shock. Her eyes widened, startled, and her jaw fell slack. Her head swiveled around as she cast her gaze on a sea of unsmiling faces.

But Maryanne's bewilderment lasted all of two seconds. Like a championship fly fisher, she reeled in her poise, picked her jaw up off the floor, and flashed a wide, frosty smile at the assembled crowd. "Giles! What a pleasant surprise."

"The feeling's not mutual." The investor's frown stayed solidly fixed in place. "Have a seat."

"Oh, thanks. I'd really love to stay and chat, Giles, but…" One red-tipped finger tapped the watch on her bony wrist. "I'm rather busy. As is Mason."

"As am I." Autumn's voice was strong but calm as a lake. "But this is important. So sit the fuck down."

"What did you—"

"You heard me. Sit. Down. You, too, Mason."

For the moment, perhaps shocked into submission, Maryanne stiffly pulled out a chair and took a seat opposite Chase and Autumn. Mason dutifully followed.

Autumn slid a manila folder across the table toward Maryanne. "Open it."

"Excuse me? Your attitude could use a little—"

"Can it. For once in your life, keep your mouth shut. I'm leading this meeting; I'm doing the talking. And trust me, you're gonna want to hear what I have to say. So I'll repeat myself just one more time. Open the folder."

Maryanne grumbled beneath her breath but complied. The open folder revealed several sheets of neatly stacked paper. Staring out from the top was Autumn's juvenile arrest record.

"How did you—" Maryanne's mouth clapped shut. "I mean…ah…what *is* this?"

"Don't you mean how did I get it? That's what you started to say."

"I did no such thing."

"You can't lead a witness," Mason said.

Autumn frowned and turned to Mason. "I don't think we've met, though I'm pretty sure you know exactly who I am. But just in case, I'm Autumn Rivette. I head up IT for the White Ibis. I'm not a lawyer, although even a monkey could tell this isn't a courtroom, and Maryanne's not a witness. Not at the moment anyway."

"I'm not sure what you—"

"And neither are you a witness. For the moment. So I'm not leading any damn witness. What I'm doing is showing information to Maryanne to find out why the hell she was in possession of it."

"Your accusations are baseless," Maryanne shot back. "You can't just place something in front of me and say it's in my possession."

"Technically, it's now in *my* possession," Autumn clarified. "Once Liesel found it in your office and gave it to me."

"Liesel!" The designer's eyes bugged from her head. "She had no right to go searching through my office."

"And what? Take something you shouldn't have had in the first place?"

"I—"

"And *you*"—Autumn pointed a finger at Mason— "broke about a thousand different rules by giving this information to her. You realize your law degree's bust now, right? Along with your job. And your life outside of jail. Holy shit, dude, she must be one ferocious tiger to lose everything you had for a few awesome fucks."

The lawyer's face and ears flushed chili-pepper-red as he sat steaming in his chair.

Before he could spit out a response, Autumn shifted her focus to Maryanne. "I have to admit, I never would've pegged you for that good of a lay. Didn't figure you had it in you."

"You obnoxious *bitch*."

"But enough with the compliments," Autumn continued, ignoring the outburst. She pushed back from the table and walked around to stand directly behind Maryanne, who immediately swiveled around in her chair. Autumn stood facing her nemesis directly, for once in her life towering over someone.

"I wondered how you found out about my record," she said, hitching her thumbs in her jeans as she faced the enraged designer. "The whole point of having it expunged is to prevent just anyone from looking it up." She leveled her gaze at Mason. "You need an unethical douche like Mason Reed to get it for you."

"You have no proof—"

"Shut your trap, Reed. I'm the one doing the talking." Again, she turned to Maryanne. "On top of just *knowing* about my expunged record, you used what you dug up to try blackmailing me."

"I did no such thing."

"You said, 'I'll make sure you never work again in the entire state of Louisiana. I'll end your career as you know it.'"

"I never said any such thing."

"Yeah, I might have the wording a little wrong," Autumn agreed calmly, "although it was something like that."

"You don't—"

"Luckily, we don't have to rely on just my memory." With calm deliberation, she reached into her back pocket and withdrew her phone.

Nervous tension seeped into the room. Not a single person spoke or moved or even seemed to breathe as Autumn tapped the screen. Seconds later, she found what she wanted, and quietly set the phone on the conference table as Maryanne's recorded voice piped from the speaker.

"I told her that if she continues throwing herself at you, I'd make damn sure she never works again in the state of Louisiana. All I'd have to do is release her little juvie record that Mason uncovered. And I would, too. Easy peasy!"

With a soft click, the recording ended.

Fiery blotches of red splashed Maryanne's cheeks in a mottled patchwork of embarrassment to accompany her public shaming. She sat ramrod straight in her chair, not moving a single muscle, frozen in place like a petrified fossil.

Giles stepped forward, his entire face bunched in a furious scowl. "What the hell were you thinking, Maryanne?"

Her lips twitched, but she ignored Giles and instead turned a furious gaze on Chase. "How *dare* you," she spat. "That was a private conversation."

With slow, deliberate movement, Chase pushed back from his chair to walk around the table to Maryanne. He stopped two feet in front of her, a hovering, scowling, leather-clad mountain of intimidation. She visibly shrank in her seat. "Did you take a trip to stupid town, Maryanne?"

"I don't know—"

"That's exactly right," he said quietly, cutting her off. "You don't know *shit*." He bent forward, his face inches from hers. "I used to think you had a brain in that head of yours. But putting together unethical business deals with slime like Reed proved me wrong damn quick."

"Unethical?" Mason Reed finally found his voice. "Erroneous and baseless charges will get your ass thrown in jail, Durand."

Chase shot a glance at Mason. "You should know, Reed. After all, your name is on the contract that Maryanne gave me. The multi-hotel deal. The five million dollars. Easy to give out money you don't have, isn't it?"

"I don't know what—"

"You're paying me on a business deal that doesn't exist."

He straightened and shifted to stand in front of Mason, his mammoth biceps crossed in front of his chest. "Did you actually think I was going to sign that contract without making sure it was legit? After Maryanne mailed it to me, I took it straight to my lawyer. His head almost exploded when he saw it. Used toilet paper is worth more than that deal."

"What?" Maryanne's shrill gasp pierced the tension. She whipped around in her chair and glared at Mason. "What the hell is he talking about, Mason? You assured me that deal was finalized."

"It was *about* to be finalized. The financing was supposed to be coming through any day now. I'm sure of it. The lawyers were certainly going to call me, to iron out last-minute details…" Mason squirmed in his chair like a scolded child.

"*About* to be finalized? What the hell, Mason? You said it was done, you lying, filthy—"

"Takes one to know one, Maryanne." Autumn pushed off from the wall she'd been leaning against to stand directly in front of the designer, ticking off items on her fingers. "Illegally obtaining court records. Illegally obtaining private personnel files. Coercion of a fellow employee. Blackmail. Offering a fraudulent contract. Being a bitch."

"Why you—"

Autumn shrugged. "Whoops. I guess that last one isn't technically a crime."

Maryanne pushed at the armrests and sprang up. "Shut your mouth, you little tramp. I've had about enough—"

"So have I." Detective Ramos, who'd stood silently in the shadows during the entire exchange, placed a hand on Maryanne's shoulder, stilling her. "I'm placing you under arrest for criminal possession of illegally obtained property, coercion, and blackmail. You, too, Reed." Ramos nodded to the cops waiting in the wings to step forward.

"Get your filthy hands off me!" Maryanne twisted away from Ramos, but her effort to move out of his grasp was blocked by a scowling, leather-clad mountain.

"Keep it up, and they'll add resistance to your rap sheet," Chase informed her, standing like a brick wall between the enraged designer and the door.

"Now, we can do this the easy way or the hard way, Ms. Boudreaux," Ramos informed her in a dry tone. "You play nice, and we'll forgo the cuffs. But if not…"

"Go to hell!"

"Get the cuffs on, boys."

In seconds, cops descended on both Maryanne and Mason, pinning their arms behind their backs and slapping on handcuffs. All pretense of the designer's composure slipped as fury rushed in to take its place. Maryanne twisted and hissed like a captured, hysterical vampire trying to escape the sun as strands of hair sprang free from her tight bun, whipping at her face as she shook.

"Let me go!" she hollered.

Ramos paid her no attention. "Book these two," he told his men.

Giles stepped over to open the door as the team of cops led their prisoners away.

As Autumn stepped from the conference room and into the hotel lobby, Maryanne's assistant, Liesel, sped toward them, carrying a silver tray heaped with her boss's favorite raspberry cakes.

"I saw a meeting on your calendar, Ms. Boudreaux, so I thought you'd like your—" The words died in Liesel's throat with one look at her frenzied, handcuffed boss. Her mouth fell open as an audible gasp ripped from her throat.

The tray filled with raspberry cakes went crashing down, the plates and silver slamming against the floor like a gigantic vat of marbles dropped from the sky. The tray itself clanged, silver forks hit the floor and bounced up, plates smashed into tiny shards. The giant mound of raspberry cakes hit the ground with such force that bits of frosting splattered everything in sight. Like a sugary red paintball missile, one particularly large blob shot up and landed with disastrous accuracy straight on Maryanne's nose.

"Ugh!" she screamed, shaking her head.

The commotion of the dropped tray silenced the room as every last employee and guest in the hotel turned their collective attention toward the ruckus. Hundreds of staring eyes watched in astonishment as the once stylish and impeccably put-together interior designer was reduced to a handcuffed and raspberry frosted fiasco.

"Ms. Boudreaux?" Liesel croaked in wide-eyed astonishment.

"Get out of my way, Liesel!"

Ignoring her dutiful assistant, Maryanne forged through the ruined heap of frosted cakes, her stilettos clicking on the floor. But the treadless heels were no match for a butter cream frosting slick. Without warning, her foot kicked out wildly from beneath her. Letting loose a helpless shriek, Maryanne went down like a sack of potatoes into a sticky pile of smashed raspberry cake.

"Damnit!" With hands still cuffed behind her back, she tried twisting to get her legs beneath her and regain her footing, but all she did was grind her skirt deeper into the cake pile.

Two officers finally stepped forward and lifted her to her feet as snickers from the crowd bounced around the lobby.

"All right, get her out of here," Ramos said, directing his team around the accident as Maryanne and Mason were led away.

As Autumn looked around the lobby, it was evident by the way some people pointed at the spill that they were talking about what had just happened. But others were already going about their business, the activity in the White Ibis resuming.

She looked up at Chase, who stood quietly by her side. Her guardian; her protector; her lover.

"Let's ditch this hotel, Mountain Man."

"You got it, babe. Where to?"

"Your place."

****

There were very few tough situations where beer and pizza didn't help. But now that Autumn and Chase were sprawled out on his couch, the pizza box nearly empty and their stomachs full, she wasn't so sure her usual remedy was doing any good. Her nerves jumped like popcorn. The beer bottle slipped in her sweaty hands. Her heart slammed wildly against her ribs. She took a last long swig of beer for courage and set the bottle down on the end table.

With reluctance, she pulled her feet off of Chase's lap where he'd been giving her the most amazing foot massage known to man. Heaped on top of the deep tissue kneading, Chase added a sprinkle of kisses on her toes, a dash of caresses along her inner thighs. He was dialing up the heat between them as familiar warm tingles started revving between her legs and her breaths came quicker.

How tempting it would be to slip down deeper into the couch cushions and tell Mountain Man to strip off her top and start sucking her aching nipples. But before she let herself get caught up in him, she had something to say.

Chase raised a questioning eyebrow when she pulled away her feet but said nothing. That was the thing with Chase. He sensed her better than anyone. Even when he didn't know exactly what was *in* her mind, he knew when there was something *on* it.

"I, ah. I got something to say."

"Okay."

She clasped her fingers and twisted them around, stalling.

"Is it something bad?" he asked.

"No." She shook her head. "Not bad."

"So how come you look like someone about to deliver last words before the hangman's noose gets slipped around her neck?" he asked.

One side of her mouth curled up. Chase was right. She wasn't delivering bad news, but it was *important*. And something she'd never said before.

She popped up from the couch and paced. She

wanted this to come out right. Her gaze traveled around the room, landing on the manila folder Chase had tossed on a table. Confusion struck her. "Is that the contract?"

Chase nodded, mild amusement crinkling around his eyes. "It's pieces of paper with official language on it that's pretending to be a contract, but until the financing is secured, it's worthless."

"And when it does get secured?"

"Then I suppose I'll have a contract."

Nausea gripped her stomach. If Chase had a contract, it meant he'd be leaving. So what she'd been planning on saying was pretty much pointless, right? Maybe it was better if she just kept her mouth shut. If she just said nothing—

Chase rose from the couch, and in two long strides, he stood right in front of her. Without warning, he wrapped both arms around her, swallowing her in a mammoth bear hug. "What's up, Autumn? I know when something's stuck in your craw. So spit it out."

With both arms pressed against her ears, his rumbly voice was muffled, but she heard him well enough. She sighed and slipped out from his grasp.

"Nothing's up," she lied. "I'm just, you know, still wound up from everything that happened."

"You expecting me to believe you? A snake oil salesman is more convincing. Now tell me what's going on."

"Okay, okay." She wrapped her arms around herself and strolled across the room, gathering her thoughts. When she reached the far wall, she turned and looked up at Chase, calmed by the patience in his eyes. He'd wait all night if that's what it took. As long as she eventually told him what was on her mind.

"I *am* still amped up from what happened. That's no lie," she began, "but it's 'cause I have something to tell you."

"I'm listening."

She released a long breath. "You know how people talk about having a partner in their lives? Someone they can tell stuff to, and count on. Someone who gets them. Who's there for them?"

"Yep."

"I never had that before, mostly 'cause I never allowed anyone to get close enough."

"'Cause when anyone did, you got screwed."

"Yeah," she said quietly. "I did."

Chase turned his back, and for a half a second, fear knifed her heart that he was walking away. But all he did was settle back on the couch and pat the empty spot next to him. "C'mon over here and sit down, Autumn," he invited. "Let me hold you."

Never had she felt so secure, so wanted. So *loved*. Willingly, she walked over to her Mountain Man, easily slipping into the empty spot next to him. Her back to his front. Hand in a glove.

His warmth surrounded her and calmed her. Gave her the courage to finally say what she wanted. As his arms circled her and held her close, she swallowed against the lump that had unexpectedly formed in her throat. "You're that person for me, Mountain Man. The one who gets me."

"The one who loves you," he replied easily.

"Yeah," she said, her voice growing shaky. "And the one who I love back."

His embrace grew tighter, holding her close like

he'd never let her go. She leaned back and felt the thump of his big heart rumbling against her.

"Thank you, babe. I know how hard it is for you to say those words."

"Took me awhile to get there," she admitted. "Mushy stuff is way scarier than I first thought. It's tough being vulnerable."

His palm smoothed her hair along the top of her head and slipped down to caress her cheek, his touch surprisingly soft coming from a hand so powerful.

"You never have to feel that way with me. I'll always keep you safe." He chuckled. "Got rid of Maryanne, after all. So you know my word's good."

She shifted in his embrace, turning so she could look at him. Her big Mountain Man, so kind and hot and all for her. She grinned up at him, enjoying the moment until a sobering thought robbed her levity.

Chase sensed the change immediately. "What is it?"

She kept her mouth shut, but he wouldn't let it go. "No secrets, Autumn. Tell me what's bothering you."

"The contract," she finally admitted. "I know it's not done yet, but when it is…"

"When it is…what? It's no big deal. We might even make a good amount of cash."

"*We*?" She shook her head. "It's only for you, Chase. I'm not getting any damn contract."

He frowned. "Has the summer heat melted your brains, Autumn? I told you, we're a team. I don't do my art anywhere without you. That's the deal."

"But the deal means you'd have to move. To leave."

"And if you don't want to go, then I don't go.

Period."

"I…you." She paused, started over. "Really? A team?"

"Forever."

His thumb and forefinger lifted her chin. He looked down at her, green eyes sparkling in the last of the early evening sun streaming through the window. The corners of his full lips tilted upward as a smile lit his face. "And forever means forever," he rumbled. "As in you're going to be my wife someday. And don't give me shit about it, 'cause that's the way it is. You're going to have to deal with hearing mushy stuff not just from me, but from my whole damn family. They're going to love you, and they're going to tell you that. And you're gonna tell them the same thing. When you're ready."

The arrow of fear that normally would have flash-frozen her on the spot never came. Her stomach didn't churn. Her hands didn't shake. Instead, what she felt was more a spring day, the kind where the wind holds the promise of warmth, and buds start opening on the trees. When the cold, slushy winter finally took a hike and summer was just around the corner. That kind of feeling.

"I'm ready now, Mountain Man. I think so, anyway."

"Yeah?" He leaned forward, dropped a soft kiss on her lips that lingered, then deepened, the hint of what they'd be doing before much longer.

"Then start practicing." When she was slow to respond, he feigned annoyance. "I'm waiting."

"I…um. I love you."

He raised an eyebrow, but she saw the twinkle in

his eyes. "That the best you can do?"

"Not by a long shot." She twisted in his arms and rose up to meet his mouth, planting him with a long, sensual kiss.

"I love you," she whispered.

"Again."

"I love you."

"And I love you, Techie."

He met her kiss, slipping his tongue between her lips as he wrapped strong arms around her and held her tight. Flames of desire licked their way down her body.

At last he parted, leaving only inches between them. "Since we're on the topic of mushiness, I have something for you," he said.

She grew instantly wary. "What is it? You're making me nervous. This mushy thing is new to me, you know."

He laughed. "You need to trust me." He paused. "Do you?"

Without hesitation, she nodded. Because she did. "Hundred percent."

He stepped away from the couch and over to a bookshelf to grab a box about the usual size that held shoes. "For you."

She took it in trembling hands. It was light, far lighter than any pair of shoes would be.

"Open it," he said.

She lifted the lid to reveal the most intricate, glass-blown lily she'd ever seen, set on a bedding of fluffy cotton lining the box. A perfect lily, bursting with streaks of yellow and orange. Inside the open bloom were the delicate stamens, the glass so beautifully blown that they looked real. At the base of the flowing green stem he'd dotted small drops of dew on the open leaves.

"I know you're not a real flowers kind of girl, but I thought a glass one might work."

She stared at it, speechless. "It's perfect," she whispered.

"I made it orange and yellow. Like the fall," he explained. "Like autumn."

Her heart swelled. "No one has ever brought me flowers before."

"Now someone has."

She drew her fingers along the delicate, flawless petals. "You know me so well, Chase," she said quietly, wonder coursing through her. "This is the exact right flower."

"'Cause I'm the guy who gets you," he said, placing a soft kiss on her lips. "Forever."

Elizabeth Shore

About the Author

Wisconsin native Elizabeth Shore will always consider herself a Cheesehead at heart, but for the past twenty years, New York has been home. She also travels frequently to Finland, her husband's home country. All that time in cold climates means she's shivering a lot, but finds no better way to shake off the chill than by writing erotic romance—the hotter the better.

Elizabeth likes brooding, complicated heroes and is also a fan of thrillers and horror. One of her geekiest moments was traveling to Bangor, Maine so she could have her picture taken in front of Stephen King's house. She writes both historical and contemporary romance, is passionate about Renaissance art, and a devoted animal lover. She's grateful to her husband for his ardent, unyielding support, and to her passel of cats for allowing her to live and write in their home.

~*~

Visit Elizabeth Shore at
www.lizshore.com

Hot Bayou Nights
By Elizabeth Shore

When corporate consultant Carla Saunders' work takes her from the skyscrapers of Manhattan to a research facility in Louisiana filled with king cobra snakes, she sees her dreams of a job in Paris sinking into the swamp. But unexpected desire burns hotter than a sultry bayou night. The snakes terrify her, but lust for the scorching hot research scientist has her dreaming less about the Champs Élysées and more about being coiled in his arms.

Obsessed with finding a cure for multiple sclerosis, Jackson Rivard's got zero time for relationships. But when a lush, efficient business advisor sweeps into his lab, zero spikes to a hundred before he can shut off the engine. In theory, no-strings-attached sex is scientifically feasible, but having an ex whose fangs make a cobra's seem modest brings new meaning to the phrase "once bitten, twice shy." How can he protect his heart when Carla's charming it out of hiding?

Catching the Cajun
By Ursula Whistler

Paranormal blogger Felicia Li wants to show she's more than an Internet flash in the pan. Her Paranormal Pest website is taking off as she debunks ghosts and monsters across the country. Her next gig involves busting a New Orleans tour group for a fake Loup Garou haunting the swamps. But the formidable tour owner kicks her off the boat, and she's not above cozying up to the sexy Cajun to catch the fake monster.

Jacques Mercier, owner of Cajun Boy Tours, isn't about to let petite Felicia bring down his family business. He's overcome oil spills and hurricanes, but something about the feisty Internet phenom tells him she's going to be trouble for his business—and his heart.

Thank you for purchasing
this publication of The Wild Rose Press, Inc.

For questions or more
information contact us at
info@thewildrosepress.com.

The Wild Rose Press, Inc.
www.thewildrosepress.com